Viral Intent
Jihad in the Big Easy

Judith Townsend Rocchiccioli

Bluestone Valley Publishing

HARRISONBURG, VIRGINIA

Judith Townsend Rocchiccioli/Bluestone Valley Publishing
Harrisonburg, Virginia 22801
www.judithrocchiccioli.com

Publisher's Note: This is a work of fiction. Names, characters, places, and incidents are a product of the author's imagination. Locales and public names are sometimes used for atmospheric purposes. Any resemblance to actual people, living or dead, or to businesses, companies, events, institutions, or locales is completely coincidental.

Book Layout © 2014 by Eric Blumensen

Viral Intent/ Judith Townsend Rocchiccioli -- 1st ed.
ISBN-13: 978-1499304367
ISBN-10: 1499304366

This book is dedicated to my sister Sally Townsend Poarch of New Orleans and Pass Christian, Mississippi. My sister has always been there for me, whether I needed a bed to sleep in, a home cooked meal, or some homemade wisdom. Sally, your support of me over the years has been phenomenal and I love you for it.

Narbeth

Enjoy!

Judiah

"And kill them wherever you find them, and drive them out from where they drove you out....and fight not with them at the Sacred Mosque until they fight with you in it, so if they fight you in it, slay them." and, "Such is the recompenses of the disbelievers."

(Surah 2:191, the Quran)

ACKNOWLEDGEMENTS

I would sincerely like to thank all of my friends and family who helped me complete this manuscript. I would especially like to thank Tracy Coyne, Cammie Tutwiler, and Jennifer Mandell for their review and editing of the manuscript. I would also like to thank Eric Blumensen for his cover design and final editing of **Viral.** Also, I'd like to give a shout out to Lt. Tommy Kain (ret) of the Richmond Police Department and my friend, John Cassara, author of **Demons of Guadara**, for his review and assistance with the manuscript. Most of all, I would like to thank all of my readers of the Alexandra Destephano Series for their continued support and the success of this series.

Chapter 1

"Sandy! Sandy! You have got to come here right away! Something horrible is happening to the guy in bed three. I have no idea what's up with him but I think he is going to die," Kelsey Saunders exclaimed, her voice shrill with anxiety as her vivid green eyes exploded with fear.

Sandy Pilsner, emergency department nurse manager of Crescent City Medical Center's level one emergency department, looked up from the nurses' station and said, "What's up, Kelsey? I just saw him 20 minutes ago when I was making rounds."

Kelsey's face was white with fear. "It's awful. He has blood coming out of his eyes and his blood pressure is low. He's also shaking all over. I don't know if it is a seizure or his fever. He's having trouble breathing too. "

Sandy rose from her seat so she was eye level with the almost hysterical Kelsey, her new nursing graduate intern from LSU, and said gently, "Kelsey, it's OK. I just checked on him a few minutes ago. He seemed fine, except for his fever and the fact that his blood work is really screwed up."

"I know, I know. But I'm telling you that things have changed quickly. Please come and take a look at him!"

Sandy shook her head emphatically as she looked at her student.

"Hurry up. I think he's gonna die any minute. There is just something very wrong! He is totally going bad." Kelsey's green eyes were huge and Sandy could see anxiety and worry reflected in them.

"All right, let's go check him out," Sandy said rising from her chair as she thought of the ideal teaching moment they would have when suddenly an urgent voice barked "CODE

BLUE, CODE BLUE, ED, Bed 3" over the hospital voice system.

Sandy grimaced and said, "Well, Kelsey, you called that one right! Let's see what we can do," she suggested as the two nurses rushed toward the opposite end of the ED, pushing an extra crash cart.

The code team was in action, and two amps of bicarb had already been administered with no response. The patient was blue, with circumoral cyanosis surrounding his mouth. His nails looked as though someone had painted them with a pearly blue nail polish. His eyes, open and staring, were blood red from petechiae and broken blood vessels. A bloody drainage seeped from the right eye, staining his cheek. Sandy noticed the flat red rash on his chest. She could swear he hadn't had that rash 30 minutes ago. The ED doc in charge, Dr. Fred Patterson, saw Sandy and hollered, "What the hell is wrong with this guy? He's bleeding from everywhere and I have no idea what's wrong with him! Give me a history and for God's sake, get us some protective gear in here."

Sandy stood quietly, paralyzed for a second. She had never seen Dr. Patterson anxious or even tense. She panicked for a moment but didn't know why. Suddenly, a dark sense of foreboding fell over her and she was afraid.

Dr. Patterson glared at her. "For God's sake, Sandy! Give me something. What's the history? He's bleeding out and I don't know why. This is, at the very least, malaria, typhoid or perhaps one of the hemorrhagic viruses - maybe even something worse. Holy Shit, I don't like this! Get us some protective gear, NOW!"

Sandy's stress soared exponentially. Fred Patterson was their calmest ED doc and he was freaked. She grabbed the chart from the medication nurse and said, "Fred, not much to tell. The guy came in several hours ago; he was staying at the Hotel Burgundy in the Quarter. He's part of the staff for the Democratic Caucus that starts tomorrow. The friend who brought him here said he started feeling sick last night, had some nausea, some vomiting and a sore throat. Then, this morning, his temperature got higher and he couldn't stop vomiting, so his friend brought him in. We started some IV fluids and gave him some Tofran for his nausea. That was several hours ago. He was OK an hour ago."

"Well, he sure isn't OK now. I think he is in liver failure at the very least and probably multi-system failure. Any recent blood work? Does he have any friends or family here other than the guy who brought him in? Any idea where he's been? Do you know if he has been traveling?"

Sandy shook her head as she and Fred watched as the Code Team continued CPR compressions as the Respiratory Team intubated the patient. There was no cardiac response at all. Flat line. A nurse rolled the defibrillator closer.

"I've no idea. His friend stayed about 30 minutes and took off. Said he had a bunch of stuff to do. You know the politicians are here for the next few days, right? They are trying to clean up their act in Washington, you know, Operation Fix America," Sandy added in explanation.

"Yeah, goody, goody and the President is coming over the weekend, right?"

Sandy could detect the sarcasm in Fred's voice. She really couldn't blame him for his jaded and sarcastic nature. Just this year, his twin brother Ron, also an ED doc for CCMC had died working in the ED. No one had recovered from it, particularly Fred. Nevertheless, he was a great ED doc and he knew his stuff. Besides, almost everyone in America had lost respect for the politicians in Washington D.C., and Fred wasn't any different.

"Yep, that's what the papers say," Sandy responded as she addressed Fred's jaded remarks and continued, "I think a food service worker from the same hotel was admitted earlier with similar symptoms. I'll need to check."

"Find out where he's been from his friend that brought him in. Call the hotel too. I think he has some kind of lethal virus. Get the infectious disease people in here too. I'm bringing in Tim Smith in Tropical Medicine over at Tulane as well. Those people over at the Tropical Medicine department are good with this stuff."

Sandy could hear the tension in Fred's voice. She paused for a second to respond, but he glared at her and said, "STAT, Sandy, we need to know what we are dealing with. If it's bad, we need to contain it. Be sure we have gathered all available blood samples for diagnostic testing. Get a tube of everything."

Sandy, an old hat ED nurse who thought she had seen everything working while in New Orleans, was disturbed and frightened by Fred's behavior and the wild look in his eyes. She could feel her anxiety escalating, something she hardly ever experienced as an expert practitioner.

"Got it Fred, I'll take care of it," she calmly replied, pushing a reluctant Kelsey forward so they could get to work. Sandy could feel the slow but increasing thud of her heart. *Oh my God,* she thought, *suppose we have an outbreak of Ebola or some unknown hemorrhagic virus.*

She looked at Kelsey, who was, once again, white with fear and said, "Have central supply bring in full gowns, masks and booties for all staff in the ED. Get face shields as well. We need to start isolation on all patients and close the ED to further traffic. We'll have to close down and transfer what we can, and divert to other local EDs. I'll call and let administration know. This could be bad. We don't know what this guy's got."

Kelsey recovered and responded quickly. "I'll take care of it, Sandy. I'll get the gear and report back to you. I'll call the CCMC infectious disease docs here at the hospital."

"Thanks, Kelsey. You're the best," Sandy said as she patted the shoulder of the young graduate and rushed toward her office to call administration and report a potentially biologic threat to the medical center. In route, she had a near-collision with general surgeon Robert Bonnet, the interim chief of medicine at CCMC.

Robert smiled brightly at Sandy, "Whoa! What's up, girl! Why are you hurrying so fast? I heard the CODE BLUE so I came down. What's going on?"

"Come into my office, Robert, so we can talk. We have a guy, the code, who looks like he has some type of really weird virus. Fred said typhoid or malaria at the best and perhaps something much worse. Maybe even a hemorrhagic virus of some kind. The patient works for the Democratic Party. He was bleeding out, has a significant trunk rash, and high fever. Also, his kidneys and liver are shutting down."

Robert's smile disappeared as he processed the information Sandy gave him. His handsome face reflected his concern and he said, "This could be bad. Get me Dave Brodrick, head of infectious disease here at CCMC and get him over here. If it looks like a hemorrhagic fever, we will need to call the CDC as well. Has anyone else been admitted with similar symptoms?"

"Yeah, but he was transferred to Intensive Care, which is where this guy was headed before he coded. I think the guy in the ICU is South African and I believe he was food service staff at the Hotel Burgundy. He had a temp of 103.2, as well as nausea and vomiting. His blood platelets were whacked and WBCs were way up. Short of breath, too, but we treated that with oxygen. Just like the guy that coded, but the South African guy stabilized and was transferred to ICU an hour or so ago."

"Find out how he is, then call me. I think we have a serious situation, a viral outbreak at the very least." Sandy nodded as she noted the etched lines of concern on Robert's handsome face as he left her office and started down the hall.

Robert Bonnet is drop dead gorgeous....If I were a few years younger...Sandy had just picked up her phone to call infectious disease when Robert returned, framed her doorway and asked, "Sandy, when does the political convention start, Operation Fix America? Do you know?"

Sandy shrugged her shoulders and said, "I don't know, sometime this weekend. I think it's mainly Friday and Saturday, but I think the President speaks on Saturday." She gave him a reproachful look and added, "Really, Dr. Bonnet, you should know. Your father is a Senator!"

Robert cracked a half smile. "Find out," he said as he stared at her steadily, his eyes unwavering and holding hers.

After several seconds, Sandy got the message and asked, "Dr. Bonnet, you don't think someone is?"

Robert interrupted her, "I don't know, Sandy, but we have to think proactively. There are gonna be a lot of very powerful people in the city this weekend. We've got to consider it."

"Oh my God, Robert. We've had enough this year, please not this." Sandy's voice was shrill with fear as she rubbed the chill bumps from her arms.

"Yes, we have, but I have a bad feeling that this may be the worst. Close the ED to further traffic, have everyone wear protective gear, and for God's sake, don't allow anyone to leave until we figure out what we are dealing with. Implement our full bio-containment protocol and divert traffic, except patients with flu-like symptoms. It's better to be safe than sorry," Robert added.

Sandy stared at him, her eyes wide. She nodded and said, "I've already closed the ED and we are transferring everyone out that we can. I just need to contact administration."

Robert smiled and said, "You have. These days I am administration and trust me, I'd much rather be in the operating room. I'll talk to Alex. We're the administrators in charge while Don is away on vacation. Keep this viral thing under your hat. It may be nothing more than a bad bug. But just to be safe, I'm calling CDC."

Sandy watched Robert leave for the second time as a dark, ominous feeling of dread permeated her body. *Oh my God, what are we in for,* she thought as she wiped the chill bumps from her arms.

Chapter 2

In the back of a shotgun house off Chartes Street in the Faubourg Marigny, a colorful revitalized neighborhood close to the French Quarter and the Mississippi River, Ali, a thin, frail, 23 year old Muslim graduate student stared at his older brother, 31 year old Nazir and asked, "Nazir, are you sure we know what we are doing? I don't trust Vadim at all." Ali's tousled dark curls and expressive brown eyes were intent.

"Ever since I hacked into his email and saw the exit plans he sent to his comrades in Russia, I have been suspicious," Ali continued. "Maybe you should abort this mission or at least, postpone it." His young face looked scared and uncertain.

Nazir's face remained unchanged and he rolled his eyes with impatience. He looked at his little brother with impatience and said condescendingly, "Ali, stop it. I thought you were ready for this. I thought I could trust you to be strong. We are doing the work of Allah." Ali seemed to shrink in stature, to retreat into his skin, at his brother's criticism and impatience. He felt very small as he stared at his feet.

"I am ready, I really am," Ali replied with all the bravado in his voice he could muster. "I just don't like working with others, those that are not dedicated to our cause."

Nazir's impatience continued and it was clear in his voice. "You have been training for over three years, and I have been planning for a mission such as this for many years. Sometimes, in order to get the job done, we have to work with others. This is one of those times."

Ali still looked doubtful, uncertain. His brother's words did not sway him. Nazir moved toward his little brother and put his arm around his thin shoulders. Ali certainly wasn't a warrior, but he was a brilliant scientist and computer genius. Nazir's voice was reassuring, "Vadim is OK. He's just different from us. He is Russian, just as we are, but he is from another part of Russia where the culture is different and where they do things differently. But he is a Muslim and worships as we do.

He is one of the highest, most revered leaders in the Red Jihad movement in Eastern Europe," he said gently.

Ali nodded as Nazir continued, "Remember, we need Vadim and his connections to get us the virus. The Russians have been holding that strain of the virus for decades. It would have taken us years to produce a similar one with the same kill rate. In fact, as I may have told you, the virus was mutated here in New Orleans in the 1960s. The Russians stole it, so the story goes."

Ali nodded. He remembered the story well. There was even information on the famous virus in the archives of the school of Medicine and Tropical disease at Tulane University.

"You more than anyone know we haven't been able to produce the more virulent strain in our laboratories," Nazir eyed him reprovingly.

"I know, I know," lamented Ali. "But we are very close to a virus that could be more potent. If you had just given me six more months, I could have had the very same thing or perhaps something even better, with an even higher kill rate. Maybe even a virus that would be harder to detect. Nazir, you have to understand that these things take time, believe me. I haven't been doddering." Ali's dark eyes were brooding and angry.

"No, of course not, my little brother. I certainly don't think that at all." Nazir continued to talk softly and reassure his brother how much he and the local Jihad cell appreciated his talents and contributions. "I know that, I know that, little one. But you know how the Americans are. Very seldom are there so many of them from all parts of their leadership gathered together in an iconic, easily compromised city such as New Orleans. This Operation Fix America meeting is a perfect time for us to strike. Washington is just too difficult to infiltrate. It is a fortress. But New Orleans? What can I say? It lives up to its name as The Big Easy for a terrorist attack. Ali, the place is a sewer, and half-underwater. It cannot be secured. Besides, they'll have a hard time figuring out if the virus is endemic to New Orleans."

Nazir smirked and continued, "They have so many bacterial and viral samples growing over there in Tulane's lab, not to mention all that stuff they're growing since Katrina, they'll never detect us. Besides, we have hundreds of places where we can hide here, for years if needed."

Ali was listening and nodded his head, but he was not in agreement with his brother's message.

"The time is right and the place is perfect. Imagine the terror and fear it will cause in the hearts of Americans when we are successful so soon after Boston." Nazir smiled and rubbed his hands together in anticipation of killing thousands of Americans, not to mention senior leadership and the President of the United States. "This mission will make 9/11 seem like child's play."

Ali was being stubborn. "I like New Orleans. I like our friends here and where we live. I have fun. I am happier here than I have been anywhere, since we left home, after our parents died. I like going to school at Tulane, too, and studying with Dr. Smith. I like being his lab rat, and he says he can get me financing for my PhD if I decide to continue my studies. He's taught me a lot, and, in some ways, he has been helpful to our cause."

Nazir's face had darkened and he shook his younger brother violently until Ali's teeth chattered and his dark curls danced in the sunlight. He gritted his teeth and barked at the slightly built young man in a hoarse voice, "Ali, for the last time, *don't you remember* that it was the *Americans* who killed our parents and all of our friends. It was their drone that killed them. *These* people are our enemy. We are here to KILL them, not become their friends and help them in their labs. Do you get it, or do you need to go back to the Cadesus for a refresher course?"

Ali was shocked at his brother's words as he wiped the tears from his eyes, "I get it. I get it, Nazir. I am sorry. Now let me go. I must get to work. My shift starts in less than an hour." Ali pulled back and shuffled out of his brother's arms, terrified, but trying hard not to show it. He left his Marigny apartment, walking quickly toward Canal Street and Tulane Medical Center.

As Nazir watched his brother leave the house, he shook his head in exasperation. *What could he do to make his brother understand their cause. Perhaps he was too young to remember the death of their parents*

Ali's heart was heavy on his way to work. He didn't like the business of hurting others, even though his parents had been killed. Hadn't the Taliban killed the parents of many American children during the 9/11 attack? Weren't the Jihadist's being just as destructive as the Americans had been over the years? He guessed his western education had made him question his supposed "mission." He was startled when his phone alarm sounded, signaling a text. The text was from Dr. Smith. It read, "ALI, CAN YOU COME ASAP? WE HAVE A VIRAL OUTBREAK IN ONE OF THE HOSPITALS. Tim."

He quickly texted back, "I AM ON MY WAY. Ali." He didn't feel good about this at all. There was nothing good about a viral outbreak that could be good for Nazir, Ali or even Vadim, for that matter. At least, not today. He wondered what was up. His heart began to thud with anxiety. Things were just not right and that bothered him. It bothered him a great deal.

Chapter 3

Alex could hardly contain her excitement as she stared across the table at her dear friend and head of CCMC psychiatric services, Dr. Monique Desmonde. Monique was sitting quietly in her wheel chair, her shoulders surrounded by the big, beefy arm of Police Commander Jack Francoise. Only six weeks ago, Monique had been in a coma, having sustained a potentially terminal head injury when a nefarious CCMC employee attacked her with a lead pipe. But, that was six weeks ago, and Monique's recovery was amazing. She was even better than last week when Alex had taken her dinner and spent the evening while Jack was working. Each week Alex marveled at her progress.

Monique was alert and seemed to be back to almost normal. By her own admission, she was still a bit forgetful and knew she couldn't return to her position as chief of psychiatry at the Pavilion, CCMC's psychiatric facility, for several more months, and frankly, that was fine with her. Her luxurious long dark hair was beginning to grow back from her craniotomy and her face was unblemished from the massive trauma she had sustained. She looked beautiful, happy, and content. Alex was thrilled with Monique's progress and anxious to have her back full time at the hospital.

Jack was happy as well. The lines of worry, anxiety, and fatigue were temporarily erased from his face as he moved closer to protect Monique. In the background hovered Chef Henri, the executive chef of the Cajun Café, who loved having Alex and her friends at the Café for lunch. Jack motioned Chef Henri, who immediately appeared at the table.

"Commander, Dr. Monique, Alex, it is wonderful to have you back. Dr. Monique, you look very lovely. My heart is happy for you and the Commander," Henri gushed and continued, "No one would ever know you had been ill!" Henri's sincere voice exuded warmth as he welcomed them to his café.

"Thank you, Henri," Monique was gracious, but her speech was slow and focused, her smile a little crooked. "It is wonderful to see you, too," she said in a halting voice. "I am so happy to be able to come in to lunch." Alex loved Henri's subtle French accent and his long slender fingers, which could have been those of a great pianist. Instead, she could picture Henri slicing and dicing vegetables for his city-renowned French dishes.

Henri touched her shoulder warmly. "Dr. Monique, when will you return to work? We all miss you here."

Monique appeared a little hesitant as she responded, "I don't know for sure, yet. I am still a little slow talking and remembering things. I hope by the end of the year."

Jack glanced over and said, "Don't worry, Henri, she will be back before you know it. Look at how well she has done and how quickly she has gotten better."

Monique glared at Jack and said impatiently, "Jack, you know it may be a while. I won't continue to get better as quickly as I have so far. I believe I still have quite a lot of work to do on my speech and ambulation, not even to mention my memory. I cannot practice psychiatry without a short-term memory and who knows if that will ever come back." Monique was matter–of-fact, but Alex could detect the impatience and anxiety in her voice.

Alex nodded her head but was startled by Monique's impatience. Prior to her injuries, Monique had been the most patient woman on earth, spending hours of time carefully listening to every word in group sessions of her acutely and chronically ill psychiatric patients. Alex had wanted to shoot herself in the head as she had listened to only one group session.

"I know, honey," the Commander said with assurance, "but it won't be that long. We'll continue to work on it every day and we'll get there."

Monique brightened a bit and nodded, "Sure we will, Jack, but just remember that it will take some time." Jack nodded and squeezed her hand in response.

Alex stared at the two of them and shook her head. "Wow, you all freak me out. Even now, I still have a hard time thinking of you guys as a couple. Remember, we had only known for several days when you got sick, Monique."

In truth, Alex had been surprised, almost shocked, when the beautiful, elegant Monique Desmonde and the gnarly, often officious, tough, and stubborn Police Commander Jack Francoise had fallen in love. Of course, they were both old New Orleans and had dated in high school, but that still hadn't prepared Alex, the beautiful legal counsel for the medical center or Dr. Bonnet, Alex's former surgeon husband, for the unanticipated declaration of love between their two friends. They had happily celebrated the news just a few days before Monique had been critically injured by a sick and unhappy employee .

Alex noticed the confused look on Monique's face as she said, "What do you mean, Alex? I thought you were happy with our relationship. You always said you were. Hearing this makes me kind of sad."

Alex reached to take Monique's hand in her own. "Of course I am happy, Monique. I couldn't be happier for the two of you. I was just teasing. You took me too literally." Alex felt guilty for failing to remember that patients with head injuries often don't understand colloquial speech or slang. She admonished herself to be more careful until Monique could differentiate between the seriousness and teasing that occurred in conversations.

Jack backed Alex up. "Monique, you know she and Robert couldn't be happier. Remember, they are standing up for us at our wedding! Maid of Honor and Best Man. Remember?"

Monique laughed, "Of course, I do. You all had better go with us to City Hall. Nobody else even likes us."

"Don't be so dramatic, silly. Everyone likes you and besides, you're covered. Just tell us when and we will be there." Alex turned her attention to Chef Henri who remained patiently waiting by the table. "Henri, what do you have today that is good for lunch?" Alex asked, giving the Chef a bright smile.

"Why, Miss Alex, it is all good." Henri looked hurt, crushed in fact.

Oh my gosh, I am really striking out today. Maybe I can hurt Jack's feelings too and then I'll be three for three, Alex thought. "Of course it's all good, Henry, but what is the special? You know I eat here all the time because I love your food."

Henri's crestfallen face brightened. "Gumbo, Seafood Gumbo! It's the special today. I made it myself. The roué is from scratch," Henri announced proudly.

Jack looked at Monique and Alex who nodded, and he said to Henri, "Three Gumbo and sour dough bread with ice tea. Then we'll order dessert."

As Henri hurried off to fill their order, Alex's cell phone rang. As she checked the digital display, she noted it was Robert, her ex and the interim CCMC chief of medicine who was covering for Dr. John Ashley, who was on a clinical sabbatical.

"Hey, Robert, I am over in the Cajun Café with Jack and Monique. She was here for rehab this morning and we are having Gumbo. Can you join us? Henri just took our order."

Robert's heart quickened and warmed as it always did when he heard the soft, gentle, Virginia accent of his former wife, Alexandra Lee Destephano, the legal counsel for CCMC. Every day when he awoke, he chastised himself for divorcing her years ago when he had been a surgical resident at the University of Virginia Hospital in Charlottesville. He had been so young, dumb, and arrogant in those days. He had wanted Alex, a registered nurse pursuing a law degree, to quit school and stay at home to become a hausfrau like his mother had done for his father, a former Louisiana Governor, and current Senator. For a brief moment, Robert shifted his thoughts to better days. Robert and Alex had married in a lavish wedding ceremony on the Lawn at the University of Virginia and had settled in Charlottesville. Their marriage represented one of the most powerful political unions in the South, the Lees of Virginia and the Bonnets of Louisiana. Alex's grandfather was Senator Adam Patrick Lee of Virginia, and Robert's father had been active in political circles in Louisiana for years and was currently the senior United States Senator from Louisiana.

"Oh, wonderful, how is Monique?" Robert asked, delighted that his friends were all together. Jack and Monique had known Robert for years, and even though Jack was older, they had all grown up together in New Orleans.

"She is wonderful, looks beautiful. Can you make it?" Alex persisted, even though her feelings about Robert remained unresolved.

"I can stop by, but I cannot eat. We have a worsening situation over here in the ED. I need to fill you in. I'll stop in shortly."

"Oh, no, not again," Alex said dismally.

"Damn, now what," Jack demanded, looking angry that someone could mess up his almost perfect lunch. When Commander Jack Francoise was angry, a big black cloud hovered over everyone in his presence and everyone was affected. Monique gently touched his sleeve to calm him down, a frequent gesture for her in her constant effort to control his stress.

Alex looked apologetic. "I don't know. There is something going on in the ED, and he said he needs to come over to update me. I am sure it's nothing, probably some irate patients, someone screaming law suit, or complaining because they had to wait more than 15 minutes."

"Well, I hope it's medical and doesn't concern police work. CCMC needs to hire me two new detectives to help solve their crimes," Jack grumbled. "I spend more time here than I do anywhere."

"Except for the French Quarter," Monique reminded him. "You were there again last night."

"Yeah, yeah, yeah. Damn stupid people getting themselves mugged and beaten up. At least we haven't had any murders lately. If they would just follow the safety guidelines located in all the hotels and restaurants and stay out of the deepest parts of the Quarter after midnight we could cut the crime rate in half. Ain't nothing good going on the Quarter after one a.m. Trust me." Jack's face darkened as he remembered the mugging several nights ago. It was particularly horrific. St. Germaine-like. The victim had survived but was still in shock and couldn't tell the police anything. Damn, he'd like to get that bastard. He was brought back to reality when he noticed Robert Bonnet entering the Café.

Tall and thin, with sandy hair and chiseled features, Robert was particularly handsome in his physician's white coat. He was on the radar of every woman in the Cajun Café. Alex was well aware of the attention her ex was generating as he walked toward their table. She smiled brightly as he kissed her warmly on the cheek. "Monique, you look good, great in fact. How is therapy?" he inquired, as he maneuvered around Jack to give her a gentle hug.

"Rehab is the hardest thing I have ever done, Bonnet. When I graduate, it will be better than getting my medical degree," Monique lamented. "I've never known how painful fatigue could be. Sometimes, I get so tired I cannot remember anything, and that is so frustrating," Monique answered, with tears in her eyes.

Robert nodded his head in understanding as his grey eyes connected with Monique's dark ones. "I'm sure, Monique, but it is paying off. You are doing incredibly well. What you are experiencing is normal, and I know you know that," Robert consoled, his gentle eyes holding her green ones.

"I do. I am just ready to close this chapter in my life. I'm really OK, don't worry," Monique offered as she gave them all a hopeful smile. "Now, what's up in the ED?"

Robert motioned Henri for some iced tea which Henri promptly delivered with their meals. After a few sips, Robert looked at his friends. His voice was low. Jack, half-deaf in one ear from the rifle range and too stubborn to wear a hearing aid, leaned in close. "I'm not sure, but it is potentially very bad. We have a man in the ED, probably dead by now, who has some sort of bad virus. He came in earlier this morning with a high fever, vomiting, and a sore throat. He just got worse and worse until he coded. They were working on him a few minutes ago, but they were about to call it."

"What the hell did he have? The flu? I didn't know the flu could kill you so quick," Jack commented between slurps of gumbo. The police commander's eyes were wide with fear.

16

Hospital germs and things he didn't know about scared him, but no one was braver in a pursuing criminals and advocating for victims than Jack Francoise.

"I hope it's only the flu," Monique said. "We would be really lucky if that's the case. Robert, what do you think it is? Are you thinking what I am thinking?" Robert noted the intense fire in Monique's eyes. She was absolutely putting it together. Robert briefly thought about just how well Monique was doing. Not many physicians recovering from a serious head injury could have put the possibility of a viral contamination together as quickly as Monique.

Alex stared at Robert and Monique, paralyzed with fear. "Oh my goodness, Robert, you all don't think .... Oh, no! Please tell me you are not thinking we have a hemorrhagic virus?"

Robert shook his head. "I don't know, Alex. I certainly hope not, but we have called the CDC and the military. Jack, HAZMAT is on their way."

Jack pushed his bowl away, stood and grabbed Monique's wheel chair. "We're getting the hell out of dodge, Monique. If there is something going around, I surely don't want you to catch it. I'll get you some gumbo to go," he added, noting Monique had eaten only half of her food. With Monique's wheelchair handles firmly in his grip, Jack turned to Alex and Robert and added, "Be back soon. This could be bad. Don't forget the President is due here in two days. You know, Operation Fix America and all that crap. I've already met with the advance team and they're rattling on about some terrorist stuff."

Alex felt her stomach sink. She'd forgotten the President was coming. But, so was her grandfather, and half of Congress. Adam Patrick Lee was one of the most influential Congressmen in Washington and was part of a powerful bipartisan ad hoc committee assigned to clean up Washington. In addition, he was a critical member of almost all committees for national defense.

Robert nodded, turned to Alex, and said, "He's right. The infectious disease docs are meeting me in a few minutes in the ED conference room. Can you gather up administration and attend after you finish your lunch? "

"I've had enough to eat. Hopefully Chef Henri won't be mad because there are leftovers. Yes, of course everyone together. There's not many of us. Don's on vacation, but I will get the others. Pretty much it's just Liz." Alex smiled, showing Robert her beautiful smile and added, "Ain't it nice?" she said jokingly, as she referred to missing CEO, Don Montgomery.

Robert gave her a half smile and said sardonically, "Don's on vacation, huh, perfect. He's generally a pain during these kinds of things anyway."

Alex nodded and added, "Oh no, Robert, what are we going to do if we have a bioterrorism threat?"

"The very best we can, Alex, just like we always do. Come on, we've got work to do."
Alex followed him out of the Cajun Cafe, visibly upset about what could be happening.

Chapter 4

The mood in the ED conference room was highly charged and palpably tense. Seated around the table were Dr. Dave Broderick, the head of infectious disease at CCMC, Dr. Tim Smith from the Tulane Medical Center Tropical and Infectious Medicine Division, Elizabeth Tippett, media relations specialist for the hospital, Robert, and Alex. Missing were Dr. John Ashley, chief of medicine, who was on sabbatical and Don Montgomery, the supercilious and obnoxious CEO who was on vacation in the Caribbean. Also absent was the useless chief of nursing, Betty Farve. Rumor was that she was on the trip to the Caribbean with Don.

"Tim, what do you and Dave think we're dealing with here?" Robert asked, his face grave. He was feeling the full weight of his responsibility as interim director of medicine for CCMC in John Ashley's absence.

Dave shook his balding grey head. "I'm not sure, Robert. It is a viral outbreak of some type but it doesn't appear to be Ebola or Marburg due to the onset of symptoms and hasty death of the one patient. Generally, it takes several days to develop and for the symptoms to become so severe."

"Could it be quickly mutating and that's the reason the guy died so quickly?" Alex questioned.

"Possibly, but I don't think so. And I certainly hope not," Dr. Smith replied. "If it is,
we're in for a really bad time. There are currently six species of Ebola that are named for where they occurred. Bundabugo, Ivory, Cossi, Reston, Sudan, and Zaire. Of course, the very worst species, the one with the 90 percent kill rate, is Zaire. The Reston case is the only US outbreak and that occurred in Reston, Virginia in 2005."

Robert nodded his head. "Yeah, I remember that well. I was a resident at UVA in Charlottesville . That outbreak was near DC and there was a childcare center next door. It was pretty hush-hush."

"Yeah, it was, but they were quickly able to identify and control it. That's what we have to do here," Tim replied to Robert. "When does the CDC get here?"

"Should be here in about 20 minutes. They are coming by helicopter from Atlanta. The folks from the Special Pathogens Branch. They will also be sending their mobile unit up as well. The mobile unit can handle quick testing with the most current technology for virus determination and testing. That will take another five hours." Robert paused to answer his cell phone.

"Sandy, what's up?' Robert's faced grimaced as he listened to her words.

"What, Robert, what," Alex persisted as she stared at Robert's anxious face.

"There are two more patients who just came into the ED. Same symptoms, nausea, vomiting, high fever. Fred Patterson needs help so I'll go over there if you guys will meet and direct the CDC when they get in. Their ETA is momentary." Robert turned to Alex and Elizabeth, "Can you all figure out the best way to handle this with the staff and media? Frankly, I am more worried about our own staff than the media," Robert added on his way out.

"We will, but we aren't saying anything until we talk to the CDC," Alex assured him. "We are doing this right!"

Just then the hospital overhead page center announced, CODE BLUE, CODE BLUE, ICU. Tim and Dave stared at each other. Tim said, "Well, Dave, that's probably number two, the second patient that was admitted. Let's get up there and see what we have." Before he left the room, he turned and said to Alex, Robert and Liz and said, "Remember, it could be many things other than Ebola. It could be Marburg, Lassa, Dengue fever, who knows? I feel pretty confident, at this point, that it's a hemorrhagic fever, but it could also be something that we have never heard of."

Alex and Elizabeth shared a stunned look. *This couldn't be good,* Alex thought.

"Alex, phone up there and make sure they are using HAZMAT including the positive pressure personnel gear with the segregated air supply." *God, I hope they are*, Tim prayed silently. "Also, make sure they have two extra pressure suits for Dave and me. Thanks."

Chapter 5

The medical center was bustling. CCMC was going pretty well, under the circumstances, with a viral outbreak and potential bioterrorism threat. The medical and surgical units were quiet, but the emergency department was frenetic with activity. Emotions were intense and staff moved at a feverish pace. ED physicians, nurses, respiratory therapists and other staff were dressed in full hazmat gear, while the hospital ED was closed to all outside traffic and only admitting patients with viral-like illnesses.

Alex was amazed as she looked through the glass at Sandy Pilsner. Sandy appeared relatively calm in the wake of a potential disaster. She had adjusted well to her hazmat positive air pressure suit and air hose, and seemed in control as she directed the ED and the Center for Disease Control personnel. Alex was convinced Sandy could handle anything, and she pretty much had over the past year. *Boy, we are lucky to have skilled folks like her*, Alex thought.

"Hey girl, what's up?" Sandy asked through the glass partition.

"You tell me, Sandy. How's it going in there?"

Sandy shrugged her shoulders. "Pretty good, I guess, considering. The CDC team leader is Dr. Yvette Charmaine who is from, guess where, New Orleans."

Alex was surprised, "Great, how is she?"

"Yep, she's one of us. She's an LSU undergrad, Harvard Medical School and an infectious disease resident at Johns Hopkins. Doesn't get much better than that, huh?"

Alex, always the Virginia girl, gave Sandy a quick smile. "Well, not too bad, I guess. But a stint at University of Virginia wouldn't have hurt her," Alex smiled playfully. "Give me a report, can you?"

"Sure, CDC hasn't named the virus. They are meeting with all of you, with administration, shortly with an update. We have three new admissions, one is currently meeting the criteria for the virus we saw earlier today and he has been isolated in the first trauma room. The other two are being worked up. We have a total of two confirmed, one dead and a total of five admissions, including the deceased patient. CDC decided to keep the known viral patients together to decrease any chance of contagion and have set up an infirmary in trauma rooms 2 and 3. Trauma 4 and 5 are available if we need them."

Alex nodded. "I sure hope we don't need then. How about the staff?"

"Stressed, but OK. They are getting tired. You know that no one can leave the hospital, right? We're working 50 percent now and have let the others rest. The stress of the staff is the worst part."

Alex nodded as Sandy continued,

"It would be good to keep the same staff working until we figure out what's happening, less chance of cross contamination and besides, I am sure all of the lucky ED staff who are not working today will be happy to have a few extra days off, right?"

"Yep, I am sure. I wish I wasn't here," Alex admitted.

"Yeah, me too. How's Don taking this? I know how he is in emergencies and he is probably beside himself thinking of the impact of bioterrorism on our image." Sandy shook her head.

Alex gave Sandy a great big smile and said, "Don's on vacation, in Aruba. So help me, we cannot reach him and that's just fine. Of course, he wouldn't come back anyway because he is such a chicken."

Sandy gave her a big, wide grin. "I think that's a blessing for you, Alex."

"Yeah, it is. Robert and I are running the place. Scary, isn't it! Wish us luck."

Sandy gave Alex, 'the look' that Alex immediately recognized as she added, "Al, you and Robert really need to be running a life together. You know how much he loves you," Sandy began.

Alex cut her off. "Not now, Sandy. Let's talk when this is over. I don't have time for this right now. Anything else I can do for you?" Alex's voice was curt.

Sandy looked a little hurt with Alex's reaction, but said, "No, I'll call you when the CDC wants to report."

"Thanks, girl. Love you," Alex said as she hurried off, aware she had been rude to Sandy. *I just wish they would all leave me the hell alone about Robert. I am sick of it. But I shouldn't have been mean to her, on this day especially.*

Chapter 6

Ali ducked into an equipment storage closet and dialed his brother's cell phone, a dread fear thudding in his heart.

"Allo," Nazir answered on the second ring.

"Nazir, there is a bioterrorism outbreak here at CCMC and it's not us," Ali said softly into the phone.

"Whatever are you talking about? How could there be?" Nazir was stunned.

Ali was careful with his response. "I don't know who it is. We haven't isolated the virus yet, but it has already killed at least one person that I know of. There are others who are sick. The CDC is here."

"Who could this be?" Nazir demanded, fear in his voice.

"No idea but I'd guess Vadim. Gotta go," Ali said, and hung up the phone.

Nazir could not sit, and paced incessantly around his Marigny apartment. Could Ali be right? Was Vadim not to be trusted? Surely, he wouldn't be a big enough idiot to double cross Nazir and the cell members. They were his countrymen. They were fighting for the same cause. Besides, a double cross would be a confirmation of an immediate death. Should he call his fellow cell members and ask for a meeting? No, he thought. This was his mission and he didn't want anyone to doubt his ability. Better just to wait and see what Ali finds out

He stuck his memory card into his cell phone and began to listen to Jihadist hymns to settle himself down, calm his fears, and renew his commitment. The real truth was that he would need to run away if this mission failed because they would murder him and his brother without reservation. He would no longer have any respect or trust. *Allah, please guide me* he prayed. Finally, the Jihadist hymns singing of victory and a new world calmed him and he dozed off. It didn't matter that the memory card was merely propaganda for recruitment into Jihad. To Nazir, it was a lullaby giving him comfort and confirmation of his cause.

Chapter 7

Dr. Yvette Charmaine calmly surveyed the group of medical professionals, hospital administrators, community leaders, and politicians seated around the ED conference room table. Their stress was evident and the cheat sheets provided them by the CDC had only increased their anxiety. This was the part she hated the most about her job with CDC. She would rather care for a dozen patients with Marburg, Ebola, or Simian virus than tolerate the inane and often dim-witted questions of hospital administrators and politicians.

She had already pegged the Mayor of New Orleans as a total pain in her butt who was needlessly sucking up energy that she desperately needed. His anxiety was uncontained and infectious, but she guessed a lot of that was because of the political Operation Fix America brouhaha scheduled to begin tomorrow. He had attempted to call her six times on her cell phone while she was assessing ill patients and even having her assistant return the call hadn't satisfied him.

Alex examined Dr. Charmaine with interest. Dr. Charmaine was strikingly lovely. She wasn't beautiful in a classical sense, but she had magnificent cheekbones, a beautiful mouth, and the most expressive, green eyes Alex had ever seen. Alex likened her eyes to Columbian Emeralds and guessed her eyes appeared even greener due to the green surgical scrubs she was wearing. She had long, curly red-blonde hair that she had pinned up in a haphazard chignon with curls that were dying to escape and tendrils framing her face. All in all, she was a knockout. At 42 years of age, Robert said she was the youngest section leader in the Special Pathogens Branch of the CDC and destined to do great things.

"Alex, come here. I want to introduce you to Yvette Charmaine," Robert said, as he motioned her forward.

Alex moved toward the front of the room with her hand outstretched and a smile plastered on her face.

"Dr. Yvette Charmaine, I'd like to introduce you to Alexandra Destephano. She is the legal counsel here at the hospital and a close friend. Alex is also a registered nurse."

Yvette accepted Alex's hand thinking to herself. *Hmmm, so this is Robert's ex-wife. Why in the world would he divorce her? She's a knockout.* She smiled at Alex and said, "Alexandra, how wonderful to meet you." She lowered her voice and asked with a tight-lipped smile, "Any idea how this group is gonna be? This is the worst part of my job. Should I expect anyone to freak or fall out?"

Robert looked around the room and deferred to Alex who asked, "Dr. Charmaine, it's hard to say with these folks. Most of them are OK, but I barely know Stuart Tansill, the Governor's assistant. I do think the Mayor will most likely be a pain. What do you think, Robert?"

"I think Alex is on target. There's nothing we can't handle here so we best get started."

Yvette nodded and eyed the group once again. They were an impressive bunch that included Jack's nemesis, the newly elected mayor of New Orleans, Anthony Devries, a mousy looking guy with an obvious comb-over; the special assistant to the Governor of Louisiana, Stuart Tansill; Commander Jack Francoise of the Eighth District, and Jack's boss, Theodore (Ted) Scott, the NOPD Police Commissioner who was in charge of and accountable for the security, safety and welfare of all of New Orleans' citizens and visitors to the city. Also included in the meeting were Elizabeth Tippett of CCMC media relations, Alex, Robert and Drs. Broderick and Smith from infectious disease from CCMC and Tulane. All of them looked expectantly to Yvette for answers. The mayor, however, only looked impatient and angry.

Yvette looked at her watch, cleared her throat, and began slowly. "Good afternoon. My name is Dr. Yvette Charmaine, and I am from the Center for Disease Control in Atlanta." She looked around the room and continued, "I have the pleasure of knowing several of you, Dr. Bonnet and Commander Francoise, as I am a New Orleans native and graduated from college at LSU. It is good to see some old friends in the group." Yvette smiled warmly at Robert and Jack. Both men responded in like manner.

Elizabeth and Alex glanced at each other and rolled their eyes, thinking again how small the medical world, and indeed the world at large, seemed to be in New Orleans. Just earlier this year they had learned that Jack, Robert, and Dr. Monique Desmonde had grown up together. Now, it was old home week again at CCMC.

Yvette continued in her clear, well-modulated voice. "I received a call this morning from your ED department about a viral outbreak and came up via helicopter from Atlanta to help you determine what was doing on."

She really doesn't sound like a native New Orleanian, Alex thought. *I wonder how she got rid of that telltale accent?*

The mayor held up his hand to stop her, but Dr. Charmaine continued, uninterrupted,

"Let me tell you a little bit about me and the Special Pathogens Branch of the CDC. The SPB works with hemorrhagic fever viruses that are classified as bio safety level four. These viruses are generally Ebola, Marburg, and Lassa. Sometimes, they are difficult to identify because they change and mutate constantly. Currently, we are treating three individuals with some type of a hemorrhagic virus."

"So, which virus do we have here," Elizabeth interjected, frantically taking notes. As media relations director for the hospital, Liz was responsible for all media statements, press releases, and responses to the press. Already news outlets had gotten wind of a potential catastrophe at the prestigious world-class hospital and TV vans, cameramen, and reporters were gathering outside the ED area.

"I don't know," Yvette said flatly. "I don't have any answers yet, but we are fairly certain we're looking at a viral hemorrhagic fever, or VHF, that has possibly mutated. I have not yet narrowed it down to a specific virus. Does everyone understand what hemorrhagic fever is?"

The mayor erupted, "I don't give a damn what it is, I just want to know when you and the CDC are going to fix stuff around here and get these people out of New Orleans. Do you realize the President of the United States, along with dozens of senators and congressmen, are arriving here today and over the next few days for the Operation Fix America political summit? We cannot have people dropping like flies from some sick, perverted disease probably caused by a monkey or something."

There was an audible gasp around the table. Alex was shocked, but Jack Francoise was absolutely furious. His face was suffused red with anger. It was a known fact to Jack's close friends that he and the mayor didn't really get along well. Frankly, they hated each other. Alex could literally see Jack's temper flaring up as she watched his eyes narrow and glitter. Robert, always the mediator, noticed it as well and intervened,

"Mr. Mayor, why not let Dr. Charmaine give us a report so we can all understand exactly where things stand now. We need for her to bring us up to speed." He gave the mayor a deprecating, yet challenging look. Only Robert could get by with such behavior because his family was so politically powerful in Louisiana. Alex gave Robert a furtive thumbs up and noted a ghost of a smile on Jack's face.

The mayor didn't respond verbally to Robert, but cut his eyes toward the CDC special pathogens leader and said, "Go ahead, Doctor. Tell us your plan." His voice was tinged with sarcasm.

Yvette Charmaine seemed unruffled by the mayor's rude behavior. Alex was amazed. Had Devries been that rude to her, she'd have jumped across the table and ripped out his carotid arteries. *What a jerk,* she thought to herself. Plus, he was gross with his slick baldhead and comb-over. His half-beard made him look like a rodent. She couldn't stand to look at him. How in the world had he been elected mayor of New Orleans.

Dr. Charmaine continued, "Viral hemorrhagic fevers are a group of illnesses that are caused by several distinct families of viruses. In general, the term 'viral hemorrhagic fever' is used to describe a severe, multisystem syndrome or simply said, a disease that can affect many parts of the body. It can cause major parts of the body to break down, like the heart, liver, kidneys, and so forth. The vascular, or blood vessel system is damaged, and the body's ability to regulate itself is impaired. These symptoms are often accompanied by hemorrhage or bleeding that can be very frightening but the bleeding itself is rarely life-threatening. What happens is that the walls of the tiny blood vessels become leaky and the patients may bleed from their mouth, eyes, ears or any other body openings," Dr. Charmaine added, noticing the look of confusion on the faces of several men in the room. Mayor Devries face was dark as thunder and he clearly wasn't up for a lecture in virology.

"How did this virus come to be at Crescent Center Medical Center? This is one of the finest hospitals in the world, and certainly the best hospital in New Orleans. I don't understand how this could have happened," persisted Mr. Tansill. "Also, can we catch it? I know the Governor is going to have hundreds of questions. In other words, what caused it?" Mr. Tansill's voice was hesitant. He was frightened. Alex didn't blame him. She was a bit frightened as well. She suspected they all were.

Dr. Smith from Tulane interjected, "Mr. Tansill, it is hard to know where the virus came from. These attacks occur all over the world at any given time. Sometimes they are devastatingly horrific, and at other times, they do little damage. Viruses causing hemorrhagic fever are generally transmitted to humans when humans come in contact with an infected reservoir host, such as mosquitoes or ticks. The virus can also be carried by rats, and house mice. The list is limitless."

Tim Smith grinned inwardly as he noted the incredulous looks on the faces of Mayor Devries and Stuart Tansill as he continued, "The virus can also be transferred to humans through urine, fecal matter, saliva, or other body excretions from infected rodents. For instance, a human can become infected when they crush a tick or pick up a mouse from a trap if secretions are spread to the human's hand."

Mayor Devries paled. Alex was sure he was thinking of all the roaches and enormous palmetto bugs that lived in the city. She smiled to herself. *Let 'em have it, Tim,* she thought as she cheered the Tulane doc on.

"Oh my God, any of us can get this! This is frightening," exclaimed Stuart Tansill, his voice moving up the scale toward hysterical. "I never knew. Why are we sitting in here when those sick people are only a short distance away. This is preposterous, unsafe even." He looked accusingly at Dr. Charmaine and added, "You could be infecting us now, correct?"

Alex sneaked a peek at the Mayor. He was pallid, visibly colorless. If she were honest, she'd have to admit that she was enjoying his discomfort. Devries was a pompous ass and she really didn't think he was very bright. He struck her as being very self-serving and not in the least concerned about the people of New Orleans.   She reminded herself that she probably needed to reel in the unkind, impatient side of her personality that often escaped when she was forced to tolerate people she really didn't want to. Her grandmother, Kathryn Rosseau Lee, of Virginia had coined it during Alex's childhood as 'the other Alex, or TOA,' that frequently escaped when Alex was frustrated, stressed, or just plain pissed off. Alexandra Lee Destephano, for better or worse, had inherited the intelligence, intolerance and impatience of her grandfather, Congressman Adam Patrick Lee. Fortunately, she had also inherited the grace, dignity, and kindness of her grandmother that counterbalanced her bad traits. All in all, she was a mixed bag.

For a fleeting moment, Alex felt homesick for her childhood home, her grandparents' horse farm in Hanover County, Virginia. *I always want to escape there when things are tough here* she thought to herself. *I want to go in the barn, sniff the hay and sweet feed and saddle up my horse, Dundee, and ride into the woods.* Yvette Charmaine's patient voice brought Alex back to reality.

Dr. Charmaine shook her head. "No, Mr. Tansill. Very much the opposite. Very few people who are exposed become ill. The virus has to get into your body through a cut, a sore, or some other portal that allows entry. It's not as desperate as it sounds. That's why we are so careful not to spread the infection. It is why all health care providers wear gloves, masks, gowns, and special air-pressure suits and are scrupulously careful when they care for these patients. The patients are isolated in two ED rooms and the utmost caution is used to prevent further outbreaks. If we need to expand, we can do so in the CCMC ED in other rooms. We are using the best science available and all of the protocols are being employed at this hospital."

"But there has to be more you can do," the mayor whined. "It's just not safe here and we have more than 100 politicians scheduled to arrive tonight for this weekend's summit. What am I supposed to tell people?" Alex was grossed out as she saw the mayor rearrange his comb over in an effort to control his anxiety. It was pretty yuk.

Robert was becoming impatient. He didn't have time for a bunch of droning politicians. As a matter of fact, Robert, from one of the most prominent democratic families in America, rued the fact that Devries represented his party in his own home town. He glared at Devries and snapped, "You're the Mayor, you figure it out. Now, let Dr. Charmaine continue and ... " Robert stopped for a moment and checked his cell phone. He had a text. "It looks like we may have two more potential cases. Dr. Patterson is in need of help. Would like one of you," Robert nodded to the infectious disease docs, "Tim or Dave - to come over and help him out in ED."

"I'll go right now," Dr. Broderick volunteered, making a beeline for the door. Robert knew he couldn't wait to get out of the meeting. Broderick, like Robert, had no need for whining, complaining, self-serving politicians. Besides, Dave Broderick was a staunch conservative and it probably frosted his ass that Devries was so ineffectual and incompetent.

Robert nodded, gesturing to Yvette and said, "Please continue."

Jack felt his cell vibrate in his pocket. He extracted it carefully and read the text. It was from his administrative assistant, Jason Aldridge, better known as Jack's right arm. *Fresh one in the Quarter. Need you* is what the text read. *Oh hell*, he thought, *We've actually gone almost a week without a murder in his District.* It was Thursday and he knew the weekend was going to be hell. A Thursday murder always predicted a hellish weekend. It never failed. He texted Jason back and said, *Will come when I can. Problems at CCMC. Who's lead* homicide? J.

Yvette felt they were getting nowhere fast and said briskly, "We currently have three cases, all housed in the makeshift isolation ward in the ED. We most likely will increase to five cases shortly if the two new admissions are positive for the virus. As you know, our first patient expired this morning. The patient in the ICU coded, but survived and we transferred him into our isolation unit."

"What are the symptoms of hemorrhagic viruses and how are they spread? I need some information for our press release and I want to be sure I am working within the CDC descriptions," Elizabeth asked. Alex nodded appreciatively at the lovely dark haired, young media relations director. Liz's network and skills had grown exponentially since her baptism by fire during Mardi Gras this past February. Alex predicted a career in Washington as a network correspondent was in the works for Elizabeth. She was well-respected, smart and highly regarded by the national and cable network correspondents. She'd also started writing as a guest correspondent for the *Times Picayune* and several papers were syndicating her column. Not bad for a media communications graduate only five years out of college. Of course, she did graduate from a Virginia school - Virginia Commonwealth University.

"Good question. Oftentimes signs and symptoms vary due to the type of the hemorrhagic virus, but initial signs and symptoms often include a high fever, fatigue, dizziness, muscle aches, loss of strength, and exhaustion. Patients with severe cases of VHF often show signs of bleeding under the skin, in internal organs, or from body orifices. This is what happened to your first patient earlier today. Severely ill patient cases may also show shock, nervous system malfunction, coma, delirium, and seizures. Some types of VHF are associated with kidney failure. All three of your cases here at CCMC are exhibiting some of these symptoms. Does this help you Elizabeth? I can offer you the CDC fact sheets on hemorrhagic viral disease if you would like," Dr. Charmaine offered kindly.

"That would be great. Thank you so much," said a visibly relieved Elizabeth.

"Have you been able to isolate our virus yet," Alex inquired.

Dr. Charmaine shook her head. "No, we have not. Our mobile lab is on the way here and we have been gathering samples on all three patients. We should have a response about Ebola by this evening as Ebola is easier to test for. Currently my assistant is data mining all of the information we have gathered. We still need to know more about the first victim, particularly his personal and travel history. We have gathered a fairly complete history about the other patients. The patient that survived in the ICU is from central Africa, Zaire, or the Congo and could potentially be the source of the outbreak although it is too soon to tell. He is a local food service worker. We are trying to locate people who know about him, how long he has been in the US and more personal information."

"Data mining? What does that mean?" questioned Stuart Tansill who was still freaked out and looking around like a germ might crawl up his arm at any moment.

"Data mining allows us to enter data in a statistical format that helps us look for patterns that can predict information to better define the outbreak. Many organizations data mine. For instance, the police data mine to predict crime patterns, marketing executive's data mine to market their services, and so on. We will create statistical charts, histograms and prediction models once we have completed our mining. Hopefully, this will help us identify the virus and control it. We are entering information about the patients, their travel history, health history, physical symptoms, and then try to predict a pattern of the organisms."

Elizabeth had a couple more questions. "Dr. Charmaine, how long can we expect this outbreak to continue? How long will we be getting in new patients? I know the newspapers are going to ask and I just need your opinion."

Yvette Charmaine looked apologetic. "I don't have an answer for that. It could end today or last much longer. I would simply suggest to the media that we are doing everything we can to isolate the virus and are hopeful it will be contained soon. That's the best information I have available."

"Well, that's just not good enough for me," Mayor Devries retorted in an angry voice. "Surely you have a better answer than that. How do you expect me to be able to protect my city and all of those politicians if you can't tell me when this mess will end?" Mayor Devries ranted. "You've got to have a better answer that that."

Alex was alarmed by the Mayor's disrespect and Robert looked ready to throttle him. Commander Francoise wanted to beat his ass, but that was pretty much what Jack wanted to do every day to Anthony Devries. Alex even noted that Jack's boss, Commissioner Ted Scott, was giving Mayor Devries the evil eye and looked ready to speak but the Mayor kept whining.

Commissioner Scott interrupted the peevish moaning of the mayor and said, "Mr. Mayor, I think the lady has told you everything she knows. We all have a lot of work to do. I suggest we close this meeting and get to it." The Commissioner looked around the table and noted heads nodding in agreement. He also noticed Alex had her hand raised. "Ms. Destephano, do you have another question?"

"Yes, and I agree with you, Commissioner. We all have work to do." She turned toward Dr. Charmaine and asked, "Is there an incubation period for these viruses?"

Yvette nodded, "Yes, the mean incubation period calculated currently for Ebola, and remember, we haven't determined this to be Ebola, is 12.7 days with a standard deviation of 4.3 days but can be as long as 25 days. I'm not saying this will be the case in New Orleans, but this is the best evidence we have on the cycle of Ebola. The incubation periods are similar for other hemorrhagic viruses. Just remember, we haven't isolated the virus yet. It could be different from Ebola or other hemorrhagic viral diseases." Yvette voice was cautionary.

An audible gasp emerged from the conference table as the participants considered the possible month of incubation and potential outbreak. The Mayor was outraged. "You cannot possibly think this degree of uncertainty can continue in New Orleans for a month. That is preposterous. You'll have to take care of it sooner. I demand it." Devries looked around wildly at each participant at the table.

Jack detected a glimmer of anger on Dr. Charmaine's face but she covered it quickly. He did however note the tell tale blush of annoyance creeping up Yvette's neck and he smiled. He'd seen her get mad and it really wasn't pretty. He'd known her older sister pretty well. The two of them used to antagonize the young Yvette in their youth and she would become furious with them. As Jack remembered, she was pretty spirited and had the vocabulary of a sailor. He was about to intervene, but Alex beat him to it.

"Mr. Mayor, certainly you understand Dr. Charmaine cannot actually 'control' how quickly the virus spreads, nor can she accurately predict how long this will last. Our immediate attention is centered on containing the virus and identifying exactly what kind of virus it is. I suggest we end this meeting and I assure you all we will send email updates as we have information. Any other questions?" Alex's voice signaled an end to the meeting.

Even though the Mayor was still flustered, he growled at the Police Commissioner Scott and ordered him to be in his office at five to review security for the weekend. After everyone finally left, Alex turned to Yvette and Robert and asked, "Well, Dr. Charmaine, welcome back to New Orleans. Has it changed much?"

Yvette laughed heartily shook her head, and asked, "Where in the hell did you all get that Mayor? He is a total idiot. I prefer our politicians crooked as opposed to stupid. You're going to have to keep me away from him or I'm liable to kill him!"

Robert chided her, "Now, Yvette, you know you haven't been gone that long. You know how colorful our local politicians are. Just remember back to Governor Huey P. Long to Edwin Edwards to Dutch & Mark Morial, just to name a few."

"Oh, I know. I remember very well," Yvette said throwing her head back and laughing. Alex loved her laugh Yvette Charmaine laughed with her entire body and it was an infectious laugh. Alex smiled as well.

Yvette continued, "My favorite political crook currently is former Mayor Ray Nagin, who campaigned against fraud and corruption and was just indicted on 21 counts of fraud, money laundering and wire tapping, and God knows what else."

"Unbelievable, isn't it." Alex commented, thinking about how honest the politicians were in Virginia compared to Louisiana. Well, most of them were honest. It had been something she had needed to get used to.

"Not really, I am beginning to think most of them are crooks. I sit in my office in Atlanta and I read the *Times Picayune* and I feel a bit home sick for corruption. Of course, you'll have all of those questionable politicians in the city in a few days. You're bringing them all from Washington to New Orleans. Way to go, right in the midst of a viral outbreak. Way to go, Bonnet," Yvette quipped.

Robert smiled at his old friend and touched her hand. "Yvette, we've got to be serious for a moment. Do you think we should step up security at the hospital, particularly in view of everything that is going on?"

All traces of fun and gaiety left Yvette Charmaine's face. She turned serious. "I absolutely think you should. And more than that, you must. By the way, do the two of you have a few extra minutes?"

Robert and Alex nodded just as Yvette's text alarm sounded. "We've got more trouble. Can I get back to you all shortly? Can we reconvene?"

"Of course," Robert and Alex said in unison. Robert continued, "I want your personal take on this, Yvette."

"Well, let me get back with you after I check in at the ED. However, I will be letting the Secretary know so she can inform the White House. The President needs to know of the danger here and that we don't know yet where it is coming from. Gotta go."

Robert and Alex and stared at each other, the stress evident on their faces.

Chapter 8

As New Orleans top cops Jack Francoise and Ted Scott left the hospital, the Commissioner admitted he was blown away by the Mayor's behavior. "Jack, what the hell is up with Devries? He was a total asshole in that meeting. I know he's a jerk, but he was at his absolute worst today."

Jack gave his boss a sly grin. "Why, Ted, Where's the surprise?" Jack answered in mock astonishment, "You know he's a SOB and every time he sees me, he's a bigger SOB. I think the sight of me raises his blood pressure 30 points," Jack added with some pride. "I work hard to piss him off. Why would he be any different today?"

Commissioner Scott laughed and said, His attitude was surprising to me. It was political stupidity on his part, possibly political suicide. There were a lot of very important people in that meeting. What do you think Stuart Tansill is going to tell the Governor? Tansill is pretty powerful. Some suspect he may be our next Governor. Did you see the look Tansill gave Devries?"

Jack was admiring how impressive Commissioner Scott looked in his dress blues. His brass and shoes were positively blinding in the October New Orleans sun. He shielded his eyes. "Damn, Commissioner, you could cut a rug all dressed up in your zoot suit. Your brass is hurting my eyes. Can you tone it down some?"

Scott smiled at the Commander. "You have one, too, Jack. Have you ever worn it?"

"Only at my big party, the night you all swore me in ... again." Jack rolled his eyes.

"Oh yeah, I remember, the celebration in your honor where you managed to attend for 11 minutes before you vanished, right?"

"That would be it, but don't worry, Commissioner, it's all spit shined and in my closet, ready to go. You know I hate crowds and shindigs," Jack added unnecessarily.

Ted Scott nodded tolerantly. "Yeah. Have known that forever. Now, what about Tansill?"

"Yeah, he's OK. But I think he's sort of an asshole too. I liked Andre Renou better, but of course, he's history."

Ted agreed. "For sure, he went the same way as Governor Raccine. Good man, Andre, but totally dedicated to the Raccine camp. It's a shame we are judged by the company we keep, right?"

"Yeah, how come you keep company with me?" Jack grunted.

"Beats me, Francoise," Scott joked. "Now, what do you think about Tansill?"

Jack thought for a moment. "As I said, he seems OK, but he's pestering the hell out of me about the murders of Beau LaMont and Hayes Hunter."

Commissioner Scott nodded. "Yeah. You and me, both. Plus, I get it every week from the Mayor. Are we getting anywhere, Jack?"

Jack gave an audible sigh. "No, sir. Not yet. Nothing. It's not for lack of trying. My guys have turned over the entire Vieux Carre and harassed the hell out of every crack addict and wino for miles around the scene. So have the feds who are involved because of Hayes Hunter, the Democratic Party Chairman. Nothing. It's just one of those murders, you know."

"Yeah, I know, but it is hard to believe it was purely random. Do you think it was?"

"Hell no! I absolutely do *not* think it was random. Just like I don't think those kids getting murdered in the wee hours of the same day in the same exact way was random. The perp is the same, no question."

As Commissioner Scott considered the possibilities he asked, "So, what do you think it means, Jack?"

Jack shrugged his shoulders. "I think someone is sending us a message. They are suggesting they can kill anyone - kids, punks, and nationally important people without leaving a single clue. They're getting by with it and will probably do it again. It is uncanny how clean the crime scenes were."

"Crimes were vicious, too. There has got to be someone who knows something somewhere."

"Yeah, you would think. But, they're not talking. Never fear, if they are out there, we'll get them. In the meantime, if they strike again, hopefully, they'll get careless and we'll get them on evidence at the scene, if not before."

"Good plan. Keep me in the loop. You know the Mayor's on my ass constantly as well?" "Huh, really? What a surprise. I was totally clueless that he was riding your tail too," Jack joked.

"The bastard ruins my week, every week. Driving me nuts, just as you'd imagine," Scott offered.

"No surprise there. Personally, I can't stand the man and I know you can't either but he's your first report. Just keep covering for me, Ted, and I promise you I won't kill the SOB."

"I'd appreciate that, Jack. I worked hard getting you your job, you know, the job you didn't want and I had to beg you to accept," Scott teased. "Don't want you to end up in Angola Prison. It would be bad for my reputation."

"Yeah, it would," Jack admitted. "In the meantime, I gotta go. I have a body down in the Quarter. First one this week and you know how I hate Thursday murders in the Quarter."

The Commissioner shook his head. "Well, all good things must end. Let me know what you find. Don't forget, we have that final security meeting about this weekend today at five downtown in our buddy's office. We've got to coordinate with the secret service."

"Oh my God," Jack sighed. "I hate working with the Feds. It's always a problem and they'll probably send some prick to be in charge. I'd like to miss that meeting for sure." He shook his head and continued, "Maybe we'll know more from CCMC by then because I am afraid this viral stuff could add another huge component to our current security plan. If there is any chance of terrorism, we're on a slippery slope."

Commissioner Scott groaned, "Yeah, I thought about that. Oh, I hope not but I've thought about it too. Hey, keep an open mind with the Feds, promise? Some of them are actually OK."

Jack nodded. "Yeah, yeah, yeah. I'll be there. Bells on. Good to see you, man. Next time, let's just meet at the bar and go drinking."

"Got it," Ted Scott waved as he left the health sciences center parking lot. *Francoise is a good man,* he thought. *Glad I pushed him into the job. Damn, I hope he is wrong about the stuff at CCMC. But...we'd better call the feds just to let them know what's going on. Some of the politicians are arriving as early as tomorrow.*

Chapter 9

Mohammed Abdu, the thick-bodied official leader of the Red Jihad cell in New York City slammed down his phone in anger. *Where was Nazir? Why wasn't he answering his phone.* It was critical for him to know what was happening in New Orleans. He had seen some blip about a virus in a hospital on CNN, and it bothered him. He'd never trusted the Russians. Never. He had experienced enough of their duplicity in Chechnya to last a lifetime. *The Russians hadn't changed a bit. They were always pandering to the enemy, sucking up and then pulling back. You could never trust them. Bastards.* Mohammed's thick frame tensed with anxiety as his powerful hand crushed a plastic glass in anger as he contemplated the situation at hand.

After some consideration, Mohammed dialed in the number of his second operation commander and lifelong friend, Omar Hassan, and barked into the phone, "As-salaam-u-alaykum. Come quickly. We may have problems."

A few seconds, later there was loud knocking at the temporary Brooklyn flat of Mohammed Abdu. Omar Hassan, a devout Muslim Jihadist of long standing, framed the doorway. A tall man with a long beard, Omar was an eminent professor of Middle Eastern History at a Brooklyn University where Mohammed Abdu taught Middle Eastern Religion. Both men had been under the watchful eye of the FBI, for years and they were aware of the scrutiny of government officials. In fact, they often laughed about it. Omar's eyes were gentle, but piercing, as he stared at Abdu, his own anxiety increasing as he studied the wild eyes and lined face of his good friend. Mohammed Abdu's anxiety was palpable and since he did not upset easily, Omar Hassan felt significant concern. Omar and Mohammed had been friends all of their lives. Both were members of a Russian Muslim Jihad group based out of a Russian region near Chechnya. Both had experienced and suffered from the horrific crimes of the Russians and deceit of the former Soviet government but had remained faithful to the Russian Muslim quest for Jihad. Omar had been a confidant of Osama bin Laden and his Al-Qaeda network and had participated in the planning and execution of the murders at the World Trade Center in New York in 2001. Mohammed Abdu had played a central part a few years later in the destruction of the U.S. embassies in Kenya and Tanzania. They had gloried in the deaths of over 3,000 Americans in New York, the destruction of US property all over the Middle East, and had celebrated the death of the American Ambassador to Libya. The duo had joyfully celebrated the Boston Marathon Bombings and more recently the work of the Red Jihad in Russia as they used suicide bombers to blow up a train station and other public transportation carriers.

"Assalaim-u-alaimuk. What is it, my brother? What is wrong?" The concern in Omar's voice was unmistakable as he addressed Mohammed. He could read his friend's body language and Mohammed's distress and angst were clearly displayed. Some terrorists were expert at reading body language and visual cues, and Omar was one of them.

"There is a virus at a hospital in New Orleans. I heard about it on the TV."

"A virus? What kind of virus? Our virus is not ready yet. How can this be?" Omar was confused and noted a sick feeling in his stomach. "Are you sure, Mohammed Abdu?"

"I don't know, I don't know," Mohammed Abdu replied with desperation in his voice. "It was not meant to be this soon, my brother. I am very troubled."

Omar nodded, his long beard moving up and down. "What of Nazir? What does he say?"

"Nothing. He is not answering his burn phone. I put in our code but I have tried and tried. Later, I sent a courier to look for Ali and him. I cannot reach either of them. I am bothered by this."

"Is it possible Ali perfected the virus and it has been released early?"

Mohammed Abdu shook his head. "No. Never. He was weeks, maybe months, away from perfecting what the Russians already have. It could be that Vadim has double crossed us."

"If that is true, it is bad for us because that would mean we have lost control of the mission." Omar Hassan's concern was etched onto his thin, ascetic, face, but his dark eyes remained calm.

"Yes, I know that. If so, our work here is done. I hope we are wrong," Mohammed lamented.

"I wish the same. We will see. Let me know. I must go," said Omar, looking back at a very apprehensive Mohammed Abdu. "Get some rest, my brother. We will know soon enough," Omar softly closed the door.

Mohammed Abdu repeatedly dialed Nazir's burn phone without success. Finally, he texted Ali's cell phone. He typed in his coded message but knew he probably wouldn't hear back. He'd had little to do with the younger brother of Nazir, but knew him to be an untouchable asset for the cell. The young man was a brilliant scientist and had managed to clone a virus that was practically endemic to New Orleans that the Russians had held for years. However, the other leaders had wanted another attack quickly, an attack in the United States to quickly follow the attack in Boston. *Another attack would show the war-mongering Zionists that terror was everywhere on American soil. Boston, New Orleans, San Francisco, Las Vegas. It would not stop until it was over. Praise to Allah.*

Judith Townsend Rocchiccioli

Chapter 10

The early afternoon traffic was bumper to bumper on Jefferson Avenue as Jack left the medical complex. A free-floating fear consumed Jack as he drummed his fingers on his padded steering wheel at a stop light. He'd felt his anxiety level escalate as he reviewed the situation at CCMC. A bioterrorism threat to an open city such as New Orleans only hours before a political convention could only mean major trouble. The person who had died had worked for the Democratic Party and the person in the intensive care unit worked at the hotel where many of the politicians were staying. They had both been at the same place. He picked up his cell phone and called Alex. She answered immediately

"Commander, I just left you. What's up? Jack could hear the smile in her voice. "You didn't kill the Mayor on the way out, did you?" she quipped.

"Nah, I wanted to but Ted wouldn't let me. Maybe later," Jack offered.

Alex smiled. *I love this man. He's a lot like my grandfather but different. He's made of good stuff.* "Good," she offered up. "I don't think you'd last long in Angola. You have a lot of enemies there."

"Funny, that's what the Commissioner said. Hey, I'm sitting in traffic and thinking. Do you have any idea what kind of work the guy did for the Democrats? You know, the political operative that passed away?"

"No idea, Why?" Alex's voice was worried and displayed her curiosity.

"I don't know exactly but I got real bad feelings about this bioterrorism threat over there. I just wondered if he was an aide or special assistant to some big political muck and if he could have been sought out to infect others, maybe as a warning to his boss."

Alex mulled over Jack's words. "Let me check it out and I'll get back with some specifics. Frankly, Jack, I'm worried too. Dr. Charmaine admitted to Robert and me that she is concerned about the rapid escalation of cases. We now have seven potential cases with three of them confirmed as viral hemorrhagic disease but the type is unspecified. The guy in the intensive care unit has taken a nosedive but they have managed to resuscitate him once again. It seems like his lungs are giving out. Dr. Charmaine isn't sure why. In fact, she's puzzled because it's not typical."

"Is it Ebola? Or does she know yet?"

"They're not sure. They should know soon. She is meeting with Robert and me in a little while when things calm down over there. CDC is sending in another physician by helicopter which makes me think they are looking for a big outbreak."

"Now, that's not good to hear, Alex. Keep me posted, will you?"

"Yeah, but I have to go. My grandfather is calling on my cell phone. He's probably having a fit because of the viral outbreak. He's due here tomorrow."

"Oh hell, he'll probably abduct you and take you home to Virginia. I'll wait to hear," Jack said, as he clicked off and began to search for a parking place.

Parking in the French Quarter was worse than usual. He couldn't find anywhere to park, legal or illegal. *What is happening down here?* Jack was getting agitated so he picked up his cell phone and speed dialed Jason.

Jason's voice was distant, controlled. Jack was immediately suspicious. "Commander, where are you?

"Searching for a parking place. But screw that. I'm just coming down. How's it going? You sound uptight as hell."

A large sigh on Jason's end of the phone confirmed Jack's supposition. "Yeah, it's tense. The State Police are here and they are calling in the FBI. Oh, and the Mayor is on his way," Jason Aldridge's voice was muffled, and Jack was having difficulty hearing due to background noise. "So," Jason continued, "it basically sucks down here."

"I'll be right down. Hang tight, dude." Jack cursed under his breath. It seemed like all hell was breaking loose.

Jack surveyed the police vehicles and obvious undercover vehicles around the scene. *Holy shit, what in the hell was going on?* Jack knew his blood pressure had just jumped 50 points. As he tripled parked and walked toward the scene, an ominous feeling and a sense of déjà vu overcame him. He knew what he would find before he ever saw it.

Jack walked another block until his anxiety overpowered him. Finally, he saw him. *Mary, Mother of God. It is exactly like before. The exact same location.* A well-dressed man was hanging upside down from an ornate wrought iron balcony. It was the same balcony. It was another hideous murder and it was unbelievable it was happening again. *This is too soon.* Generally, they had a little time between the murders. Sometimes months and oftentimes years. But not now, not today. *What the hell?*

His shoulders slumped in defeat and he was overcome with guilt and remorse. He was culpable. He was to blame. It was his fault the monster had struck again. He felt weak and dizzy and thought he would black out. Then he spied Jason and Detective Vern Bridges, the night detective who had been called in as well. This revived him for a moment until he was swamped by the press who pressed in on him and seemed to suck the last breath out of him. He moved quickly, before they pissed him off, and he felt revived from adrenalin flush.

"Commander Francoise, what can you tell us about this murder? What's going on? Why are the State Police involved? What's going on at CCMC? Is the dead man upside down? Will you be making a statement?"

Jack muttered, "No comment, no comment," repeatedly until has was rescued from the press by several uniformed officers and escorted inside the crime tape where he was hailed by Jason and Captain John Houser of the Criminal Division of the Louisiana State Police. Jack was pleased to see John Houser. The two were old friends.

Captain Houser pumped Jack's hand incessantly. "*Commander* Francoise, congratulations on your promotion. I heard they forced you into it. How's it going? What's it like to be a big cheese?" John Houser teased as he continued to pump Jack's hand endlessly.

In spite of current conditions, Jack gave John a big grin and said, "You tell me! You are the State Cheese. What the hell are you doing here? Can't you just take care of your part of the State? We'll handle New Orleans."

John Houser shook his head, "Hell no. The rest of the state is boring next to this hellhole. What's going on down here?"

Jack gave him a perplexing smile and retorted, "What the hell isn't. Let's go take a look," he suggested, gesturing toward the body that had been painstakingly and grotesquely wired to the balcony. "By the way, Vern, who is the victim?"

"You ain't gonna like this, Commander."

"Oh, shit, Vern, who is it?" Jack snapped, dreading the reply.

"It's a Republican Congressmen from Arizona. He is apparently the darling of the Republican Party. Name's Benjamin Blankenship. He came in town yesterday for the convention this weekend. Last seen mid-morning having coffee and beignets at Cafe du Monde. He was alone and reading the newspaper."

"What the hell, did anyone see him leave? He couldn't have vanished into thin air." Jack's voice was impatient and his temper was short. *Shit, a politician. This situation was getting out of hand.* He looked over at John Houser, grateful for his old friend's presence and help.

"Commander, we're checking. We're questioning every derelict we can find, every crack addict on the streets and everyone in the Congressman's traveling party. So far nothing." Vern's voice matched the impatience noted in Jack's voice.

"Who's he traveling with?"

"His aide and his wife. Also several political staffers. Wife's pretty torn up. Sedated at the Hotel Burgundy. Two little kids at home with their grandparents. This just sucks We've gotta find this son of a bitch."

Jack shook his head sadly. It was a hell of a way to die, much less to tell your children, even when they grew up. "We'll get him. It will take a little time, but we *will* get him. The bastard will screw up and we'll nail him. That's a promise," Jack pledged with more bravado than he felt. *Get back Jack had returned.* He had earned that nickname the hard way.

Vern Bridges shoved an evidence bag with a small piece of paper in it at him. "Commander, we found this on the victim."

Jack donned a glove and pulled the paper out of the bag. Jack read the note aloud. The threat was chilling.

"I'm back. Watch for me. I'm everyone you see and I am everywhere you go."

"What does that mean?" questioned Jason Aldridge.

"Exactly what is says," Jack replied. "The bastard isn't finished. He still has work to do. We'll get the son of a bitch." Jack ended on a ferocious note, was quiet for a moment, and then scratched his head as he put things together and said, "I don't like this. Somehow, this is turning out to be very political. LaMont, Hunter, and now this guy? We've got to figure this out. I am gonna ask for a special task force to study these murders. I want the state, the FBI, anybody that can help. The murders are politically motivated."

"Yeah, we need to discuss this at that security meeting this afternoon," Houser added.

"Houser, can you come to my office after we are done? I have a lot to catch you up on." Jack turned to Vern, "Get this note to forensics will you?"

"Yeah, man. Let's go check out the body," Vern suggested.

Jack didn't want to, but he did. He knew what he would find.

Even the beautiful, cool New Orleans day couldn't overcome the pall of the group reviewing the body strung over the railing. It was a gruesome and hideous sight. It was as if a dark cloud had blanketed and shrouded the blue sky from the team of police officers. Finally, Captain Houser spoke, "OK, gentlemen, I've seen some weird stuff in my time but I have never seen anyone with their throat slit from side to side with no blood at the crime scene. What's this all about? Also, why is the body upside down? Anybody have any idea what this means?"

After a moment Jack spoke. "The killer is a serial. We had four murders just like this in a 24-hour period less than two months ago. Two of them were Senator Beau LaMont and Hayes Hunter of the Democratic Party. The other two were just kids. In addition, we believe there are more. Potentially many, many more. There was a similar, almost identical case in 2009 and some in the 1980s. There are no clues, no murder weapons, no suspects, and very little evidence."

Captain Houser was thoughtful. "OK, but where is the blood? We do not know much at all, do we, but there should be some blood here. The cause of death is pretty obvious."

Vern responded, "There is no blood at these scenes. The victims die from exsanguination. They bleed out. The murderer bleeds them to death."

Houser hesitated and moment and scratched his head. "I understand that. But, let me ask again, where is the blood?"

Vern Bridges was exasperated. He was very short on sleep. His response was short and clipped. "We don't know. They are killed somewhere else, we have no clue where and then the bodies are always brought to this location. Sometimes they are hung upside down, just to be sure all the blood has come out. I am surmising that is what has happened here, once again."

Houser nodded, "Unbelievable. It's like a ghoul, a monster. Are you serious, no evidence, nothing?" He gave Jack and Bridges a look of disbelief.

Jack nodded. "That's right. We unofficially call them the St. Germaine murders."

Houser's face was blank. "What's St. Germaine. It's a place?"

"No, it's a man. Where the hell have you been? Jacques St. Germaine was an eighteenth century nobleman, purportedly a vampire, who allegedly still roams the streets of the French Quarter feasting on the blood of its residents...only now he seems to be feasting more on the blood of tourists."

Captain John Houser's jaw dropped with disbelief. He looked at Jack as though he was an idiot. "What? What in the hell are you talking about? Are you nuts?"

As Jack was about to answer, he heard the grating, whiny voice of Mayor Anthony Devries over his shoulder. For Jack, the sound was worse than fingernails scratching a chalkboard.

"Francoise, I *told* you to catch this man. What in the hell have you been doing?" The mayor's complaining, moaning, voice was more than Jack could handle. He was about to jump out of his skin. He couldn't tolerate the mayor for one more second.

The commander gave Jason a wild-eyed look and said to everyone, "I gotta get out of here. I just got out of a meeting with that sleazy combed-over son of a bitch an hour ago plus I have to see him again at 5:00. Jason, please update him for me."

"Francoise, do you hear me," the mayor intoned. "I am talking to you."

Jack faced Devries and said abruptly, "Office Aldridge will update you. I just received a call from CCMC and must leave." He turned to Captain Houser, "Meet me at my office on Royal ASAP."

Houser nodded and Commander Francoise ran toward his silver Cadillac with the speed of a 15-year-old kid. He jumped into his car with the prowess of an Olympic gymnast, roared out of his parking place and raced to his office on Royal. *I'll give Jason a gift certificate to Commander's Palace. Anything he wants for dealing with the mayor. Anything he wants. I just couldn't handle him again so soon...The whiny son of a bitch makes me crazy.*

..

Chapter 11

Alex clicked on her cell phone with a bright smile on her face and said, "Granddad, how are you?"

"Alexandra, what the hell is going on in that damn sin-infested hellhole city you insist on living in?" Congressman Adam Patrick Lee's voice literally roared into Alex's ear. His voice was so loud that Alex held the receiver away from her ear.

"And hello to you as well, Granddad. How are things in Virginia?" Alex asked pleasantly, attempting to relieve some of the stress in her grandfather's voice.

"Things in Virginia are fine. Things in Virginia are *always* fine. We don't live with cockroaches the size of automobiles, enough germs to infect the Mississippi River, or incompetent, elected officials who steal from their own citizens," Adam Lee spat into the phone. He smiled. His granddaughter was the light of his life. "Why you insist on living in that heathen hellhole is beyond me. You could be anywhere in the world but you choose that dump. It's beyond me."

"Be careful, Granddad, there's always a first time. Disaster is never far behind. Things in Virginia can go bad at any moment. When does your flight arrive tomorrow?" Alex's voice was cheerful, placating as she deftly changed the subject.

"What the hell is this I hear about some bad virus at the hospital? Your grandmother just heard it on CNN. They said the CDC was there. Is that true?"

Alex groaned inwardly. "CNN? What did they say?" *How did the news always find out information, most of it accurate, before the hospital issued a statement?*

Congressman Lee's impatience was explosive. "Exactly what I said, young lady. Now, stop stalling and spit it out. What the hell is going on at the damn hospital you work at?"

"Granddad, it's CCMC now. We're a premier hospital. Show some respect, will you." Alex admonished cheerfully.

"I don't give a damn if it is ABCDE or FART hospital. What is happening there? Do you have Ebola or something worse?" Adam was insistent and was getting angry. Adam Patrick Lee was a crusty old codger and used to getting his way. He had never been blessed with patience.

Alex sighed and said quietly, "We don't know and I didn't know it had been on CNN. Yes, the CDC is here and whatever it is, we have seven cases. The CDC is trying to isolate the virus and should know something by late afternoon."

Adam Lee was quiet for a moment and said, "You've got to get out of there. I won't have you there when there is such a danger. I will send a jet for you later this afternoon." Adam's voice was firm and final.

This time is was Alex who was angry. She hated that tone of finality in his voice and remembered it well from her rebellious teenage years. She retorted angrily, "Granddad, there is no way I am leaving New Orleans. If we have a viral outbreak, then we have one. I can't leave. Robert and I are the only administrators at the hospital and as the hospital legal counsel, I couldn't leave if I wanted to. I am not leaving New Orleans, not anytime soon." Alex's tone left no room for negotiation.

The Congressman was trying to be patient but he was used to getting his way. He was also incredibly stubborn. "Alexandra, this could be much worse than you think. This could be an act of bioterrorism in view of the political convention this weekend. Things could get much worse, violent in fact. You must leave. I demand it."

By this time, Alex was seething. "Granddad, you need to understand that I am not 8 years old anymore. I'm an adult and I have an adult job and adult responsibilities. Even if I wanted to leave, I wouldn't. If you want to blame me for my ethics and sense of responsibility, you'll have to look at yourself. It's been ingrained in me since I could walk." Alex was more than a little pissed and she knew he could tell by her voice. An angry silence followed.

"I told the old fool you wouldn't come home. I knew I was right. How are you darling?" Kathryn Rosseau Lee's voice was warm and soothing on the phone. Alex's spirits lifted at the sound of her warm, Southern drawl.

"Grand! I am fine. I promise you." Alex was thankful for her grandmother's intervention and understanding. Her grandmother was always there for her and possessed the wisdom she needed, and the comfort that she seemed to need a lot of these days. Alexandra Destephano's grandmother was her rock and her fortress in life. "Things here are complicated but we will get it all worked out. Please don't worry."

"Is Robert around?" Kathryn Rosseau Lee always asked about Robert Bonnet. She felt Alex was safe and cared for when Robert was close by.

"Yes, as a matter of fact, I just saw him. Believe it or not, the two of us are in charge of CCMC. All the other administrators are away. Scary, isn't it?" Alex joked.

Her grandfather grunted but her grandmother said, "I believe the hospital is safer than it has ever been. You two are a good pair."

Alex smiled into the phone. "I may need to call you for advice, Grand. Adam, when do you arrive? Are you staying at the Palm Court?"

"I have reservations at Hotel Burgundy, in the Quarter. I'll have a cab just drop me there."

Alex shivered with fright for a moment and asked, "Granddad, please stay at the Palm."

"No can do, Alex. My mentee, a young Congressman, needs to meet with me and we are both at the Hotel Burgundy. You know him. Ben Blankenship. He was here at the farm a few years ago. I'm supposed to teach him the political ropes," Congressman Lee's voice was firm.

"Granddad, please," Alex pleaded. "The first admission with the virus worked at the Hotel Burgundy. Can you get a reservation at Palm Court? Would you like me to check?"

Alex's grandmother intervened, "He'll be at the Palm Court, Alex, or he won't be at the convention. You can be sure of that. The old fool doesn't need to catch anything, much less a bad virus." Her voice was strong and decisive.

Adam Lee started to protest, but Alex could picture her grandmother glaring and waving her index finger at him. Alex interrupted and said, "Good. Have to go guys, I have another meeting. I love you."

"We love you too, Alex. Your grandfather will be at the Palm Court tomorrow afternoon."

"Got it, Grand. Love you, Bye."

"Bye, Alex," her grandparents said in unison.

Alex smiled and shook her head as she clicked off her cell phone. Would her grandfather ever realize she was grown up? *Probably not, her inner voice answered. And somehow that worked for her but sometimes it did make her mad.*

Chapter 12

Robert and Alex were ushered into the Emergency Department conference room by a fully garbed CDC nurse who had been friendly but either unwilling or unable to answer Alex's questions. Alex's best guess was that the CDC staffer was trained not to answer their questions. The nurse assured them that Dr. Charmaine would join them shortly. Alex looked around at the conference room. It was cluttered with crumpled papers and dirty cups. A large carafe of coffee and dried out fruit and doughnuts stood on the credenza at the far side of the room. The place was a mess and it was fast becoming her home away from home. She busied herself cleaning up and realized how much she missed her larger, beautifully appointed conference room in the legal counsel's suite with its well-stocked refrigerator and comfortable padded chairs. In comparison, the ED conference room was utilitarian and crowded. Besides, the chairs were dreadfully uncomfortable. She made a mental note to ask Sandy how to deal with the leftover food. She doubted housekeeping or dietary wanted to enter the ED area or that CDC regulations would even allow it.

After a few minutes, Yvette joined them with a container of iced tea, lemons, and three glasses with ice. Alex accepted, realizing for the first time that she had missed lunch. Her stomach growled. Yvette laughed and offered saltine crackers 'on the house.' Alex smiled, but declined, and the three got down to business. Dr. Charmaine put on her official CDC hat and began.

"Well, I do have some news – both good and bad. It's not totally Ebola, so that's the good news but the bad news is that we still don't know exactly what we are dealing with and that concerns me. Dr. Tim Smith from over at Tulane will be joining us in a few moments. He has a brilliant virology grad student who has been running permutations and predictive models and is helping us identify what we are working with.

Dr. Broderick has been working non-stop in the ED." Yvette shook her head and added, "Folks, I don't know what to tell you. We may be in for a long haul here."

Robert was listening carefully. "Yvette, have you ruled out Lassa and Marburg? Wouldn't those be the next two most logical viruses?"

Yvette shook her head. "No, Robert, not completely. I haven't ruled out anything except Ebola as the primary virus. Ebola is easy to test for and I have tested twice. It is definitely not Ebola. Whatever this thing is, it's not a totally hemorrhagic virus. There is a hemorrhagic component, but I think it is bigger than that. It doesn't appear purely hemorrhagic under electron microscopy. It's mutating quickly and that is alarming."

Alex interrupted, "Bigger? I don't understand, Yvette. I thought we were talking about a hemorrhagic virus. Has that changed?"

Dr. Charmaine shook her head. "No, Alex, not totally. My original thoughts and suspicions have just changed a bit."

The three turned toward the ED door as Dr. Tim Smith entered. He sat down, nodded at Alex, and gave Yvette a dispirited look.

"What's up, Tim?"

"Not good. Our first patient, the one in the ICU just died."

"From the virus, I suppose?" Robert asked.

"Indirectly, I presume. But it's strange. He developed an incredibly virulent pneumonia. He had a respiratory arrest earlier, we revived him, but then he coded again and once again we revived him. But, his lungs just gave up. Filled with fluid. His films and CT are suggestive of some type of pneumonia, but none of us has seen anything like it. The pneumonia appeared viral. It's important to note that the films were not clear. We'll have to wait for autopsy."

"Robert, who is your best forensic pathologist?" Yvette asked.

"Madeline Jeanfreau."

Yvette interrupted her voice incredulous. She hooked, "Maddy Jeanfreau is a pathologist? A medical examiner? Oh, wow, I didn't even know she was a physician! That's amazing!" Yvette's voice displayed her surprise as she turned to Alex. "Can you get her over to post this guy STAT? We have to isolate this lung virus."

Alex nodded. "I'll call. She reports to Jack Francoise because most of her work is criminal. Let me call over to the Coroner's office. I suppose, for containment reasons, she must come here, right?" Alex questioned as she went outside to make the call.

"Yes, Alexandra, absolutely. Tim, anything from the grad student?" Yvette was all business.

"Ali is working on some prediction models and slides. Hopefully, he will come up with something. He's the best I've seen at this. If we keep feeding him data, we'll get something."

Yvette nodded and turned to Robert. "We are under a bioterrorism attack. I need you to triple your security here at the hospital. We also need to call the NOPD for more manpower. We need stairwells locked, all staff easily identifiable, and all elective surgeries cancelled for fear of contamination. Also, be sure all radioactive materials are accounted for and under strict surveillance. I would recommend that you discharge or transfer all patients you possibly can in an effort to decrease traffic into and out of the hospital. Please be sure the parking lots are secure and all cameras are working properly. Have hospital security patrol them more often."

Robert nodded grimly. "OK, what else?"

Yvette continued, "I'm going to have to notify the Governor's office and ask for more help. I will ask him to involve the Louisiana National Guard. They can help secure the hospital along with CCMC security and local police."

Tim Smith shook his head, "Unbelievable. This is a medical center's worse nightmare." His voice was dour. Robert and Yvette nodded in agreement.

"This is anyone's worst nightmare," Robert added.

"Yeah, for sure and we need to be prepared for anything and everything. Things could go badly here at a moment's notice," Yvette added bleakly as Alex returned to the conference room.

Yvette questioned her, "Is Dr. Jeanfreau available?"

Alex nodded. "She'll be here in several hours. She'll come over here to CCMC. Robert, Yvette, Tim, I had to talk with Jack to free Maddy up. She's pretty busy." Alex hesitated for a moment.

Robert knew Alex well and asked, "What else, Alex? I can tell there's more by your face."

"Yes, there is. We have another problem," Alex announced, and gave the trio a depressing look. "Jack will be here soon but he told me to alert you in case he got tied up."

"What the hell else could go wrong? Dr. Charmaine just declared us to be under a bioterrorism attack. We're calling the Governor and he's sending in the National Guard, so what else could be worse?" Tim Smith was emotional. In fact, Alex thought he sounded pissed.

She turned to Tim, "Dr. Smith, you are going to be sorry you agreed to help us and left Tulane Medical ..."

"Alex, what is it," Robert persisted. He knew she was stalling.

"Another murder in the Quarter. It was a Republican this time. Another gruesome murder. He was killed just like Senator Beau LaMont and Hayes Hunter. It was a young Congressman traveling with his wife and aides."

Yvette Charmaine digested this information, turned to the others and said, "While I was in Atlanta, I read about the murders of Senator Lamont and Hayes Hunter. They were horrific, brutal. I'll have to report this. We may have more than a virus problem in New Orleans. It seems to be that someone is after politicians as well. There are too many coincidences to be ignored."

The others nodded as Dr. Charmaine left to call her offices in Atlanta and Washington, and the Governor's office in Baton Rouge. Seconds after she left, Sandy Pilsner entered and alerted them to three additional admissions to the ED. "They all have the same symptoms and two are political operatives. What is happening here?" Sandy was grey with fatigue and the fear was etched into her aging face. She continued,"Dr. Bonnet, Dr. Smith. Can you help? We are swamped. These folks are really sick and the staff are getting tired. The care is just so complex and intense," Sandy added, her voice emotional. She looked scared and frazzled.

Alex's heart sank when she saw Sandy's anxiety. Sandy was a tough old goat and she was freaked. What could this possibly mean for all of them? In a moment of honest reflection, she wasn't sure she wanted to know. She sighed as Robert and Tim left the conference room and stared into her iced tea glass. *I'm terrified! How is this going to end? Please, God, help us get through the next few days."*

CHAPTER 13

"Alex, what are you doing? Where have you been? I have been looking for you all day! How come you aren't answering your cell phone or texts?" Bridgett was grouchy and clearly irritated with her boss as she pushed long, blonde curls behind her ears to show off her long, orange and hot pink dangling chandelier earrings.

Alex couldn't help but grin at Bridgett, her beautiful, blue-eyed bombshell of a secretary, or administrative assistant as Bridgett now preferred to be called. Noting that Bridgett was obviously displeased with her, Alex decided to diffuse her anger.

She gave her a big smile and said, "Whoa, Bridge, you look really, well, really... bright. You know, your eyes are so much more blue when you're mad at me and where in the world did you get that orange dress and those hot pink heels?"

It was working. Bridgett's eyes were sending fewer daggers and there was a half smile on her face. Alex continued, "And that jewelry is stunning. You could direct traffic in that outfit, but, on second thought everyone would probably wreck looking at you."

"Are you kidding me, Alex, or what. It'd be best not to make me any madder," Bridgett warned, her temper obviously short, but her smile was widening.

"No, Bridgett, truthfully, you look magnificent. No one else could carry off orange and hot pink. How in the world do you put your outfits together? Where do you get this stuff?" Alex couldn't help but admire how amazing the outfit was for Bridgett. The orange sheath was perfect for Bridge's tall, statuesque figure and fit her like a glove. The jewelry was perfect for the dress. The necklace was three strands of orange and pink glass pearls, dyed howlite and crystals. It was beautiful on Bridgett's perfect skin. She looked flawless.

"Well," Bridgett puffed up and said, "I sure don't shop at those boring stores like you. I'd rather be gagged than have to shop at Ann Taylor and Victoria's Uptown. Besides, those stores are way above my budget. I got this outfit at Dressed to Kill over on Dauphine. I forgot where I got the shoes, but they do match perfectly." To prove her point, Bridge lifted her long leg up for Alex to survey them better.

"I have to hand it to you, Bridge. They are perfect. You're perfect. Your lipstick and nails even match."

"Check these out, Alex," Bridgett said, obviously pleased. "See, my toes. They have little pink stars on them." Bridgett easily slipped out of her four-inch heels and held her leg with perfectly painted pink toenails up for Alex to view.

Alex was amused as Bridgett revealed her foot. *How fun,* she thought. Sure enough, they were painted bright pink and had orange stars all over them. "Wow," was all Alex could muster.

Bridgett gave Alex a bright, dazzling smile. "You know, Alex, if you would like, one day we could go shopping. I could show you all the good places and we could brighten you up for sure. You know, get you some good stuff. Great clothes, not boring like all of those tailored clothes you wear all the time. I know where all the deals are too," Bridgett volunteered as she critically appraised Alex's conservative navy blue silk suit, white blouse and very proper pearls. "I could fix you right on up! I could take you to my nail shop and we could get you some great nail color," Bridgett added, delighted at the prospect. "You know, there's more to life than French manicures. You'd be surprised at what I could come up with!"

Alex laughed, "No, Bridge, I wouldn't be surprised. You know, we'll have to do that. It would be fun. Just know that I can't come to work in an orange dress and chandelier earrings like you. Don would have a duck fit."

Bridgett rolled her huge, blue eyes. "Forget Don Montgomery. He's a pain in the patooty. By the way, he's phoned for you several times from wherever he is in the Caribbean. Said something about something on TV. I told him I'd have you call back. So, will you please do it? I don't want to have to talk to him again today," Bridgett groaned as she handed Alex a fistful of messages.

Alex's face soured. "I guess I'll call him but I'd rather not. Anything else," she questioned as she moved toward her office.

"Nope, but I'm leaving shortly. Got to go shopping." Bridgett's blue eyes danced as she glanced over her shoulder. "Angela is going with me. We're hitting the sales at Dillard's."

Alex immediately felt jealous. She wished she were going shopping and not managing a viral outbreak. Bridgett's simple life was looking pretty good right now. "Great, how's Angie?"

"She's doing super well. Almost back to her old self. She should return to the ICU next month."

"Wow, that's wonderful, Bridgett. I am so happy for all of you. We've all come a long way," Alex added, remembering how Bridgett's twin sister, Angela, a CCMC nurse had been brutalized several months ago. What a nightmare all of that had been. "I'm going into my office to catch up and call Don."

Bridgett made a face, her blonde curls dancing around her face. "Yuk. Lucky you. OK, I'll see you tomorrow. Have a great night," Bridgett gushed, back to her happy, cheerful, wonderful self. Alex said a prayer that things were back to normal in Bridgett's family. Bridge was the best, she was her friend and the best secretary ever. She couldn't imagine existing at CCMC without her fun-loving secretary.

"You too, Bridgett," Alex said happily as she closed her office door and settled into her luxurious desk chair that fit her body perfectly. She dialed Don's phone number and was instantly barraged with a dozen questions from CCMC's irascible, self-centered, and petulant chief executive officer.

"Destephano, what the hell is going on there. It's been all over CNN and network TV that you have some sort of a bad viral disease in the ED. I can't leave for one week that things don't go to hell there without me and Bette Farve. What are you doing about all of this?" Don's voice was snappish and grumpy.

Alex rolled her eyes, put the phone on speaker and placed it on her desk while Don continued to bitch, gripe and grumble about how he could never take a vacation and trust "his" hospital to anyone because everybody there, Alex included, was incompetent, except for him, and blah, blah, blah. For a moment Alex considered hanging up on him, telling him she dropped the call and it must be his phone but decided against it. She'd have to talk to him sometime so she might as well get it over with. Finally, he quieted down and demanded an update.

"Well, we are having a problem in the ED."

"Well spit it out. I don't have all day. I'm on vacation, remember?" Don was complaining again, truly a pain in Alex's ass. She decided to do just that.

"We have a virus. It's not Ebola, and it's still unidentified. The CDC is here and we are working on it. Things are under control."

Don was ready to get off the phone. "OK. Call me but only if it is absolutely necessary. If you and Bonnet can't figure it out, then I guess it's worth a call to me. But remember, I hired you to be competent," Don replied, his voice sneering.

Alex said nothing else and offered no other information. She had told the truth as he had asked. She just wanted to hang up. "I'll call if I need you, Don. I won't bother you unless there is no other way," Alex promised as she heard him ordering rum punch specials and fresh fruit for two on the background. She swore there'd never be a reason she would call him.

"OK." Don clicked off, CCMC out of his mind for at least four more days. Alex was delighted but only for an instant when her cell phone rang and she noticed her grandfather's number on the display.

"Granddad, what's up?" Alex's voice was curious. It was very unusual for her grandfather to call her twice in one day.

Alex heard a strangled sob on the other end. She became alarmed. "Granddad, please speak to me. Are you OK?"

After a few seconds, Congressman Lee composed himself and said, "It's about Ben Blankenship. He's my friend. He's like a son to me. New Orleans killed him. He's dead."

Alex was confused. "What, who? I don't know who or what you are talking about. Who is Ben Blankenship? I am sorry, granddad. I don't have a clue."

"Congressman Benjamin Blankenship. The young congressman from Arizona. He was murdered in the French Quarter. Just several hours ago. I thought you would know."

"Oh Granddad, I am so sorry. I did know about the murder, but I didn't know who it was. I am so sorry. So very sorry. Ben is the young man you call your adopted son, right? What can I do to help you?"

"Nothing, Alexandra. Nothing. Ben was like a son to me. I have been grooming him in Congress. He and his wife Beth were here at the farm for July 4th. They have two little children. Beautiful children, 7 and 5 years old. They lived in our swimming pool for three days. Such wonderful children, so well behaved. Your grandmother and I are devastated."

Kathryn Lee spoke for the first time, "Alex, you know the Blankenships. You met them here at Wyndley two years ago at Christmas just after he had been elected. Remember, it snowed and you grandfather got into the White Lightening and thought he was going to die the next day."

"Oh my God, Grand. Oh, no. What a wonderful family. This is so tragic. Of course I remember them." Alex was stunned with the news.

"Yes, Alexandra, I thought you would, " her grandmother replied.

"I remember them well. I envied them for their love and devotion to each other. I was really lonely for Robert then and wanted a family just like that," Alex said as she remembered the handsome, square-jawed, all-American guy and his lovely, demure brunette wife. She recalled he had been some kind of American hero but then most of her granddad's friends were. She especially recalled the two tow-headed children to whom she had read *The Night Before Christmas* at least a dozen times during their visit. Her mind flickered back to the Christmas Carol sing when her grandfather had placed the little girl on the grand piano while her grandmother had played *Frosty the Snowman* and the little boy had sat beside her grandmother on the piano bench where Alex had sat for years and years singing the same songs. It would have been a perfect Christmas that year except that Alex was so lonely and it was the first

Christmas after her split from Robert. It was just before she moved to New Orleans. And now, the handsome, young congressman was dead, leaving a lovely wife and two little children. How sad and unbelievable. Alex could feel her chest constrict.

"I am coming with your grandfather tomorrow to be with Beth. Her parents are deceased and Ben's mother has the children. She is alone in New Orleans and I am sure very frightened. If you have time to call her or stop by the Hotel Burgundy to see her, it would mean a lot to me. I know things are crazy at the hospital, but if you could, " Kathryn's voice faded out and Alex could hear a sob.

"I will go there now, Grand. I will call you back after I see her. I would take her to my home if we didn't have the crises at the hospital. Maybe I will anyway."

Adam Lee interjected. "She needs to be with Ben's aides. They are overcome with grief as well. We will be there tomorrow. We will move all of them to the Palm Court with us."

"Granddad, you are all welcome to stay at my home. You know that. I have lots of room."

"Thanks, Alex but we need to be with the other Congressmen and our friends. Ben Blankenship is a huge loss to America. Decorated war veteran, Iraq, Army Ranger, hero, perfect. My party was grooming him for great things. It's tragic for all of us. Many called him the hope of America." Alex could imagine the grief stricken, tearful, lined face of her grandfather. She wanted to reach out and hug him and tell him things would be all right. Just like he'd always done for her. She heard another stifled sob.

"I know, Granddad. I am so sorry and I'm distressed. Will you please call Beth and tell her I am coming and let me know what you need."

"One more thing, Alex. Could you ask Jack Francoise to release the body as soon as possible? I know Beth will want to take him home as soon as she can." Adam Lee had recovered some of his usual "take command" control.

"I'll try Granddad, but it may be hard."

"Why?"

Alex was slow to respond. "Well," Alex was having difficulty telling her grandparents how their friend had died.

"What, Alex, what the hell. What is going on?" Adam Lee's voice thundered. He was distressed, irritated, and impatient. Not a good combination.

Alex sighed and said, "I spoke to Jack briefly, but there is some thought that the murder may have been politically motivated. It was similar to the killings of Senator LaMont and Mr. Hunter several months ago."

"Oh my God. Sweet Jesus. He died like they did?" Adam Lee's voice was barely a whisper. Alex wanted to reach out and hug her granddad. She could hear the torment and despair in his voice.

"I'm afraid so, Granddad. That was what Jack said, but our conversation was brief. I will see him later this evening."

"What about these killings? What's different about them?" Kathryn Lee asked.

Alex spoke quickly, "They were particularly brutal, angry, like the killer had an agenda. I can tell you more when you get here and I know more. I love you both. I will go see Beth."

"Thanks, Alex. I love you. See you tomorrow," her grandmother's voice was soft.

"Bye, Grand. Granddad, are you OK."

"Yes, Alex, I am. At least I think so." The anguish in his voice was heartbreaking.

"I love you Granddad and I'll see you tomorrow." Alex knew he wasn't OK but there was nothing she could do. She was worried about both of them. At their age, information such as this was crippling, stressful, and demoralizing. She was concerned for both of their health. Alex knew she would have to return to Virginia soon. She just hadn't been able to figure out how to do it.

Alex felt her own despair mounting as she considered the congressman's death. Her heart was heavy as she called for Martin, her faithful cab driver to take her over to the Hotel Burgundy to see Beth Blankenship. She had tears in her eyes as she left the hospital and noticed the guards at the doors and the NOPD police presence all around the medical center. The parking circle was loaded with press and media vehicles and several reporters ran toward her barking questions when they saw her. Their presence just depressed her further. She waved them away, and repeated the standard, "no comment, no comment" as she returned to the hospital foyer to escape their questions.

Chapter 14

Traffic in the circle of the CCMC pickup/discharge area was brisk. Alex checked her watch. It was a little after four in the afternoon and despite her sadness, she was appreciating the beautiful October afternoon as she sat on a bench and watched the TV and media teams in action. As she waited for Martin's Cab to pick her up, she observed a nurse assisting an elderly lady from a wheelchair into her son's car, she was reminiscent of the days when she was in clinical practice. Boy, she missed it. Alex was a caring and nurturing person and she had loved taking care of her patients. Alex continued to think back to her earlier years. Life had seemed so much simpler then. She had been working at the University of Virginia Hospital in Charlottesville and dating Robert. How wonderful life had been then. It was just before her miscarriage and prior to her decision to go to law school and their marriage was perfect. Of course, a year later, things began to fall apart. She shook off her gloom and faked a smile for Martin who had just pulled up to the curve.

"Mz. Alex. What's goin' on here?" Martin looked around and shook his head. "Ain't never a dull moment here at de hospital is they? Whatcha got now? Gangsters, crazy people, sickos? Cars are backed a mile, especially the TV trucks. Why is all these police here? And all them TV trucks," Martin demanded as he opened the door for Alex.

"Well, we have...."

Martin interrupted her, not uncommon for him. "Guess it can't be too bad if you is leaving, right Mz. Alex?" Martin looked proud of himself for deducing that fact.

Alex smiled and nodded. Martin was authentic Cajun, right down to his black and orange 'Who's Your Crawdaddy' t-shirt, black jeans, and the alligator boots he was sporting. He was a memorable character and took pride in telling tourist's coming to the Crescent City all about his ancestors and the history of Naw'lins. Martin had been good to Alex over the years, teaching her much about New Orleans culture, both the positive and negative aspects. Martin knew everybody and he was a good man to know. His cab company was one of the largest, and certainly the most honest cabby fleet around. He also knew ways to get around the crowded city and of back streets that Alex couldn't have known had she been born in New Orleans. Martin's only vice was playing the roulette tables at the Casino out in Kenner where he lived. He and his wife Carla went every Wednesday night for the free buffet and a hard night of gambling. Mrs. Martin loved the slots, and confided to Alex that she lived for Wednesdays and sometime visited the Casino after Mass on Saturday evening. Alex suspected that she went a lot more often than that but never brought that up to Martin.

"Yeah, not too bad. At least not yet. We have some folks in with a virus, a really bad one, and several have died."

"That ain't good. Is it de tourists spreading germs or what?" Martin never believed any illness or disease or germ could originate in New Orleans - not even after all the sickness caused by Katrina. He was always suspicious of tourists "bringing in stuff."

Alex smiled. "Maybe. A food service worker passed away and then a couple of the political types that are coming in for the political meeting this weekend."

"Damn, I hate all 'dem worthless shitheads from DC. They have screwed everything up." He turned and gave Alex a sheepish look. "Sorry, Mz. Alex. I apologize for my language."

"It's OK. Anyway, it should be OK. The Feds sent in some experts and they are doing OK."

"The Federal Government. Oh, great. That makes me feel so much better. Goin' home?" It was easy to detect the sarcasm in Martin's voice. "I cannot believe we gotta put up with all 'dem sons of beeches this weekend. They're all coming to Naw'lins' to fix America? Figure that. Can't they do that in Washington, DC so we don't have to pay for them to come here and mess up stuff? I just don't unnerstand it." Alex had never had a political discussion with Martin and decided that she never would.

"No. I need to go to the Hotel Burgundy. To see an old friend. Her husband was killed today in the Quarter. Very sad. I am dreading the visit."

Martin stared at her. "Oh, that political guy? Yeah. I heard 'bout him. Bad, bad, bad. Whoever's killin' all these peoples is bad. Commander Jack's gotta get him. Gettin' way out of hand." Martin shook his head and repeated,' bad, bad, bad' over and over again. He continued, "You know it's the Comte, right? He usually just kills a few and leaves for a while."

"Huh, I know nothing about a Comte. You mean a Comte like a French nobleman?" Alex was surprised.

Martin nodded. "Yeah, the Comte St. Germaine. You know."

Alex gave him a blank stare with her mind really not on the subject, "Who, huh?" She was barely listening, thinking about the ordeal ahead of her.

Martin gaped at her and said, "I can't believe this. Do you mean you don't know about him?"

Alex shook her head. "No, I don't, but I'm sure Commander Francoise is doing his best to get him. I'd imagine they have a whole bunch of people working on it. They'll get him. Soon, I hope."

Martin shook his head. "I wouldn't be so sure. Rumor has it he's been killing for years. Hundreds of people are dead 'cuz of him," Martin said, his voice positive, adamant.

Alex was bewildered. She was really lost in the conversation. "Martin, what are you talking about? I didn't even know they had a suspect."

"Comte's been a suspect for years. I'll tell you about him later," Martin promised as he pulled up to the Hotel Burgundy. "Good luck in there. Lots of cops around."

"Thanks. I'll need some luck and wisdom. This will be hard. Put this on my tab?" Alex gave Martin a thin smile. "Pick me up in an hour and take me back to CCMC?"

"Always, Mz. Alex. We gotta deal. Be careful now, ya hear," Martin admonished as he pulled out into traffic without looking.

Alex shook her head and refocused as she entered the brass plated hotel doors. As her eyes adjusted to the dimness of the hotel foyer, she was approached by a clean cut, handsome man in a dark suit who asked for her credentials. Alex pegged him for FBI. She was correct. He identified himself as an FBI Special Agent.

"I'm Alexandra Destephano and I am here to see Mrs. Blankenship. I believe she is expecting me," Alex said, her voice hushed.

The man nodded and said, "Yes, she is. Follow me."

The agent accompanied Alex to the elevator and pushed the button for her. On the third floor, another good-looking man greeted her at the elevator and said, "Ms. Destephano, Mrs.

Blankenship is in her room. I'll get her. She has been waiting for you."

Alex murmured thanks and choose a seat on a sofa in the suite's living room. She chided herself for thinking how hot both of the FBI dudes were. Probably married, she thought. Everyone was these days except, a little voice reminded her, Robert. Alex forced herself to change the subject. She looked around the suite. The room was well appointed and Alex wished she were there for a drink rather than visiting the widow of the most promising young man in Congress. This wasn't going to be easy. She wished her grandmother were already here.

Beth Blankenship was tear-stained, but composed as she emerged from her bedroom and hugged Alex tightly. She wore jeans, short boots, and a cashmere sweater. Her dark hair was pulled back in a ponytail. "Oh, Alex, thank you so much for coming. It is wonderful to see you. Your grandmother called and told me you would be here this afternoon. I so appreciate it. I am so lonely."

As Beth sat down next to her, Alex took her hand and their eyes meet. Beth's eyes were empty, hollow, and tortured. "Beth, what can I do for you," she asked. "Is there anyone I can call or anything I can get."

Beth's composure left her and she dissolved into sobs, her petite body racked by the intensity of her grief. Alex hugged her as she gulped, "What am I to do without Ben? He was my life, my love, my best friend. What am I to tell the children? Alex, please help me make sense of this! What I need for you to do, Alex, is help me keep it together here in New Orleans until I can get home. I must keep my composure and not be a blubbering idiot like I am now."

As Beth's weeping continued, Alex held her tightly. There was nothing she could say, nothing at all. There were no words. Only time would lessen this pain. And then, only partially. This woman's life, the lives of her children, and most likely the history of the United States had been altered today because of the wickedness, cruelty, and immorality of one man.

"I'll help you Beth, I'll help you all I can," Alex promised as she held the thin, shaking shoulders of the new widow. Alex prayed for strength for Beth for the months ahead. As Beth's tears subsided, the two women sat and talked quietly.

Chapter 15

Commander Jack Francoise dawdled in his office on Royal Street, doing the best he could to piss away time. He had a ton of stuff to do but was blocked on all sides. He'd phoned Maddy Jeanfreau three times and had been told politely each time that she was still in autopsy and would return his call. He had driven his homicide detectives to the brink of murdering him and the crime lab wasn't taking his calls because he had called and barked up their ass too many times in one day. In fact, nobody wanted to talk to him, not even Monique. She had begged him to leave her alone to nap after their second conversation, which he had grudgingly agreed to do. To top it all off, Alex hadn't answered his phone call or his texts and he really needed her and Robert at the late afternoon security meeting. Robert had agreed to track her down. *What the hell*, he asked himself. *What's a police commander to do when no one will talk to him? How the hell could he be effective, get stuff done, catch the bad guys? This was crap.*

In truth, Jack was on his pity pot. He didn't want to go to the security briefing at the Mayor's Office because he couldn't stand the Mayor and didn't want to put up with his droning and incompetence, particularly in front of the Secret Service and God knew what other Federalas. And, he didn't want anyone else telling him what to do in his city, particularly on his beat. Finally, the anticipated knock at the door and Jack grunted an impatient "Come in."

John Houser from the State Police Criminal Division and Jason Aldridge motioned for Jack to join them. Houser smiled broadly at Jack and quipped, "Time to go, Commander. There's no way you can get out of this. The President and all of his men are coming to your Precinct and we're gonna have to make nice with them for the next three days, at least and hope nothing happens."

Jack grunted and gave Houser a dirty look.

Jason grinned at his boss and said, "Sorry, Commander, I couldn't get you out of this meeting. There was just no way. If you like, I'll listen and take notes if you'll just behave."

Jack gave Jason a dirty look as he proceeded out of the door and growled. "Make sure you do. I'll do my best to control myself but you know I hate others telling me what to do," he grumbled to whoever would listen. John Houser laughed and clapped him on the back.

"Jack, it'll be OK. We're meeting Ted there. Specifically, you'll be OK because Ted Scott, *your* boss, has a syringe with a 4-inch-needle with *your* name on it that is filled with a powerful horse sedative. He fully plans to use it if you misbehave."

Jack grinned, but looked a little crazy as Jason added, "That's truth Commissioner, and the worst part is that the horse shot makes you drool." Both men burst into laughter and continued their banter on the short walk to City Hall as Jack stared stonily ahead, dreading a meeting room full of Feds.

Perdido Street was lined with the requisite mid-sized coupes, SUVs, and minivans which Jack knew were specially equipped government vehicles. He also noted SWAT vans parked in the circle. Traffic was jammed around City Hall, the 1950s structure on Perdido and the area was buzzing with media and pedestrian traffic. Security was tight and the entrance to City Hall was virtually obstructed. Just recently, city officials had announced their plans to rehab the Hotel Dieu or the Old Charity Hospital and use it for City Hall and the new Courts Building. The old hospital, a national landmark, had over a million square feet and had only sustained flooding in the basement area during Hurricane Katrina. Jack looked over at the old building, the former "free" hospital that had cared for millions of people over the years. It'd be good to see the place alive again, even if it was going to cost millions of dollars. The Old Charity Hospital had done more for Orleans Parish than perhaps anything else. Jack spied a NOPD officer who waved them through the police barricades surrounding the building.

Police Commissioner Ted Scott met the trio inside the double doors. The place was on a virtual lock-down. He gave John Houser a firm handshake and said, "Hey John, heard you were on the list. Glad to have you since there is some speculation that our French Quarter murders and the threat over at CCMC are possibly related." He nodded to Jason and then turned to Jack and asked, "You ready for this, Commander?" What the Commissioner was really asking was whether Jack was going to behave himself or revert to his obstinate, stubborn behavior.

Jack grunted and said, "Yeah, heard about the horse shot shit so I guess I'll try to keep it down. Not like I have a choice, right?"

"Right. Are the hospital people coming?"

"I know Dr. Bonnet will be here. I haven't heard back from Ms. Destephano. Also Dr. Yvette Charmaine, the CDC lady doctor. Both of them are incommunicado at the present, or at least they won't answer my calls," Jack joked.

Ted Scott nodded and grinned, "I try not to answer your calls either, Jack. It generally means you want me to do something. On another note, Alexandra Destephano's grandfather asked her to spend some time with Beth Blankenship, Congressman Blankenship's widow. Apparently, they are family friends. I've spoken with Congressman Lee twice this afternoon. He's devastated by the murder. Congressman Blankenship was his protégé and I think he wants us to be sure nothing happens to Beth or Alexandra," Commissioner Scott offered.

Oh shit, Jack thought. In a low, sardonic voice he said, "Great, now we'll have Mayor Devries, Congressman Adam Patrick Lee, the FBI, and the Secret Service barking up our asses. It just couldn't get any better, could it?" *Actually, it was getting interesting*, Jack thought.

John laughed and said, "Congressman Lee's pretty good. He's one of the few law and order politicians left. I've great respect for him. I'll take his flack and I'll watch his back. No problem."

Ted and Jason nodded as Jack added, "Yeah, he's one of the best, old school, but you can bet your next kid that he won't leave us alone until we find who killed his friend. That's a given."

"Well, hell, we'll just have to do it since we're planning to find the SOB anyway," Ted said as he waved at FBI Special Agent in Charge Jeff Bodine and introduced Jeff to Jason.

Jeff clapped Jack on the back and said, "Well, I'll be a blue monkey's uncle. Francoise, how in the hell'd they get you here? Never saw you at a meeting. In fact, I never see you anywhere except on the news when you are pissing off the press."

Jack cut his eyes over toward Ted and said in a grumpy voice, "Figure it out. Ya got one guess." Jack liked FBI SAC Jeff Bodine. He and Jeff often worked cases together and Jack had been delighted when Jeff had been named Special Agent in Charge in New Orleans. Jeff was tall, slim, had a receding hairline, and was as thorough as a cop could be. All in all, he was great for a Fed.

Jeff grinned and looked at Ted Scott. "Aw, Ted, did you make him? Did you make the big guy show up for this meeting?"

"I did, and I am sure I'll be paying for it forever. I pulled rank, and now I'm gonna have to watch it. God knows what he'll do to me to get back," Ted joked as he surveyed the room. "Jeff, do you know the guys up in front?"

Jeff looked ahead. "Yeah, the guy in the very front is the federal honcho in charge. He is actually the advance guy for the PPD."

"Huh, what the hell is PPD? I thought I got that every year to check for tuberculosis. You know I hate letters that are all strung together, Bodine," Jack cursed under his breath.

"For God sakes, Jack. It's Presidential Protective Division. His name is Secret Service Agent Travis Stoner. He is doubling as the PPD and agent in charge. Stoner is the best, knows his stuff. I've been working with him off and on for a while. The others up there are his team. They're good."

"Stoner. That's his name, *Stoner? The dude's name is Stoner.* What the hell? I'd change my name." Jack couldn't stifle his snicker.

Bodine laughed. "Yeah, and he takes ribbing pretty good. Used to it. Laughs about it himself. Stoner is a hell of a name for a Secret Service Agent, but don't underestimate him, Jack. He's got his stuff more than together."

Jack and the others nodded as Jeff continued, "Let me introduce you." Jack grimaced as the Mayor and the Governor's aide entered the conference room. He rolled his eyes, but he was happy to see Robert, Alex, and Yvette behind him. Maybe this meeting wouldn't be so bad after all. At least there was somebody here he actually liked.

Travis Stoner greeted FBI SAC Jeff Bodine warmly. Jack liked Stoner at first pass. His eyes were direct and his handshake was firm. He also had a take-charge attitude that Jack admired. He studied Jack closely and said, "Commander Francoise, you and I are going to be pretty tight before this is over. My biggest concern in all of this is your beat, the hospital area and the French Quarter. The Quarter seems the hardest to control. Can you hang back and talk with me and my men after this?"

"Yeah, glad to." Jack seemed delighted to be included. He felt his chest puff. *Maybe the Feds weren't so bad after all.* He grudgingly admired Stoner. Stoner was correct. The French Quarter was tough to protect. There were hundreds of places to hide or escape. Jack knew the dark and sleazy underbelly of the Quarter better than any cop in New Orleans Most NOPD officers only knew a few of them but Jack had spent most of his life either hanging out there, living in the Quarter, or patrolling it as part of the NOPD.

"OK. Let's get started, gentlemen and ladies," Stoner suggested, signaling his men to round up folks to the conference table.

The loud buzz in the room quickly became silent as the law enforcement officers seated themselves and Travis Stoner moved behind the podium. He was a commanding presence as he stood at the podium of the Mayor's large, well-appointed conference room. His silver-grey hair gave him a distinguished look and his steely grey eyes were clear and insightful. Alex figured he didn't miss much. She was impressed by his appearance. She judged him to be in his mid-forties.

Stoner looked around the room. All eyes were trained on him as he began, "As most of you may know, any event of national or international perspective that is thought to be a significant threat against the United States as a potential target for terrorism is handled by the secret service. Federal law mandated that the United States Secret Service be in charge of event security, the Federal Bureau of Investigation is placed in charge of intelligence, counter terrorism, hostage rescue and the investigation of incidents of terrorism or other major criminal activities. In additional, the Federal Emergency Management Agency is in charge of recovery management in the aftermath of terrorist or other major criminal incidents, natural disasters or other catastrophic events. Federal law also requires that all Federal and local agencies work together to provide full cooperation and support to ensure the safety and security of those participating in or otherwise attending the event. Also, the community where the event takes place, in this case Orleans Parish, must be protected as well for a specific time frame. In other words, the Feds are in charge and we all work together. Are there any questions?

"It is important to note several differences in this briefing. First of all, generally, we only allow law enforcement to be present, but since we are considering the possibility of a dual threat, I have invited hospital executive personnel to attend. We also have representatives from the city and the Governor's office. Are there any questions?"

Stoner surveyed the room and noted the rapt attention on all participant faces. Since there were no questions, only silence, Stoner continued, "Homeland Security has assessed the possibility of two threats. I am going to ask Dr. Yvette Charmaine of the CDC to update us on the viral threat. Dr. Charmaine, would you come forward."

Alex leaned back in her chair to allow Yvette room to weave her way to the podium. She looked subdued, but official in her white CDC lab coat. Her voice was clear as she began, "Good afternoon, ladies and gentlemen. The virus we are examining here in New Orleans is very real and quite threatening. We have four dead, and 11 people being treated in the CCMC ED. The virus remains unknown but we have ruled out Ebola."

90

The Governor's aide quickly spoke out, 'You've ruled out Ebola? This morning I thought you said it looked like Ebola. I'm uncertain of what you mean. Is it bad because it's not Ebola?"

Yvette shook her head. "No, sir. It's not necessarily bad. As we discussed this morning, the virus does appear hemorrhagic based on its appearance but it also has a respiratory component that is generally not a part of the Ebola complex. The respiratory failure seems to be what caused the deaths."

Jeff Bodine stood and said, "Dr. Charmaine, I'm Jeff Bodine, FBI SAC and I am in charge of counter terrorism and ground operations here in New Orleans for the next few days. Do you consider this biological threat to be a weapon of mass destruction?"

Yvette didn't hesitate. "Absolutely. Yes, Mr. Bridges, it certainly could be a WMD. The potential is there. We've admitted 15 cases in a matter of less than eight hours and that number could double or triple in the next eight to 12 hours. We don't know the source, although I am sure you know that one of the victims was a political aide staying at the Hotel Burgundy and another casualty was in food service at the Hotel Burgundy. Based on the fact that many of the guests at the Hotel Burgundy are either members of the United States government or their assistants, we cannot rule out biological terrorism as a weapon of mass destruction."

"And when *will* you identify the virus?" This question came from a very irate Mayor Devries. Alex wanted to close her eyes and mentally escape each time she heard the Mayor's whiny, nasal voice. She looked over at Jack and their eyes met. Alex knew exactly what was on the Commander's mind and how much he wanted to hurt Devries.

Yvette answered him directly with composure in her voice. "As soon as we can, Mr. Mayor. We have the best minds at the CDC working on it. As I have tried to explain, this virus is not a virus that we can identify from known viruses so we are going to need to run more tests and take more time. The virus is not acting like anything we know or anything we have currently identified. It is an arduous and difficult process."

Robert intervened, "Dr. Charmaine, could you let us know how you are testing for the virus?" Alex knew Robert was highlighting the integrity of the work of Yvette and the CDC crew. She gave him a grateful smile.

"Of course, Dr. Bonnet. In addition to the routine, classical techniques for virus isolation such as cell tissue cultures and examination by electron microscopy, we are also using serologic testing, histopathologic and IHC assays, PCR; and sequences as well as metagenomics. Metagenomics allows for the isolation of microorganisms without the need to isolate and culture pathogens, thus saving us a great deal of time. Trust me, the best scientific knowledge in the world is being employed here by the CDC in an effort to identify and isolate this virus or viruses."

"Thank you, Dr. Charmaine. We appreciate you and your team's work on this." Robert gave Yvette a warm smile.

The Mayor sighed heavily and shrugged his shoulders and turned to his aide and whispered loudly. Alex could hear the word 'incompetent' on her side of the table. She thought she was going to have to restrain Jack. She could feel the anger rolling from his enormous body. She couldn't blame him for his intense dislike for Mayor Devries. Devries was an idiot. How in the world did he become Mayor of New Orleans? Of course she knew how. It was because he was an idiot and could be bought and sold to the highest corrupt bidder. Boy, she missed Virginia politics. They were a little scandalous sometimes, but nothing like this. She'd be glad when this meeting was over. She refocused her attention on Agent Stoner.

Stoner stood and stared down at the Mayor until Devries turned his head. "Are there any other questions for Dr. Charmaine." Stoner continued to stare at the Mayor, his eyes smoldering. It was as if he dared Devries to open his mouth. Devries didn't and Stoner continued, "We need to move on. Commissioner Ted Scott, NOPD, please come forward."

Alex had to admire Jack's boss. He was a tall man, heavy set, with a broad, deeply lined face, dark hair and a square jaw. He looked like the proverbial all-American jock. Commissioner Scott was highly regarded in the city. Under his tenure as Police Commissioner, he had decreased police corruption and cleaned up the murder and assault statistics in New Orleans and most of City Hall loved him except for the notable dislike of the Mayor. Scott didn't buckle for him. Alex imagined that Ted handled Devries better than Jack, who actually didn't handle him at all. He simply ignored and avoided him in typical Jack Francoise avoidance style. She shook her head as she thought about Jack's antics and the hundreds of people over the years who had tried to bully him into submission. Nothing had worked. Jack was Jack and if he liked and respected you, things would always be OK. If he didn't, well, you'd best watch out. He was not an enemy to be ignored. Hence his nickname, "get back Jack."

As Commissioner Scott shook hands with Stoner, Alex continued to inspect the group around the conference table. Standing guard at the door was a young NOPD officer of Middle Eastern descent. He was standing at attention, his hands behind him, but Alex believed he was intently listening to everything. She noticed his eyes flicker from one speaker to another. As Ted began to speak, she dismissed the young man from her mind.

"The Secret Service has asked me to update you on the murder of a young Congressman this morning in the French Quarter. He has been identified as Congressman Ben Blankenship of Arizona. He was last seen alive at Cafe Du

Monde around mid-morning reading a newspaper and drinking coffee. He was found dead in the Quarter around noon. No witnesses remember him being approached at the Cafe or seeing him leave. His death occurred in the same manner as that of Senator Beau LaMont of Louisiana and Hunter Hayes, an employee of the Democratic Party. Both were murdered in the Quarter several months ago."

FBI Agent Jeff Bridges asked, "Commissioner Scott, can you be more specific? I don't think all my agents, particularly the agents from out of state, know about the deaths of LaMont and the other gentleman."

"Yes, of course." Commissioner Scott pivoted toward and addressed the group of FBI agents in the far corner and said, "All three men had their throats slit from end to end, and there was no blood at either of the crime scenes."

"Huh, no blood? How can that be. Can you be more specific, sir?" The question came from an incredulous, young agent in the back of the room.

"Yes, of course. The victims died from exsanguination. It is still questionable, but we believe, for the most part, that they were killed at another location and their bodies moved and posed in the French Quarter. We are not sure about that in Congressman's Blankenship's case yet. Forensics is working on it. There was minimal blood at the scene but we haven't established whether he was killed in the Quarter or not. He is currently being autopsied."

Ted noted the uncertainty on several of the men's faces. He continued, "We believe someone took their blood. We don't know why but there have been other recent murders that are similar."

Jeff Bodine broke in, "It is a serial killer, but we have to be certain the crimes are not politically motivated. We've lost three politicians here in New Orleans in the past two months and we expect several hundred more politicians in New Orleans shortly for Operation Fix America. The murderer is a terrorist, no question."

"Yeah," Jack muttered to anyone close by. "A terrorist playing a Vampire. What a pervert."

The Mayor gave Jack a wild-eyed look and then looked back down at his notes. He didn't know what he'd do if he had a vampire loose on the streets of the Crescent City. That wouldn't bode well at all. It would certainly hurt tourism, and the city was only now beginning to recover from Katrina.

Ignoring Jack, Ted continued, "We aren't absolutely sure the virus at the hospital and the murders of the politicians are related, but we cannot take any chances. It seems highly suspect that a biological threat broke today within hours of another political murder. We cannot overlook that. Personally, my opinion is that they are related but we still lack evidence to make that assumption official."

Stoner looked at Commissioner Scott and said, "Agreed. It could be more than a coincidence. We must stay diligent. What's the NOPD plan?"

"We'll have triple patrols in the French Quarters 24/7 for the next few days and as long as we need to. We'll station extra patrols near the hotels where most of the politicians are staying. The patrols will be in uniform and civilian attire. We have installed more video cameras at busy traffic intersections and heavy tourist areas. We have our SWAT teams activated to work in conjunction with the federal teams. We'll also, at Commander Francoise's suggestion, place several undercover cops in the local clubs where the Vampire-Wanna-Be crowd hangs out, specifically Howl, Shadow Gallery, and a few others." Scott's report was to the point.

"Why do the clubs, Jack? Isn't it better to stick to the streets," John Houser, from the LA Criminal Division queried.

Jack shook his head and stood to reply. "No man, we need to watch the clubs. The last place Senator LaMont and the staffer had partied was a Vampire Club named Howl down on Decatur. They had a charge slip in their pocket that was time-date stamped several hours before their death. Some of the people who frequent these places actually believe they're vampires and it's rumored they drink blood. Most of them are harmless kids, but at any rate, it's worth the patrolling."

Alex could swear she saw a small smile on the face of the uniformed NOPD officer. It sent a little prickle up her spine. She made a mental note to mention it to Jack.

"OK," Stoner stood up. "Any other questions for the Commissioner or the Commander?"

The room remained silent. "Good. Special Agent Bodine, you're up," Stoner gestured toward the FBI agent.

Special-Agent-in-Charge Bodine's voice was clipped and his demeanor grave as he addressed the group of law enforcement officers and Louisiana state officials. "We're treating this as a terror threat, probably an extremist Muslim group with an additional domestic terror threat when we factor in the French Quarter murders. We've been hearing internet chatter about an 'event' in New Orleans for quite some time so we think this is it, that the time has come."

Alex could feel the fear creeping up her spine. Was the FBI suggesting a domestic and international threat? The thoughts of a dual attack chilled her to the bone.

Bodine continued, his voice clear and his manner restrained. "Based on the recent events in Boston we have

96

reason to believe that the terrorists are part of the emerging Russian Red Jihad which has known terrorist cells in the US, mostly on the west coast and in the northeast. We believe this threat involves several sleeper cell in the New York area as well as cells in the south, one here in New Orleans as well as several others in Alabama and Mississippi. We have evidence that the Soviets, now present day Russians, have a long history of cooperation with extremist groups against the west. Since the mission of Jihad is to destroy the western way of life this is not surprising. Militants from Chechnya and Russia's explosive North Caucasus region have attacked Moscow in the past but it turns out that now the insurgency has spread to neighboring provinces with Dagestan, located between Chechnya and the Caspian Sea, the epicenter of violence in that region. Islamic militants are launching daily attacks against police and authorities. The attack in Boston is the first known attack of Russian Jihadists in the US. Muslim terrorists from Russian are not a new breed, just a newer emergent threat to the United States.

Alex was confused and raised her hand, "Agent Bodine, are you suggesting the terror threat against New Orleans is the same group that attacked Boston in May?"

Bodine didn't pause, "Yes, Ms. Destephano. We believe they are part of the same group. That's exactly what we think. Internet chatter is suggesting this and we believe it. The threat is real and it is credible. The Boston Marathon bombers were Muslims from the Russian Caucasus. They have declared war against the United States as evidenced by the events in Boston and in New York and Washington on 9/11. Most Americans don't acknowledge that our country is at war, but trust me - there are thousands of civil servants who spend every day and night keeping us safe. The Boston bombings marked the first time the Russian conflict had spawned a major terror attack in the US. There is no reason to believe they won't attack us again."

Stoner interrupted, "Agent Bodine is correct. The US receives numerous threats from Jihadist extremists every day, threats from the Taliban, Al Qaeda, Hezbollah and Hamas - not to mention terrorists groups most citizens have never heard of. The threats are against US citizens, our operations abroad, such as Benghazi and other Embassies, and business interests. Of course, that includes Washington, DC, the President, and members of Congress. We believe they are using the virus as a biological weapon of mass destruction. It is possible they plan to kill people who live in New Orleans as well as some of the most powerful leaders in American. Washington and Boston are great American cities. It is logical that New Orleans would also be on the terrorist hit list."

The room was so quiet it was deafening. The enormity of what was happening stunned Alex and she thought Robert felt it too. She looked at him for comfort, but despair etched his handsome face. She reached for his hand. He gave her a brief smile and squeezed her hand back. Yvette Charmaine looked as though she had just realized her second nightmare, and even Jack appeared a little subdued by the massive amount of information they'd been given.

Jack asked grimly, "What are the plans for the FBI and Secret Service offensive?"

Bodine answered quickly, "We'll have our FBI SWAT teams in place. They are specially trained to intervene in high-risk events such as this one. The New Orleans office has 48 trained SWAT officers, but due to the potential of the threat, we may dispatch other SWAT teams from neighboring states as well as our larger FBI SWAT teams."

Bodine paused to answer a question from Yvette. "Dr. Charmaine, do you have a question?"

"Yes, I do. What is a larger SWAT team, and will any teams be available at Crescent City Medical?"

Agent Bodine responded quickly, "The FBI has teams that are known as enhanced FBI SWAT. Those elite agents are trained to assist the FBI's Hostage Rescue Team if needed. These teams are available for worldwide deployment. They are highly trained and skilled and are not unlike Army Rangers, Special Ops or Seal Teams. We will determine in a matter of hours how many of these teams will come to New Orleans."

"What do these teams do that the NOPD cannot do," whined Mayor Devries. "Our police force is very capable. We handle huge crowds during Mardi Gras and we do just fine."

Jack turned and murmured to Alex and Robert, "Holy Shit. That man is an absolute idiot. Does he really think our SWAT teams here have the same skill set as the Spec Ops guys?"

Robert gave Jack a grim smile, shrugged his shoulders and shook his head.

Agent Bodine stared at the Mayor as if he didn't hear him. In fact, he wished he hadn't heard him.

Alex decided she liked Agent Bodine. She admired his style. He had to be shocked by the Mayor's behavior but he hid it well.

"I'm sorry, Mayor. What do you mean," asked Bodine with a touch of irritation in his voice. "We will be coordinating with Commissioner Scott and Commander Francoise throughout this mission. We will use every resource you have to offer and we are appreciative of all your assets."

Devries turned to Commissioner Scott and said, "Commissioner, do you think we need all of this 'outside' help? I don't!"

Alex could barely contain herself. His nasal, droning voice was making her crazy. She wanted to rip out his carotid arteries.

Ted Scott was embarrassed and his face was flushed. He was dismayed at the Mayor's question. Jack had smoke coming out of his ears as he glared at the idiot, asshole Mayor. Alex could see the tension exploding from Jack's brain. How in the world could this man be so stupid? He's a real dumb ass. How embarrassing for Ted, Jack and the other city leaders who must suffer through his leadership.

Carefully choosing his words, Commissioner Scott said, "Mayor, we absolutely need everything they have suggested. We are talking about biological warfare, weapons of mass destruction and a terror threat against the leaders in Congress, the President of the United States. We need all of the help we can get, and then some." Ted's voice was firm, adamant.

Now, shut the hell up, Mr. Mayor, Alex thought. She'd had more than enough of him and his stupidity.

Agent Bodine nodded in agreement with Ted Scott and added, "Let me assure you, Mayor Devries, that our agents and SWAT teams are specially trained for situations such as this. They protect dignitaries, make high-risk arrests, conduct fugitive tracking, operate in WMD environments, and perform site surveys for high risk, high visibility events, and sniper operations. As I said earlier, we will coordinate with the NOPD, the Louisiana State Police, and the National Guard that I understand has been called out."

The Mayor nodded and stayed silent. Alex could see Jack relax a bit. He was as tense as a loaded sling shot ready for release, but she could see his massive biceps contract and relax through his white shirt. She could only imagine the four letter words circling through his brain.

In closing Agent Bodine added, "In addition to our ground assets, we also will make wide use of video and camera surveillance. We will have analysts trained in recognizing behavior changes, cues, and these analysts will be continually analyzing multiple camera feeds. The Feds will be coordinating with facial recognition software, person-specific identification and crowd flux congestion analysis technology. Hopefully, we have covered all bases.

Alex was impressed. These guys were amazing. She felt the breeze as Robert's hand raised.

"Yes, Dr. Bonnet, what can we help you with?"

Robert's voice was firm and clear. "Crescent City Medical is following all of the CDC recommendations for viral containment. We are using positive pressure personnel suits with a segregated air supply and have incorporated all HAZMAT regulations. Will the FBI be assisting us in managing the biological, viral threat?"

Stoner responded, "Yes, we will. Both Secret Service and FBI agents are trained in the management and containment of biological threats. We will have a team placed at the medical center. They will coordinate with Commander Francoise who in turn will coordinate with you and Ms. Destephano and Dr. Charmaine. Anything else?"

Stuart Tansill, the Governor's aide, spoke up. "The Governor wants to know if you want him to come to New Orleans earlier than Saturday. He has plans with the President on Saturday evening after he addresses the delegation from Congress. He has offered all of Louisiana's resources to be at your disposal."

Stoner replied, his tone formal, "Please reiterate our thanks to the Governor for all of your state's resources, Mr. Tansill. The Governor should stay in Baton Rouge until he plans to meet with the President who should arrive on Saturday morning. The Secret Service and the Louisiana State Police will be responsible for his security from Baton Rouge to New Orleans. I will call him later today and brief him. Please tell him to expect my call."

The Governor's aide nodded and said, "I will tell him, thank you. The Governor is thankful for the resources of the Federal government at this time." Tansill looked over at Mayor Devries and snickered. "We, the Office of the Governor, understand the severity of these potential threats and are grateful for all federal assistance." Stoner nodded his thanks.

Alex raised her hand. "I have one more question. Is the first lady planning to come to New Orleans?"

"This remains unclear at this point. She had planned to accompany her husband, but due to the dual threat, she may not be coming. I seriously doubt she will come," Stoner paused for a moment and added, "I am recommending that the President not attend either but I am sure he will insist upon being a part of 'Operation Fix America'. Quite frankly, we are working with his chief of staff and asking for his support in keeping POTUS in DC."

Alex digested this information and said, "Thank you, Mr. Stoner and Mr. Bodine and all of you in this room, for all you are doing here for us. Let us know if we need to do more at Crescent City Medical." Her voice was clear and she knew that the lives of potentially thousands of Americans were currently within the purview of these two men as well as the other police officers around the table.   "Oh, Mr. Stoner, where will be President be speaking on Saturday?"

"Currently his main address is scheduled for the Convention Center, but that could change to one of the closer hotels if the threats continue. Thank you, Ms. Destephano. If that is all, then we're dismissed."

As Alex and Robert stood to leave, Jack caught Robert's sleeve. "Can you guys get with me later? I need to find out more of the plans and pass them on to you. Yvette needs to be a part of this meeting as well."

"How about coming to my house for dinner around 7:30 or so. I'll just order in. It will get us out of the hospital for a while and Yvette and Robert probably need a break."

"Good idea, Alex. I'll tell Yvette. She left a minute ago to go see Maddy Jeanfreau. She finished autopsying Blankenship and has some interesting findings, though I don't know what yet."

"OK. We'll meet up this evening. See you then."

As Alex and Robert walked toward his car to return to CCMC, Alex's angst was clear, "Robert, I am really scared. This is very serious. Do you think the murders are part of the terror threat?"

Robert shook his head. "Don't know, Alex. Possibly. Three politicians is pretty significant and doesn't sound random to me. And you're right - this is very frightening. I never really realized the essence of terror until just an hour ago."

"Oh, did I tell you that the Congressman murdered in the Quarter was my grandfather's protégé? He was like a son to him. They have been guests at the farm many times. I met them during Christmas break, right before I moved to New Orleans. My grandparents are so devastated. I am worried for them both."

"Oh my God, I am so sorry. I can check on them if you like." Robert's voice was kind, sympathetic as he touched Alex's shoulder.

"They're coming tomorrow. I just spent time with Beth Blankenship, the widow. She's lovely, and this is so tragic. I hope to see her again. She's under Secret Service protection at the Hotel Burgundy. My grandmother is planning to stay with her. She and granddad arrive in the morning."

Robert shook his head, his grey eyes sympathetic. "I am so sorry, Alex. I know how you worry about them." He took her hand and clasped it tightly as they walked hand in hand to his car. There was something comforting about their relationship and their ability to rely on each other. They were silent during the short ride to CCMC. Alex wondered again if she should just love him and let go of all of those red flags she seemed to manufacture in her mind. It felt good to be a couple, if only for a few moments.

Chapter 16

Mohammad Abdu impatiently turned off his remote and stared into the blank screen of his large television set. The thin veil of anxiety he had felt hours before had now provided him with a pounding headache. *What was wrong? Why wasn't Nazir communicating with him.* In desperation, he picked up his cell phone and dialed his New Orleans operative again on his burn phone. This time Nazir answered.

"Ahlan," said the quiet voice. Mohammed Abdu thought he sounded depressed.

"Nazir, I have been trying to reach you for hours. What is happening down there? What of this virus?"

The silence on the end of the phone made Mohammed Abdu uneasy. "Nazir, you must speak to me. What do you think of the virus at the big hospital there?"

"I do not know. I am afraid that Vadim may have double-crossed us. I have been trying to reach him, but he is not to be found," Nazir's voice was distant and sounded as if he were speaking from a deep hole.

Abdu was silent for a moment and then said, "What does Ali think? Is he working on the virus at the hospital? Does he have any insight, any knowledge?"

"He is there, but he doesn't know. The CDC says it is not Ebola. It is a combination of viruses. Ali is working on models to identify the virus. He said it is difficult and it is not anything like the virus we were planning."

"Nazir, you must find Vadim. It is critical to see if he has betrayed us or has in any way altered the virus."

Nazir sighed deeply and said, "I have been trying and trying, but he is not at home nor does he answer his phone. For all I know he planted the virus and left New Orleans. I never trusted him. A Russian! Blah! Kalet! Naqual! Dirty bastard!" Nazir had recovered from his apathy. He was furious, ready to kill. Then he remembered how he had contradicted Ali a short while before and felt humiliated.

"Ibn haram! Filthy bastard indeed, but we must find him to learn what he has done," said Mohammed. "I am sending several brothers down to assist you. The brothers are close by and will be there in several hours. Stay where you are and meet them. They know the plan. They know our mission. I am coming this evening with Omar Hassan on a plane. Be prepared for us. We must be ready for this. It has been in the plans for years and we must not fail."

"We will not fail." Nazir sounded more pumped than he felt. "Please wear Western dress. I am sure they are looking for us."

"Yes, I am sure they are. What does our NOPD police informant say? Is he loyal?" Mohammed Abdu certainly hoped he was. He was the only insider in the cell that had any fix on what the Americans might do to protect against the Jihad plan.

Nazir's voice was bolder now. "Yes, he is loyal. I just spoke with him. He is part of the American FBI and Secret Service security plan. He will report to me later. He has a lot of information. I will share it with you later tonight."

"We will be there by midnight. Wait up for us. Please have more information for us when we arrive. And nourishment. We will be hungry. As-salaam'alaykum."

"Peace with you as well," Nazir added as Mohammed Abdu clicked off. Nazir looked around his shotgun house apartment that would soon become a full-fledged terrorist cell.

The peaceful, planning, dreaming days for he and Ali were over. Of course, who knew where the neighboring sleeper cells were. He could have mortal enemies next door or down the street and not know it. It could be the man at the market who sold him the taboule. He supposed that was what made terrorist organizations so powerful and successful. It certainly should scare the infidels, especially since it scared him so much.

Chapter 17

Alex was exhausted by the time she reached home, arms piled high with food from Napoleon's, flowers and cheese from the French Market, and wine from Martin's Wine Shoppe. She quickly set five places for dinner in her dining room. She had decided to serve informally from the kitchen. She had originally planned for six, but Jack had phoned to let her know that Monique wasn't up to a long evening and had declined her invitation. Alex had to remind herself that Monique was still very fragile and certainly in no need of the stress of a terrorist strike, as well as the fear of more murders in the Quarter. Besides, Monique didn't need to be pressured with the problems occurring in the city and at CCMC. Her major focus and energy needed to be directed toward her recovery. She would pack a doggie bag for Jack to take home for Monique. Monique loved food from Napoleon's.

Alex had just finished arranging flowers for the table when her home phone rang. It was her grandmother. It was a little after 7 p.m. local time, 8 p.m. in Virginia - almost dark. Alex visualized her grandmother sitting in her glass sunroom watching the horses graze in the pasture that surrounded the house. Her heart ached for Virginia and her home. Things seemed so sane there, so easy and predictable, so unlike her life in New Orleans. In her mind's eye, Alex saw Dundee, her horse, running down the river path toward the river. Her loneliness was palpable. She wanted to cry at the sound of pain in her beloved grandmother's voice.

"Grand, how are you? Is everything OK," Alex asked, a little concerned to hear from her grandmother again so soon.

"Yes, honey, things are pretty well. Your grandfather has gone to bed. He's exhausted and really upset by the events in New Orleans today, but even bigger than that, he's worried about Beth, her family, and the future of America. Apparently,

Ben Blankenship was a shoe-in for the vice-presidential nomination next fall. I had no idea about any of that. How is Beth?"

"As well as expected, I guess. She's very sad. It's tragic. I stayed with her for over an hour. She is pretty much in shock right now." Alex paused for a moment, thinking, and then continued, "She cried a lot but I guess she is doing OK considering what has happened. I wish I could take her pain away. I tried to get her to come stay with me, but she wanted to stay at the hotel. I'll try to see her tomorrow."

"That's one reason why I called you. Do you think Beth and I could stay at your house? It would be so much more comfortable than the hotel. Of course, that would mean Ben's aide would need to come as well, and there would probably be Secret Service in your home. I think the White House has ordered that."

"Of course! Absolutely, Grand. I would love for you all to be here. I can make up the Carriage House for the Secret Service and NOPD, as I am sure they will be here as well. I will pick up all kinds of food for you all early in the morning. Maybe I will just order it online. I can also ask Martin if one of his daughters or Carla, his wife, will come over and help prepare meals and clean up. You know they are the best Cajun cooks in the world. Will Granddad be staying?"

"I suspect he'll be in and out. He'll keep his room at the Palm, but he'll probably sleep at your house. He also kept his room at Hotel Burgundy. Could you arrange for Martin's cab to take him back and forth? That would be helpful."

"Not a problem. Martin will be happy to be of assistance. Is there anything else I can do for you, Grand? You sound so tired."

"No, Alex. I'm just a little worried about your Grandfather. He's really depressed about all of this. He feels he has lost the son he never had and I cannot alter what only the passage of time can heal."

Alex felt tears spring into her eyes. They were getting so old. The anchors in her life were aging and she was powerless about it. She needed to be closer to them. She could feel her grandmother's pain through the phone line. Her stomach contracted into a huge knot when she considered life without them. She couldn't wait to see them in the morning. "Robert said he would be happy to check Granddad out when he gets here if he is still under the weather."

Grand laughed and said, "We would love to see Robert. How is he doing these days?"

Alex smiled and said, "We are both up to our eyeballs in this virus stuff. It's huge to have the CDC in your hospital. We're the acting administrators since Don is away. Actually, I am glad he's not here. He'd just get in the way."

"I know you are both working very hard. How's Monique doing?"

"She's continuing to improve, much slower than before, but she is getting there. Jack is very patient with her. She tires easily, but she is really together intellectually. She is actually amazing. I never would have believed she'd be this good so soon."

Grand sighed audibly and said, "What a gift. Who'd have thought several months ago she would have even come out of her coma. God is really good, isn't he, Alexandra?"

"Yes, He is. Yes, He is. I learn that more and more the older I get. I'm having Robert, Jack, Dr. Yvette Charmaine, and

Dr. Maddy Jeanfreau over for dinner. I picked up pasta and a salad from Napoleon's. Monique begged off because she was tired. Anyway, it's just take out but it should be good."

"Hmmm, Robert? You know how I feel about that, right?" Alex could hear the hope in her grandmother's voice. Kathryn Lee loved Robert Bonnet.

She sighed and replied, "Yes, Grand. You know I do, and you know how I feel. This is sort of a business dinner about security for CCMC." She loved her Grand more than life, but sometimes she could kill her. She knew her voice sounded exasperated.

"Alexandra Destephano, I can see you rolling your eyes from here. Show an old lady, who only wants your happiness, some respect." Kathryn Rosseau Lee's voice was sharp, a little acidic.

"Sorry, Grand, I really am. I do need to get going. These people will be here shortly. Give Granddad a hug for me. Love you." *Holy Cow, she will never give up on Robert and me. But I need to remember that she is rarely wrong. Actually, can't even remember when she has been wrong, ever.* That little voice she often hated to hear, the inner or the other Alex, spoke to her and suggested her Grandmother was most likely right.

"Love you too, Alex. See you tomorrow. I should be at your house around noon. Please have Martin pick up Beth. She will love to come and see you. Just wish it were all different. " Alex could hear the strain in her Grandmother's voice as she clicked off. Almost immediately, Alex heard her front door chimes. She gave her dining room one more quick look and satisfied that things were in place, moved through her living room into the foyer to greet her guests.

Chapter 18

Nazir paced up and down the Riverwalk as his anxiety mounted. He had a premonition that something bad was going to happen. He prayed for peace but it just wouldn't come. Surely, things would work out. After all, he was doing Allah's Work. Jihad was a Holy War and he was on the side of the righteous. Of course, Jihad was an inner spiritual struggle as well as a physical struggle. His greater Jihad, the inner struggle and religious faith, was unhampered. Nazir was having no difficulty with his inner Jihad, but the lesser Jihad, the physical struggle against the enemies of Islam was terrifying him. *Where was Yahwa?* The NOPD informant was supposed to meet him an hour ago, but hadn't shown up yet. *Certainly he wasn't betraying him like the still elusive Vadim? The thought of another betrayal robbed his breath. But then, who knew?* None of the terrorists knew each other until several days before the event was to take place. That was when the cells were activated. That was how Al-Qaeda and Hamas operated. It was all secret, but it was unnerving at times. *Praise be to Allah.* Allah helped him trust other people of his own kind.

The sun had set as Nazir sat on a bench overlooking the mighty Mississippi River . As always, he was appalled by the muddy color of the huge body of water. He likened the water to the infidels, to Americans and the other Western cultures -- dark, dirty, and ugly. It was nothing like the pristine, azure Mediterranean Sea in his country that was perfect, with its beautiful sandy and rock beaches. He was jilted out of his thoughts when a little girl with blonde hair approached him and asked, "Would you like some of my peanuts to feed the seagulls? They really like them. I have popcorn too." The little girl held out her bag. He just stared at her, examining her pure smile and sweet face.

The little girl's big blue eyes were staring at him, imploring him to share her popcorn and peanuts. He was momentarily confused, and intrigued. She seemed to be an innocent. He had never spoken to an American child and was surprised she had approached him. He shook his head when he heard a female voice behind him say, "Kirsten, come here right away. You know you are not supposed to talk with strangers. " The voice was stern and scolding.

Nazir turned around to see the child's mother, a young woman who was a tall twin to her daughter. His dark eyes met her blue ones and locked in place. The mother was scrutinizing him and it unnerved him. Finally, he broke the stare and quickly shuffled away from the child as the mother said, "Kirsten, I have told you over and over again that not everyone is our friend. Not everyone loves you. You have to be careful."

As the woman and child moved back into the crowd in the French Quarter Nazir realized, for the first time in his life, that the children were innately good, at least until adults corrupted them and taught them to hate. He was surprised that he was so affected by the incident when suddenly, a strong hand grabbed his shoulder.

Nazir turned quickly, prepared to defend himself when the voice said in Arabic, "Brother. What is wrong? You look as though you have seen a spirit!"

Nazir smiled in relief when he saw Yahwa. "Where have you been? You are late. I was worried." His voice sounded angry and Yahwa laughed at him.

"Relax, Brother, all is well. I had to work late, then go home and take off my police uniform. I came as quickly as I could. Traffic was heavy, so it took longer to get here."

"You could have texted me. You could have let me know." Nazir's voice was irritated, accusing. "I did not know what to think."

"Calm down. We have a lot to do, a lot to talk about. In Western speak, 'take a chill pill'. Besides, we are cautioned against texting. The American's have eyes and ears everywhere. We have a lot to do. Let us walk and talk."

The men walked a short distance without talking, then stopped to look at an ornate calliope, complete with an organ grinder and a monkey. The organ grinder looked Slavic with dirty blonde hair, blue eyes, and a broad forehead with wide-set eyes. His body was short, powerful and resembled a tree trunk. He was dressed gaudily in bright colors with lots of fake gold jewelry and chains. He stared at them as he played his instrument. Yahwa laughed outright at them and said, "Nazir, I heard monkeys carry a lot of diseases. A lot of viruses. Did you know that?"

Nazir said nothing but continued to examine the organ grinder carefully. He was vaguely familiar. Yahwa went up to the monkey, made lewd gestures at him, and poked a finger in his face. The monkey screamed a blood-curdling yell at Yahwa, jumped from the organ grinder's shoulder, and in an instant, bit Yahwa on the arm. As the monkey jumped to bite Yahwa again, the organ grinder pulled at the leash around his neck. halting the angry primate. The organ grinder growled at Yahwa and said, "Keep away! My monkey bite again." The organ grinder made a menacing gesture with his arm.

Yahwa was shocked at the monkey's actions but recovered quickly. He screamed every curse word he knew in Arabic, and then a few in English, and enraged, moved toward the organ grinder who said in broken English, "No come closer. Will bite again. You be sorry."

Nazir, who had recovered by this time, jerked Yahwa back and said, "Let's go. Your hand is bleeding badly." Surprised, Yahwa checked his arm and hand. The monkey had bitten him twice. The monkey's teeth had pierced the radial artery in his wrist and blood was spurting freely. Quickly, Nazir pulled out a white handkerchief and tied it around Yahwa's wrist. Then he ran over to a street vendor and came back with an ice-cold bottle of water, which he held against the wound. The blood flow seemed to slow down, but did not stop.

Nazir shook his head. "You need to go to the hospital. You may need stitches and some injections. Monkeys can cause a lot of diseases. I can take you. My car is close. We can talk on the way."

"No, never. I want no Western medicine. Let it bleed freely. It will take all of the germs away. Let us go and eat. I am hungry." Yahwa was fiercely adamant and defiant. Nazir shrugged his shoulders and said nothing else.

The two men stopped at a small cafe and went inside to escape the late afternoon heat. The cafe was empty. Yahwa grabbed several white napkins and held them against his wounds. The bites were hurting and stinging. He couldn't believe the pain. He focused on the menu and prayed to Allah for the pain to stop.

After they ordered and were served, Nazir asked the inevitable. "What about security. What do you know."

Yahwa grinned and said, "I know a lot. I know it all. Triple patrols and video surveillance cameras everywhere. I know the details, and I know where the undercover police officers will be stationed and where the FBI snipers will be located. I even know who they are. There is FBI, Secret Service and I can identify those agents as well and can point them out to our brothers. I also know the route for infidel the American President, so we can station our people so that they will not miss. It will not be a problem."

Nazir nodded. "Excellent. Tell me more. The leaders are coming from the North tonight and meeting at my apartment. They will want details. I need all of the specifics."

Yahwa continued, "There are plainclothes police all over the hospital and National Guard on the outside. I also have the electrical design and detailed plans for the hotel where the American President will most likely speak, but the exact location remains uncertain. I will pass it on to our people."

"What makes you so sure they will not change the location of the President's speech many times?"

"I know all of the possible locations as well. I have this covered. We will be successful." Yahwa was confidant and wore a smirk on his face that Nazir found discomforting.

Nazir nodded his approval. "Good, brother. Give me the details for tonight. I will trust them to my memory. Nothing will be written."

"No. I cannot. Nazir, I will be at that meeting. You need to know nothing. I will share with Mohammad Abdu and the others when they arrive. You will learn when the others learn."

Yahwa noted the look of uncertainty on Nazir's face and added, "You know what the American special forces say, 'if I tell you, I will have to kill you'." Yahwa was trying to be funny but it clearly wasn't working.

Paranoia was creeping up Nazir's back. *What was happening? Were the leaders checking up on him? Was Yahwa held in higher esteem than he was?* As the uncertainty increased and continued to crawl up his spine, Nazir did the best he could to disguise his feelings. "What do you know of the viral outbreak at the hospital? I am sure you know it is not the virus we planned."

Yawah nodded, exasperated. "I do know that, and once again, I will share tonight. As you know, the least said, the least confusion and misinterpretation. I am leaving. I am not feeling well, and want to rest before midnight. My arm is hurting still and I want to elevate it. Praise Allah."

Nazir repeated praise for Allah and watched as Yawah left the cafe and headed uptown. His heart was hammering in his chest. He was paralyzed by fear and suspicion. He needed to talk to his only friend, his brother, and quickly punched Ali's number into his cell phone.

Chapter 19

Alex welcomed Robert and Yvette warmly. She hugged Maddy Jeanfreau, who she knew only slightly, primarily from her friendship with Robert and Jack. Once again, it was an old New Orleans relationship. The three physicians had grown up together. Alex suggested wine and Robert ushered the three ladies into Alex's beautifully renovated kitchen.

Yvette was stunned by the beauty of Alex's fully restored uptown home. "Did you plan the redesign alone? It is absolutely spectacular. What a lovely blend of antiques and colors."

Alex was pleased and said, "Yes, I did. I've had many of these antiques for years. Robert and I used to study at this kitchen table. We bought it many years ago when we were in school. Other pieces are from my home in Virginia. My grandmother's attic and barns are full of old pieces from her family as well as my grandfather's family. Some of them date back to the Revolutionary War."

Robert intervened and said, "Maddy, you and Yvette may not know that Alex's ancestors are part of the Lee family of Virginia. Lee as in Robert E. Lee and that group of fine folks."

"Wow, that's just amazing. Impressive. I have never known anyone, except for maybe Robert, who could date his linage that far back. I'm in awe," Yvette smiled as she gave Alex a hug.

Alex shrugged and said, "From what I know about my ancestors, they were a bunch of stubborn old goats who wouldn't take 'no' for an answer. Horse thieves as well, though we don't tell everyone that part. They're a feisty bunch for sure. Wait until you meet my grandfather. He's coming tomorrow, and he is a Lee to the core." She turned to Robert and quipped,

"Granddad and Robert struggled with their relationship over the years but they are fond of each other, right Robert?"

Robert grinned and looked sheepish for a moment. "Yes, Adam Patrick Lee is one of the most interesting, honorable men I have ever met. He is dogmatic, ethical, impressive, and stubborn as a mule. Of course, he didn't think any man was good enough for Alex. Add to that the fact that our political views were totally opposite made life thorny for several years."

"True, but in the end, you all were the best of friends, and still are, " Alex reported, smiling warmly at Robert. She turned to Maddy and Yvette and said, "You'll meet my grandparents tomorrow most likely. Granddad is devastated over the death of Congressman Benjamin Blankenship, the young man murdered this morning in the Quarter. The Blankenship's are close family friends and he was my grandfather's mentee in Congress."

Maddy nodded and said, "Tragic, it was absolutely tragic. The Congressman's death is heartbreaking. I heard he had young children."

Alex nodded sadly and said, "Yes, two beautiful young children, a son and a daughter. His wife is lovely as well. It just shouldn't have happened."

Maddy continued, "I know. He was killed exactly in the same manner as the others who have died in the Quarter. So sorry, Alex, for your grief." Maddy touched her arm in condolence.

Alex nodded as Robert handed each of them a glass of Pinot Noir. They drank deeply. The wine was good, the bouquet enticing and the taste lingered on the palate. Alex was glad she had three bottles. She felt like drinking the first one by herself. It had been a most upsetting day. As they headed to Alex's garden room for cheese and fruit, Alex's door chimes sounded again. Robert offered to answer and Alex waved him forward.

"Oh my gosh, Alex, this is the most magnificent painting I have ever seen! It is absolutely beautiful. Where ever did you find such a beautiful work of art? It is spectacular! The colors are to die for." Yvette was awestruck by the beautiful 5 x 5 foot painting in Alex's garden room. The painting showed three lavender, pink and purple orchids that beckoned as one entered the marble-tiled room. The painting completed the immense beauty of the room.

Alex smiled broadly, pleased that Yvette had noticed. "Isn't it stunning? It is a Karen Sistek original. She's a world famous silk artist I studied with several years ago in Washington State. In my humble opinion, she is the best silk artist in the world. I love her work."

"Silk, this painting is on silk?" Yvette exclaimed as she moved closer to examine the beautiful picture.

"Yes. The painting is actually on silk. It's not watercolor as most people think." Alex was secretly pleased that her new friends had noticed. She loved the painting as much as she loved Karen and Rick Sistek. Karen was a wonderful friend, and there was nothing Alex wanted more than to return to her studio in Port Angeles and spend a week doing nothing but silk painting and eating Rick's gourmet cooking.

Maddy moved closer to examine the orchids, "Silk? I have never seen a silk painting. Is that something new? It is exquisite. I want one. Does she do commissions?"

"Me, too," Yvette chimed in. "I want one as well."

"I am sure she will. She will do anything you would like. She is a wonderful person and easy to work with. Her work is the best. And, to answer your question, Maddy, silk painting is an old art that is fairly new in the US. The number of silk painters is growing. I will give you both her contact information. I have several other of her paintings I will show you before you leave. This is just the largest." Alex turned to hear the sound of male voices entering from the kitchen. She was surprised to see Jack and Secret Service Agent Travis Stoner.

Stoner was smiling. "Ms. Destephano, please forgive me for crashing your party. Commander Francoise assured me you wouldn't mind and I wanted to hear what Dr. Jeanfreau had found in her autopsy of Congressman Blankenship." Stoner looked around the room and added, "You have a lovely home, Ms. Destephano. That picture of those orchids is amazing. I have never seen anything like that in my life. My wife would die for that!"

"I am delighted to have you, Agent Stoner. You are absolutely welcome. Would you like some wine?"

"I would love wine but had best stick to coffee. Can I have a rain check until Sunday?"

"Of course you can. Let me get you coffee. Jack, would you like coffee as well?" Jack nodded and followed Alex into the kitchen to prepare a tray as Stoner moved closer to Maddy Jeanfreau and Yvette Charmaine and greeted them formally.

"Good evening, ladies. I'm the Secret Service party crasher. I hope you don't mind."

"Of course not," they said in unison. "We all need a break after today," Yvette suggested. Would you like some cheese?"

As Agent Stoner accepted some cheese from the tray in Yvette's hand, he turned to Maddy and asked, "Dr. Jeanfreau, is there anything significant about the murder of Benjamin Blankenship I need to know?"

"Please, call me Maddy. Every time someone calls me Dr. Jeanfreau I look around for my husband. I guess that's because he was an MD before me." Maddy smiled at Stoner and added, "To answer your question, no. There is very little difference in the death of Congressman Blankenship and the deaths of LaMont and Hayes. Most likely, the weapon is the same. Same MO. Same positioning. There was virtually no blood to speak of. The victim died from exsanguination just as the others did. If there is any difference at all, it is that the killer drained this victim's blood more slowly. I could tell by the perfusion of his internal organs."

Stoner arched his eyebrows and frowned. "Why would he do that? What does that mean, in your opinion?"

Maddy answered, thinking what a handsome man the agent was as she formulated her reply. "I would imagine the killer was making a point. This time he only had one victim, he had more time, and he made his victim suffer longer. Perhaps he is sending us a message that he has great control over whom and when he kills. At least, that's my take."

Yvette shook her head. "These crimes are hideous and gruesome. The killer is a psychopath to say the very least."

"He's a serial killer. No question. He killed the two kids the same day that he killed LaMont and Hayes. I don't think the crimes are related but the MO is the same," Jack reported as he entered the Garden room, a cup of coffee in hand, "unless, of course, he was practicing his style and timing on the kids."

Stoner looked thoughtful and nodded, "Perhaps he was practicing. Timing the event with the kids. Getting the kinks out of his technique. Was the Congressman's body moved?"

Maddy nodded. "Forensics are still out, but I think so. My best guess is yes. There was minimal blood, but it's difficult to be sure because the body was discovered fairly quickly after the murder. That makes it harder to tell."

"Who found the body?"

"Once again it was an anonymous call to the Mayor's Office from a burn phone. NOPD couldn't trace the call, and they responded quickly. The killer wanted this information out immediately. And he got his way. It was all over the news channels in a matter of minutes. Has been since this afternoon."

Alex returned to the room with coffee, listened for a few moments, and handed the coffee to Travis Stoner who accepted it gratefully.

Jack nodded and opined. "I agree with Stoner. He wanted people to know he had killed another politician, perhaps sending the message of a two-pronged attack against the politicians coming for Operation Fix America. He was threatening both -- the virus and murder--assuming we find the two are related."

"Jack, do you think the two are related? The virus and the murders?"

Jack reached for some cheese and answered, "No, my gut says no. We've had these kind of murders in the Quarter for years. I think the virus is separate, but as Stoner and Bodine have said, we cannot be sure. Are they related because the last three are political? Perhaps. Consequently, I must agree with Stoner that we cannot negate the possibility. Of course there's always the chance of murder for hire, right Stoner?"

Stoner nodded, "Possibly. I'd be more likely to agree if the murders were a little different. Don't think we can say for sure."

"What about the fact that three of the murders are political?" Robert asked.

Jack thought for a moment and responded, "That would suggest to me that they are related and that there is, possibly, a copy cat killer. A copycat St. Germaine. I don't believe these murders are related to the same or similar murders in the Quarter over the years. But, that is simply my theory at this time. It could change."

Stoner nodded. "Yeah, that's a new angle."

A tingling sensation crept up Alex's spine as feelings of apprehension washed over her. "Jack, you say we have had these kinds of murders in the Quarter for years. What do you mean by that? Have there been more that I don't know about?" Alex was curious about the local murders that she had been hearing about for several years. *Hadn't Martin mentioned them earlier?*

Jack's face was grim as he turned to Robert, Yvette and Maddy and answered, "Yes, Alex, ever since I can remember. My father investigated similar murders. They've been around for years and years.

Yvette's face paled and she spoke almost in a whisper, "Jack, you're talking about St. Germaine, aren't you?"

Jack's eyes locked with Yvette as he nodded. Robert shook his head.

St. Germaine. That's the third time today. Who the hell is St. Germaine? Alex made a mental note to ask Jack after everything settled down, but for now, she had hostess duties.

"Folks, dinner is ready. Grab a plate, fill it in the kitchen, and join us in the dining room. I know you're all starved."

The banter around the dining room table was as cheerful as the cocktail hour had been grim. The food was superb and the salad fresh. Robert kept the wine glasses filled as Alex refilled water goblets and coffee cups. Finally, Yvette asked, "Agent Stoner… Travis, is there further information we need to know?" She glanced at her watch and continued, "I may have to leave soon if the hospital calls and I'd like to be brought up to date." Out of respect for each other and the need for a break, everyone had turned off their cell phones during the dinner hour, except of course, Agent Stoner.

The fun was over, and the lighthearted repartee ended as all eyes focused on the Secret Service Agent. Stoner put down his fork and said, "Yes, there is more internet chatter. The chatter suggests it's the Red Jihad and there is a definite attack planned against the President. We also think there are plans to release the virus as some sort of a gas through several hotel ventilation systems. The threat is credible. We are marshalling every asset we can to prevent it. The news is not good but we are doing all we can to defuse everything that we can. That's about all I know now."

A pall permeated the group. A dark cloud blacked out the beauty of Alex's beautiful crystal chandelier and a shroud blanketed the group. There were several long minutes of silence until Maddy piped up and said, "Alex, didn't I see a chocolate cheesecake in the kitchen. Can I get it? It's telling me to come and get it."

"Maddy, the cheesecake is talking to you?" Alex asked with a laugh.

"Yeah, it is. It wants us to eat it." Maddy smiled brightly into the group.

Robert looked at Jack and joked, "Commander, where is Monique when we need her. Your medical examiner is talking to a cheesecake. Are you worried?"

"Hell no, Robert," Jack quipped. "It's talking to me too! Actually, the cheesecake and the coffee pot are speaking to me and I'm just about to answer them."

Yvette looked at her newfound friends, wishing she lived in New Orleans and not Atlanta. Even with the threats and all the work, this had been the most pleasant evening she'd had for years.

The carefree banter continued throughout dessert, but everyone at the table was well aware of the dire, extreme threats against each of them and their way of life. Shortly after dessert,

Stoner bid everyone good-bye as Jack, Robert, Maddy, Yvette, and Alex moved into the living room for more coffee and conversation. Maddy swore she had to leave soon or she'd be sleeping outside because her husband locked the doors at 11 pm. Nevertheless, she joined the others in the living for more talk.

The evening was pleasant, the conversation colorful and the weather perfect. Each guest had put aside their dark gathering fears, at least for one night.

Chapter 20

"Ali, Ali, call me as soon as you can. I have to talk to you. I must know what you have learned. I need information for our leaders." The panic and uncertainly in Nazir's voice was obvious and the Jihadist was ashamed of himself for being so emotional. He tried over and over again to convince himself that he had done nothing wrong, that the elders and leaders knew and respected his allegiance to the cause. But he still had a little niggling of uncertainty and the feeling was bothersome and frightening to him.

After he left the third message for his brother, Nazir stopped at the Middle-Eastern market on Carrolton and picked up tons of food for his late night guests. He returned to his apartment and laid on his sofa after spending considerable time in prayer. His knees were raw from the hours he had spent on his prayer mat. Ali had not returned his call. It was 10 p.m. and Ali's shift ended at 11. He needed to know what his genius little brother had learned about the virus. Surely Ali had isolated the virus by now. Knowing him, he had probably developed an antidote. He smiled. Ali had gotten the brains in the family, but Nazir had the brawn. Together, they were an ominous duo. He checked his watch again, 10:10 pm. Nazir dialed Ali again. This time his brother answered. Ali's voice sounded worn and frustrated.

"Little brother, what do you know? The leaders are coming tonight and we must have news for them about the virus. They are concerned. What do you know?" The anxiety in Nazir's voice was palpable and for some reason it irritated Ali.

Ali's voice was impatient as he answered. "I have no answer, brother. I cannot isolate the virus. Nothing is working. This virus is mysterious and I cannot develop a prediction that is valid. It acts very differently in each patient. The only common thing is that the people that are dying from some horrible form of pneumonia."

"Have we been betrayed by Vadim? Is it the Russian virus?"

"Brother," Ali's voice was exasperated. "I do not know. They have sent tissue slides of the dead people's lungs to pathology. We will find out the kind of pneumonia and that may help."

"When? I only have two hours before I must have answers. You must get them for me Ali. Everything rides on this. Our loyalty and commitment are at stake here. We are doing the work of Allah."

Ali was trying to be patient, but he was tired. His head hurt from using the computer and looking into microscopes for hours. "I will do what I can brother. I do not know when I will be able to come home. They need me here."

"You must be home by midnight. I demand it," Nazir snapped. Ali flinched at the anger in his brother's voice. He could visualize the angry glint in his brother's eyes as he hissed the words. "Midnight, at the latest, to meet with the leaders. They are coming from the North."

Ali was sick of it. He was sick of Holy War and Jihad, and now he was sick of the one he loved most in the world, his brother. He clicked off the phone.

Nazir was speechless with anger. He couldn't believe Ali had hung up on him. His anger turned to fury and he called Ali's cell phone back repeatedly, but Ali had quickly cut his phone off so he couldn't hear the ring or the beep of a text message.

Nazir threw his phone to the ground and ground it into the wooden floor with his heel. He was furious with his little brother. He sobbed and prayed for Ali as he lay on the sofa, neglecting to put the food away he had purchased for the leaders. He felt as though he had failed at his life's work, but most of all he was tortured because he had failed to convince his little brother of the importance and power of Islam. He had failed Allah. His life was over.

Chapter 21

Alex stifled a yawn as she watched Jack push the blue button on the Keurig for his umpteenth cup of joe. She wondered if coffee did anything for him anymore. He never seemed hyped up from it like she was after several cups. If she'd had three cups of coffee after dinner, she'd be jumping out of her skin. Jack just seemed to take it for granted and it never seemed to affect him. Monique was always fussing with him about his caffeine intake, but of course, it was useless. Alex smiled as she looked fondly at Jack. Her heart warmed for him. Once her mortal enemy, Jack Francoise was one of the men Alexandra loved most in the world.

Robert had noticed Jack's caffeine habit as well and couldn't resist ribbing him about it. "Commander, it seems as though your caffeine receptor sites are either dead or broken. Does the coffee affect you at all? Keep you awake? Does it still taste good?"

Jack shook his head and replied, "This coffee tastes good, and no, it never does affect me. I've been abusing the stuff for years." Jack eyed his cup critically and continued, "That swill down at the precinct is pretty bad. Hardly ever finish it. I pretty much just pour it and then it sits around all day. Crap's so bad that it stained my coffee mug almost black and I can't even bleach the color out." Jack took a sip, smiled, and continued, "Of course, this is pretty good coffee so I am actually drinking all of it." As Jack reclaimed his seat in the recliner in Alex's living room and pushed the lever to elevate his legs, he noticed a pensive look on Yvette's face. She seemed to be contemplating something important.

"Yo, Yvette, what's up? You're lost in thought." Jack stared at the lovely CDC doc, a mug of steaming coffee in his hand. "Have you come up with something? Have a revelation or epiphany?"

Yvette gave the group a contemplative look and shrugged her shoulders. "You know, I am totally baffled by this lung condition that is killing the virus patients. They're not bleeding out or dying from the virus. Instead, they are getting this horrible pneumonia and then checking out. I just don't get it. There is something that we're just not seeing. We're missing something and it's key to this whole thing."

Robert and Maddy nodded and Yvette turned to Maddy and asked, "Maddy, do you have any idea what the lung tissue looked like on autopsy from that patient that died this morning?"

Maddy shook her head. "Not really, at least not in great depth. I briefly glanced at the histology reports and took a quick look at the slides under the microscope. It looked like a poorly differentiated pneumonia or an advanced lung disease. It was strange, different. I've never seen anything quite like it. What about your people? What have they found?"

"The CDC team found pretty much the same thing." Yvette stopped to think for a moment and continued, "We probably need to do some more tissue slices and further histological studies. The tissue should tell us what's going on. The lung changes are the key to solving this viral complex. In the meantime, I just had the craziest thought."

The group looked at her expectantly but Yvette was silent, obviously deep in thought.

"What the hell, Yvette? What gives? You know we need all the help we can get." Jack was impatient and edgy.

Perhaps the caffeine was getting to him. Alex's blue eyes met Robert's grey ones, and they both smiled. It was uncanny how each knew what the other was thinking. It had always been like that, even during their marriage. *What in the hell had happened to them? Why had their marriage ended?* Alex jerked herself back into reality, refusing to ponder this never-ending issue when the entire city of New Orleans was under siege.

Yvette glared at Jack, with eyes like a hungry wolf circling in for the kill. Her voice was icy. "Give it a rest, Jack. I'm thinking and just trying to put some stuff together." Yvette's voice was sharp and fatigue was evident in her face. She turned to Robert and Maddy and asked, "Do you guys remember the case of Dr. Mary Sherman from back in the mid-1960s?"

Maddy shook her head, but Robert responded, "Of course. Dr. Sherman was an internationally known cancer specialist and researcher at Tulane. She was Dr. Alton Ochsner's star doc. I think he recruited her from somewhere in the Midwest. Dr. Sherman was well respected as a skilled physician, researcher, and scholar. She died tragically, was murdered in fact, and I don't think they ever figured out who killed her." Jack didn't seem to be paying attention, still recovering from Yvette's scathing attack.

Alex's windows shook as Jack slammed his recliner into the floor and jumped quickly from the chair, his face flushed with excitement. It seemed as though he had returned to reality. "Of course, I know who she is! Mary Sherman. Dr. Mary Sherman. Of course. My father was on the NOPD when they investigated her murder. It was strange. She was found dead in her bed in her apartment over on St. Charles. Her arm and rib cage were burned away. She had also been stabbed in the heart. It was bad. Brutal."

Jack paused for a moment to collect his thoughts and continued, " Huge cover up, initially by the NOPD, and then the entire city and state for that matter. The Feds covered it up too. The crime was never solved. People went through a lot of trouble to cover up her death."

Yvette nodded and urged Jack to continue.

"Details of her death were withheld and officials sealed her autopsy for 30 years. Lot of cover up stuff going on back then in New Orleans. I remember it really well because my dad was so pissed about it. They pulled him off the case, well, not just him, but everyone connected to it. Basically, the Feds just came in and took charge. Totally disregarded the investigation the NOPD was doing."

Robert nodded and continued, his voice grim, "Yeah, you're right Jack. Whoever murdered her also set her house on fire, specifically her bed. I was young when this happened, but I remembered how upset my parents were about it. I think the stab wound in the heart is what killed her though, because her heart hemorrhaged suggesting she was alive when she was stabbed. The fire didn't kill her. That's for sure."

Maddy shuddered. "Oh, my God. What in the world? This is shocking. Why would someone kill a famous physician? Who would do this to her? I don't remember this story at all. When did this happen again?" Alex could see that Maddy was searching her mind as she mentally clicked through her younger years. Her face remained blank.

"It was in the mid 1960s. It was the talk of the town for years," Robert replied. "It's hard to believe you don't remember. They sort of gloss it over in med school at LSU in med school."

Maddy responded, her voice indignant, "Really, Robert? I'd like to remind you all that you're 'senior friends ' by a few years, and in the mid 1960s, I was focused on cotillions and boys. No time for something awful like murder to enter my adolescent, boy-crazy ,hormone- addled brain."

Yvette raised her finely etched eyebrows and said, "Calm down, sweet thing. No one's mad at you for not remembering. I'd rather been dancing than learning about some horrible murder as well, and, by the way, we just remember the story. We're not that old." Yvette finished a bit chagrined at the thought of being a 'senior' anything.

Maddy gave her a bright toothy smile and quipped, "If the shoe fits, wear it and stop fussing, Dr. Charmaine. You're older than my oldest sister."

Yvette rolled her eyes, as Robert looked between them, and wondered if he had started a argument of some sort. He just didn't really understand women.

Alex had totally missed the playful exchange between Maddy and Yvette. She was astounded. Crap like this in New Orleans never ceased to amaze her and it totally creeped her out. Could there be a city anywhere else in the world with so many hidden skeletons, monsters, and tales of intrigue? "What in the world are you all talking about?" she exclaimed. "Why would someone kill this poor woman? What on earth was she doing to merit such a horrible, brutal death? I agree with Maddy. Shocking!"

Maddy nodded as Alex continued.

"To be a female oncologist in the 1960s was amazing in and of itself, but to be a murdered female oncologist and Alton Ochsner's protégé to boot is astonishing, and to hear about such a heinous crime being covered up is unbelievable! What kind of bull shit is this?" Alex's voice was harsh and her face was white with indignation. She rarely cursed but when she did, people noticed.

Jack and Robert's eyes met in a gesture of understanding. Robert began his recall of the gory story. "I was pretty young when this happened, but I remember it well because my mother and Dr. Sherman were good friends. Mary Sherman was a very community-minded and generous lady. She offered medical services to the children's cancer clinic as part of Charity Hospital's outreach. My mother championed this clinic as part of her charity work. It was around the time my father was considering a run for Governor and my mother was working really hard for the city of New Orleans. She and Mary became friends and Mary often came to tea at our house."

Alex nodded, well acquainted with the elder Mrs. Bonnet's numerous good deeds. "But Robert, why did someone kill her like that? Burn her up? Stab her in the heart? What was she doing? She had to have made someone really mad."

Jack interrupted, "Yeah. She did. She had a lot of people pissed off from what I can remember. There's all kinds of stuff associated with her murder. Lots of conspiracy theories, many related to the cause of cancer and the death of John F. Kennedy. Some of them are probably true. Ed Haslam, a New Orleans native, has been documenting this case for years. His father, an orthopedic surgeon was a close friend of Mary Sherman. Ed remembered her well and probably never recovered from the agony her death caused his dad. According to Ed, Mary and Alton Ochsner were working on a virus to cause cancer. A virus to…."

Alex interrupted, "A virus to cause cancer? Don't you mean a virus to cure cancer? Why in the world would someone be developing a virus to cause cancer? That's ludicrous!"

Commander Francoise glared at Alex. His face was beet red and his eyes flashed with anger. "Counselor, if you would be quiet and not interrupt, I could finish my story! Can you put the liberal lawyer crap away for a few minutes and let me continue?" Jack demanded in a condescending tone.

Alex flushed red and was angry as well. Tempers were getting short and she knew she needed to grab on to hers. There was too much stuff going down in the next few days to be bitchy. Besides, the last person she wanted to alienate was Jack Francoise. She took a deep breath and said contritely, "Sure, sorry, Jack. I'll try to be quiet, but that being said, you know it's hard for me to be quiet," she added in an attempt to end on a light note.

"I'd appreciate that," the Commander smirked as he looked fondly at one of his favorite people in the word and realized what an asshole he had been. "Sorry, Alex, that was uncalled for."

Alex smiled and nodded for Jack to continue.

"There supposedly was a secret, clandestine lab full of mice that Mary Sherman was using to research her cancer-causing virus. The lab was run by David Ferrie, the guy you may remember from the JFK movie released some years ago by Oliver Stone. David Ferrie was played by Joe Pesci. Supposedly a good friend of Lee Harvey Oswald and Jack Ruby, David Ferrie was the 'supposed' researcher who oversaw Dr. Sherman's experiments. The story is he injected the mice with cancer-causing organisms and kept the records. In fact, Ferrie was performing medical research on the hundreds of mice he kept in his apartment at least according to New Orleans district attorney Jim Garrison."

"Jim Garrison, the legendary DA who was ousted from power?" Alex asked incredulously. "This story is becoming more and more unbelievable! It's turning into a fairy tale, and a bad one at that," Alex protested as she held up her hands and shook her head. "Wait, wait, wait! Why would a world-renowned oncologist oversee the development of a cancer-causing virus? Particularly in a secret mice lab in New Orleans. It makes no sense. The thought is simply absurd!" She stopped as she saw anger flame onto Jack's face and heard him take a deep breath. *Oh, crap. He's really going to give it to me now.*

As Alex braced for an angry tirade from Jack, Robert intervened.

Robert stood to make his point and positioned himself between Alex and Jack. He'd seen Alex and Jack go at it before, and even though they loved each other, and something good and useful generally came of their altercations, Robert was not about to let things get out of hand at this point. He continued in a reasonable voice. "I know, it sounds crazy, outrageous even, but there's credible evidence that Ochsner was part of a CIA project. Of course, back then it was called something different, INCA or something like that, to create a cancer-causing organism to use against Fidel Castro and the Communist population in Cuba. I think INCA was actually the first name of the CIA," he added.

Alex had just about had it. She kicked off her high heels and listened to them thud on the wooden floor. She was tired, her grandparents were arriving tomorrow, and this entire evening was turning into fairytale land. She sighed deeply and tried to massage away the beginning of a headache, induced by either stress or caffeine. It certainly wasn't the wine. If she'd known this story was coming up, she'd have consumed a lot more, just to tolerate the evening. All of this virus stuff was irritating her and rubbing her the wrong way. It was the stupidest, most absurd story she had ever heard. It was downright outrageous, and would be comical if New Orleans wasn't facing domestic and international terror threats and if patients weren't dropping like flies in her hospital. Alton Ochsner had been a leader in New Orleans healthcare and his legacy today, The Ochsner Clinic, was a premier facility for modern healthcare, clinical practice, and research. The organization was a paragon of excellence. What a waste of time. Alex looked around and wished her company would go home. She still had to straighten the kitchen and sort out this fantasy bullshit in her head. She wearily returned her attention to Robert who was staring at her.

"As several of you may not know, Alton Ochsner was a right-wing conservative, anticommunist who had a proven, long standing relationship with the US military and the FBI. In fact, it was widely believed that Dr. Ochsner was project chief in virus development for military applications. There was also a rumor that he was a CIA operative."

Alex smiled, figuring that Alton Ochsner couldn't have been a close friend of the liberal, democratic Bonnet family, probably the most powerful political family in Louisiana. She doubted the Bonnets' ever interacted with the arch-conservative Dr. Ochsner on a social level. Robert's dad just couldn't have tolerated it. She could hear him now raving about pea-brained, right-wing, conservatives. She smiled at the memory, a memory from the good days. *He must be dying now with the tea party movement,* she thought.

Yvette interrupted and assessed her friends around her and their reactions to Dr. Mary Sherman's story she decided to continue. "You're absolutely correct, Robert. There's believable, credible evidence that Ochsner's project was supposed to be about developing a vaccine against SV-40 to help prevent soft tissue cancer in children who were administered the Salk-Sabin vaccine against polio in the late 1950s and early 1960s. This vaccine was mistakenly grown on cancer-causing, diseased monkey kidneys . However, evidence suggests that Ochsner's true project was more akin to a 'New Orleans's Manhattan Project' and was really about developing a secret biological warfare agent to use against Communism. It is clear that Sherman and Ferrie conducted research in the irradiation of Simian Virus 40 or SV-40 in a secret lab. In fact, it is believed that the burn wound on Dr. Sherman's arm was most likely caused by the linear accelerator located in a sub basement of Charity Hospital. Some speculate Dr. Sherman had to die because of the burn, which couldn't be explained, and that she was actually killed by members of INCA. In short, the project was transformed into an effort to create a cancer-causing biological weapon to assassinate Fidel Castro and all the communists in Cuba and Latin America." Yvette looked around, and noting the response of her friends, she added, "And there you have it!"

Alex felt her mouth gape open. She hoped she didn't drool. This story was amazing, kind of like a bad mystery or something. But, her judgment was kicking in. Maybe it was true, particularly if Yvette was onboard and knew the story.

"Why, what do you mean, 'children exposed to the polio vaccine'? I'm totally confused." Alex's voice was uncertain. She was intrigued and needed answers.

Robert sighed audibly and continued. "There is some evidence that the polio vaccine, the Salk-Sabin vaccine developed in the 1950s, was grown on the kidneys of monkeys. Unfortunately, it was learned, after a few years, that many of these monkey kidneys were tainted with multiple cancer-causing organisms and were in fact diseased. This spoiled or tainted vaccine suggested that there could be a huge increase of soft tissues cancers in the future--soft tissue cancers such as breast, lung, stomach and so on."

"Robert," Alex exclaimed, her face flushed with excitement. Her heart was beating rapidly as her imagination jumped ahead. "Do you realize what you are saying? You're suggesting the US Government knowingly grew a vaccine for children on diseased monkey kidneys that could cause cancer in the future. Is that what you are saying? Do I understand this correctly?" Alex was full of uncertainty and hoping she had misunderstood.

Yvette and Robert nodded in unison and Yvette spoke, "Yes, Alex, this is exactly what we are saying. There is credible evidence to support these claims as well."

Alex felt as if the wind had been knocked from her lungs. She was breathless, speechless and couldn't respond. *Oh my God*, she thought. *Just think of the increases we have seen in the last 40 years in these exact types of cancer.* Her mind was spinning with the implications. She looked over at Jack who was looking as pissed as she had ever seen him. His face was dark and foreboding. She had a deep sinister feeling that what they were saying was true but her mind refused to accept the enormity of it.

Robert glanced at Maddy and Alex carefully and continued, "In response, the Federal Government started to put aside huge funds to prepare for a cancer epidemic when the recipients of the Salk-Sabin vaccine came of age. You may remember from your history that President Richard Nixon declared the 'War on Cancer' just about the same time. Many people believe he did this because the medical community suspected there would be a huge, increases in cancer due to the fact that the Salk-Sabin vaccine was grown on cancer-infected monkey kidneys."

Maddy, who was clearly upset, spoke for the first time. "Well, they were right on with that. There has been a dramatic increase in all of these types of cancer. I see it every day in my work, just as most of us do. This story is terrifying, and I for one hope it's just that, a story, a bit of fiction, the fodder from which great novels are born."

"Of course there has been a huge increase in breast and lung cancer in men and women as well," Yvette added." Not to mention the increase in stomach and other soft tissue cancers."

Alex was fit to be tied and exclaimed, "What the hell! Are you supporting the claim that the US Government mistakenly grew the polio vaccine on monkey kidneys that were tainted with cancer and then distributed it to millions of American children so that the country could go broke fighting the cancer epidemic?"

Robert's voice was quiet and sounded remote, far away, as if in a deep well or cave as he responded. "Yes, that is exactly what we are saying, and what's even worse, there was a political decision to distribute a second batch of tainted vaccines to children after they knew the virus had been contaminated with cancer-causing organisms. That is absolutely what I am saying. It is pretty well documented, although the US Government has never admitted to any wrongdoing for that matter," Robert added as he ended on a low note.

Alex was outraged and blustered, "You've got to be kidding! This just couldn't be true. This sounds like some third world country story, or some story about a dictator in a political state who was trying to kill children, a country in anarchy or civil war."

Robert nodded, "Yes, you might think that but there is no evidence to support that it didn't happen, unfortunately. Many people think it is absolutely true." He shook his head sadly and stared at the floor.

Alex was dumbfounded. "But, but, why? Why inoculate millions of American children with bad vaccines? American would never stand for this in 2013. Never."

Maddy was pensive and added, "I'm sure this was kept quiet, as it still is. Right Yvette?"

Yvette nodded, "Yeah, pretty much. It didn't make the front pages of any newspaper. Times were different then, as we can all imagine. And there was no Internet or social media or YouTube to allow the story to go viral in minutes."

Alex and Maddy shook their heads, still bewildered by the story. Alex thought about her mother who had become ill at 13 with an unusual form of childhood cancer and suffered neurological damage. Of course, she had suffered from a mild case of polio as a child. *Didn't Simian Virus cause neurological injury? I have to check.* Her mother had never recovered and the damage had caused her massive depression and anxiety all of her life. It still did. Her mother couldn't live as a normal person. And, then, of course, there was her father, Louis Destephano, a man she barely knew. The thoughts of her father, who had deserted her when she was barely four years old, still weighed heavily on her to this very day. A massive feeling of rejection overcame her and she shook it off. She wondered if there was a connection between the vaccine and her mother's illness. She'd damn well find out. Soon. Could the Sabin-Salk vaccine have deprived her of her mother's love most of her life. Could the greed and avarice of the Government have robbed Alex of her mother and Louis Destephano of his wife? *Oh my God. I can't think about this now,* Alex thought. *I have got to back burner this for now.* But, she promised herself, she would revisit it soon.

Yvette continued, "And it gets worse. Sherman and Ochsner were weaponizing SV, or Simian Virus 40 to kill Castro and the communists."

They *were weaponizing Simian Virus to kill Castro and the Communists in Cuba and all over the world. And they were doing this in New Orleans?* The thought was so ridiculous and even comical and she almost laughed out loud. Her mouth gaped open. She was incredulous, and skeptical to say the least. She sat there and gawked at her friends.

After a period of silence, Alex found her tongue and it was acid-sharp. "I can hardly believe what you are saying. This story sounds like a made-for-TV movie. It's hard to imagine our government being a party to anything like this."

Robert nodded at her and said, "I agree, Alex, it does sound like a movie, but I can guarantee you the story is, unfortunately true."

Alex was still unable to buy in to the story. "The idea of the United States government growing a vaccine to inoculate millions of American children against polio on diseased, cancer-riddled monkey kidneys is just beyond my belief. I'm just not buying it. Period. It's dumb."

Yvette's impatience was palpable as she drummed her well-manicured nails on Alex's glass end table. She glared at her hostess and said in a scathing voice, "For God sakes Alex, grow up, join the real world, and join the planet. There is nothing, absolutely nothing, that Robert and I are making up. What we are stating is well-documented in the medical literature, mentioned in medical text books, and described on a website developed by the United States Government that talks about a link between soft tissue cancers and the polio vaccine. Of course, they take no blame for the debacle. No blame at all, but why would we expect them too?"

Alex was silent, a bit taken aback by Yvette's biting comments. Maddy Jeanfreau, stunned by the bitterness between the two women asked timidly, "Is there more to this story or is that the end of it?"

Yvette eyed Alex and Maddy and said, "Yeah, there is more to the story if you would like to hear it. I am happy to share if you can handle it and not get pissed off. Some of it is speculative but still considered absolute truth by many people. Robert, perhaps you would like to continue. You are less confrontational by nature than I am."

Robert looked uncertain. He didn't want to cause a catfight between two of the women he respected the most in the world. He remained silent for a moment and was about to speak when Alex interrupted him, her voice apologetic.

Alex had tears in her eyes as she addressed Yvette. She was so tired that she was losing it. "Yvette, I am so sorry for my behavior. I can hardly believe I was so rude. The story just seemed so far-fetched that I guess I didn't want to believe our government would orchestrate, or even participate in, such a heinous crime. Please forgive my irritation and bad behavior and for heaven sakes, if you meet my grandmother in the next few days, don't tell her!"

Yvette smiled and teased, "Of course I am tattling to your grandmother. I plan to let her know what a horrible, deplorable and disrespectful hostess you are. Now, can I finish the story or perhaps Robert would you like to finish it?"

Robert gestured for Yvette to continue and said formally, "Dr. Charmaine, I will defer to you since you have published on the sad part of our nation's public health history. You're the expert in this case."

Yvette grimaced and said, "Yeah, and that article just about ruined my career at the CDC. Fortunately, I had a lot of good folks who respected my work and went to bat for me. By the way, we do still believe that we have freedom of the press, right? Sometimes, I'm not so sure."

"Hell yes we do!" Jack Françoise roared, recovering from the altercation between Alex and Yvette. Alex smiled as she remembered how Jack had suddenly disappeared from the living room, supposedly for more coffee. He was famous for disappearing whenever he noticed two women disagreeing.

"Okay, Jack, I'm ready to hear the rest of this tawdry tale. Now! If I don't get my carcass home soon, my husband will be calling you to come find me," Maddy threatened as she yawned and checked her watch. "It's really getting late." Alex nodded her head in agreement. She was dead on her feet.

Jack was agreeable. "Okay. Just remember what I'm telling you I'm picking out of my brain from 40 years ago. Robert, you and Yvette chime in whenever you need to. I'll probably forget stuff or leave it out."

144

"Will do," Yvette promised as Robert nodded his head in agreement.

Jack began in his typical police "state the facts" style. "The murder of Mary Sherman is multifaceted and remains so to this day. As Robert said earlier, Dr. Ochsner was clearly tied to a conservative group that was focused on eliminating communism from the globe. Dr. Sherman's murder is also tied into the Kennedy assassination, the death of Lee Harvey Oswald, David Ferrie, and the other notorious criminals of that era. There was, in fact, a mice lab located on Louisiana Avenue. Dr. Sherman oversaw it, and it is believed that David Ferrie performed experiments on the mice using cancer-causing agents in an effort to perfect a cancer causing organism. There is also credible evidence that the CIA, or whatever they were called back then, had planned to assassinate Fidel Castro using cancer-causing monkey cells. This plot fell to pieces after Dr. Sherman's death." Jack looked around at his audience for their reactions.

Alex signed deeply and sat down. Maddy looked surprised, and Robert and Yvette's faces remained impassive. Jack continued, "It is also true that there was a heavily guarded linear accelerator located somewhere uptown that was used to mutate the virus. It is also believed by some that the linear accelerator was the cause of Mary Sherman's death."

"I'm confused, Jack," Alex ventured. "How did the linear accelerator hurt Dr. Sherman?

"Good question. It burned her. You probably didn't know that linear accelerators could actually burn people. Think of a radiation burn. It's the same theory. Somehow Dr. Sherman was burned by the accelerator while working on the virus and because of that, she had to disappear or be killed."

"Because of the burn?" Maddy arched her eyebrows in disbelief.

"Yeah, there weren't that many linear accelerators around then. So the theory suggests Mary Sherman was killed because of her massive burns from the accelerator."

"Wow, is that pretty far-fetched or what?" Alex wondered out loud.

Robert nodded at her and said, "Not so much really, Alex. Mary Sherman was murdered on the day the Warren Commission was scheduled to hear additional testimony on the death of President Kennedy. There is considerable belief both Dr. Sherman and Oswald, who was on both the payroll of the CIA and the FBI according to records, played a huge part in what was happening with the monkey lab in New Orleans."

A silence engulfed the group as they considered the possibilities of what could have and most likely did happen 50 years ago in New Orleans. It did, as Alex had suggested, seem like a fairytale, a very sad and clandestine ending to Camelot.

Finally, Maddy stood and said, "It was a lovely evening, guys, but I've got to head out. Alex, you are a magnificent hostess and your house is beautiful. I may come one day and steal your silk painting!"

"Don't even think about it," Alex warned. "I'll hunt you down and hurt you."

"Yeah, right, I'm scared to death," Maddy said, grinning.

"I'd listen to her if I were you, Maddy. She sounds like she means it." Yvette warned. "I've gotta go too. I'm right after you, Maddy. I need to stop by the hospital on my way to the hotel. Jack, how about you? Can I get a lift to CCMC in your great, big, Cadillac police mobile?"

Jack was accommodating, always willing to share and show off his big silver Cadillac. "Absolutely, Dr. Charmaine. Always happy to cart the CDC around. Robert, what about you? Are you headed out?"

"Yes, I am. I want to help Alex clean up a bit. I'll be leaving shortly." He turned to Yvette and said, "If you need me, just call my cell phone. Let me know how things stand at the hospital. Hopefully, it's quiet."

"Will do, Robert," Yvette said as she kissed him on the cheek and hugged Alex and Maddy. She looked at Alex and said, "Wow, it's been a great evening. You're the best,and I won't rat you out to your grandmother, unless of course you make me mad. It was a super time."

"Thanks, you all. You're the best. We had a great evening," Alex replied, secretly glad they were all leaving. She was exhausted. It was after midnight. She couldn't wait to get in her bed.

Chapter 22

As Alex and Robert stood at the door, bidding their guests goodnight, Alex realized that Robert had his arm around her shoulders. *Hmmm,* she thought. *I hope Yvette noticed this.* Alex had a sneaking suspicion, as women intuitively do, that Yvette was interested in Robert and even though she had no claim to him, it made her mad. *Damn,* she thought. *Am I jealous? Were they an item a long time ago?*

She leaned back and embraced the warmth and gentleness of Robert's touch against her bare arms. Being in Robert's arms felt right and wonderful most of the time. *But when it didn't, well, I just can't think about this tonight... I'm much too exhausted to analyze this again.* Alex was far too tired to analyze the complex and emotionally vacillating relationship the two of them shared.

Robert was great help in cleaning up the dishes and Alex was relieved and grateful. As they worked silently, both caught up in their thoughts, Robert said, "You know, Yvette never did say what she was thinking?'

Alex looked at him quizzically, "What do you mean?"

"Remember, she said she had an idea, and then asked us if we remembered the story of Dr. Sherman. It was the same time Jack roared out of your leather recliner."

Alex smiled as she remembered. "Yeah, you're right. And Yvette ate him for lunch. She has a bit of an acid tongue, doesn't she? I'd hate to get on her bad side." Alex gave Robert a shrewd look as she waited for his reply.

He laughed out loud. "You're right, you would. I've been on her bad side and it's not a happy place to be. Anyway, she never said what she was thinking. She never put Mary Sherman and the polio virus in perspective."

"You're right. I guess she was too busy picking Jack apart and spitting me out. We'll have to check it out tomorrow," Alex said, stifling a yawn.

Robert looked around the kitchen. "Things look pretty good in here. Let me get out of here and go home so you can get to bed. If things go well, I'd love to see your grandparents."

"That would be great. Grand and Beth Blankenship are staying here. You know that Ben Blankenship was my grandfather's mentee and really close to my family, right?"

"Yes, I do. I am so sorry. You have told me several times. All of this is just terrible. Is there anything else you need before I leave?"

"No, Robert. Thanks for coming and for helping. You're such a wonderful friend and you are so good to me."

"Of course I am, Alex. I love you," Robert whispered, as he kissed her on the cheek, and turned the brass door handle, and left."

As Alex watched him walk through her courtyard to his silver Mercedes, she shivered. The night had turned cool, but the loss of Robert's warmth left her cold, empty and scared. *What would happen to them if the terrorists were successful?* The thought scared her as she headed back toward her bedroom, cutting lights out as she passed through the lovely well-appointed rooms in her house. *Life had seemed so good yesterday. What the hell had happened?*

Chapter 23

Nazir was tense and anxious as he looked at the Muslim leaders clustered in a circle on the floor in his Marigny apartment. Six prayer rugs were neatly folded by the window and the entire room was littered with Styrofoam carryout containers and papers products. Eight AK 47s had been stashed in a closet and two others were under his sofa. Nazir's eyes felt like burning torches in his head. He wanted nothing more than to lie down for a good sleep. Night prayers had not lessened his anxiety about the mission, even though it was the work and plan of Allah. The two brothers, who had arrived around 7 p.m., had done nothing to allay his anxiety. They were strange and distant and did not want to talk with him. Habib, the older one had spent most of his time on his cell phone while Syed had spent his evening checking his watch every 5 minutes, looking sullen and watching TV. They had ventured out for a while, but both had declined his invitation to tour the French Quarter and "check out" the surroundings.

Ali had arrived home shortly after 11 p.m. and had fared better with their house guests. The three had interacted well and enjoyed a huge meal from the food Nazir had picked up earlier from the best mid-Eastern restaurant in New Orleans. A short while later, Omar Hassan and Mohammed had arrived and had feasted as well. In their only moment of privacy since Ali's return from work, Ali told Nazir that he had seen Habib and Syed smoking hookah with several men at a bar on his way home from work. Nazir pondered this and wondered what it meant. *Were they part of the mission?*

"Nazir, what do you know about the Russian?" Mohammed Abdu spoke to him sharply as he locked eyes with the paranoid Nazir.

Nazir was jerked back into reality as he stared into the intent face of Mohammed Abdu. Omar was watching him closely for any reaction and once again, Nazir's paranoia skyrocketed. He shrugged his shoulder in reply. "Nothing, I know nothing. Just as I said to you this morning. I have been to his apartment many times today. I have hunted for him in the bars and restaurants where we met in town, and I have sat on benches near the River looking for him in the crowd. He is gone." Nazir realized his voice sounded apologetic and that made him mad. He knew he couldn't control the movements of Vadim, but still, not knowing made him seem weak to the leaders. "Besides, he is difficult to find anyway. He is a master of disguise."

"When did you last see him?" This question came from Omar. His voice was gentle, prodding. Nazir wondered if they were tag teaming him, playing good cop, bad cop. He was overwrought and on edge.

"Let me see, today is Thursday, well, Friday, now, I guess. I saw him Monday afternoon. We met for a Hookah at Aladdin's." Nazir rejected his good cop, bad cop theory. Muslim Jihadists, particularly Muslim leaders would never adopt the tactics of Westerners. It was unthinkable.

"How did he seem? Did he act any different?" Omar was watching Nazir carefully, or so it seemed to Nazir.

Nazir's denial was emphatic. "No. He was just like always. He said he had the virus and would call me to set up a time to meet again for the exchange. We left on good terms. All was well." Nazir looked around the group for encouragement but he saw none. Omar and Mohammed were watching him carefully, while Habib looked bored. Nazir flinched from Syed's penetrating eyes. He got bad vibes from the guy. Scary, evil, sadistic vibes. Habib pulled out his text phone to check his messages. The only friendly face in the room was Ali who gave him a brief smile of support. "I had no reason to suspect him of anything," Nazir continued, his voice uncertain and a little defensive.

"It's OK, brother. We believe you," Omar admonished as he turned to Ali and asked, "Ali, what about the virus at the hospital? Do you know what it is?"

Ali shook his head. "No, we do not. We have tested for all the normal viruses such as Ebola, Dengue, Marburg and so on. It is strange combination of viruses and the American CDC hasn't seen anything like it. They are mystified."

"What do you think," Mohammed demanded. "Certainly you have some idea, correct?"

Ali was a bit taken aback by the harshness in the leader's voice, but replied clearly, meeting Mohammed eye to eye. "I don't know for sure. I could not establish a projection model or a prediction algorithm because the virus is so diverse and quickly mutating. Some people died from bleeding, some from fever and seizures, and most others seemed to have died from a bad pneumonia. I am uncertain what it is. It will take more time."

"There is no time. Can you go back tonight, or more correctly, this morning, or even now, and do more testing?" This wasn't a question, it was an order and Ali knew it.

"Sir, I...."

Ali's response was interrupted by a pounding on the door and the sudden appearance of Yahwa. The NOPD snitch framed the doorway of the small living room, holding onto the wall for support. He looked pale, and he was unstable on his feet, and obviously sick. His eyes had a tortured look. He was sweating profusely and his hand was slowly seeping bright red blood. Yahwa raised his good arm to motion for Syed to put down his automatic weapon. Syed didn't budge, and kept the weapon trained on Yahwa's heart.

Nazir stood to help his comrade. "Yahwa, you are ill. Did you see a doctor?"

Yahwa shook his head. In a hesitating voice, his speech slow and weak, he gasped, "No, no American doctor. Will get better. I have a fever. Feel very sick, but I just had to come and report to ..." Suddenly, Yahwa was seized by a violent fit of coughing, and to Nazir's horror, Yahwa coughed up a large amount of bright red blood. Instinctively, the circle became larger as all five men moved as far away from Yahwa as possible, bracing their backs against the wall. Syed had his hands extended out, as if to block any germs that Yahwa might have expelled.

"Nazir, get him out of here before he infects us. He is contagious and we don't need to be sick." Mohammed's voice was angry as he barked orders at Nazir.

"He is OK. He has an infection. He was bitten by a monkey today and..."

Omar nodded to Habib, who rose from the circle, grabbed his weapon, and roughly grasped Yahwa by the arm and jerked him toward the door. Nazir tried to help his friend but Habib pushed him roughly to the side. Yahwa was too short of breath to speak, but his face, moist with perspiration, was frightened and bewildered. He looked at the automatic weapon with fear in his eyes.

In a quiet and controlled voice, Mohammed spoke for the first time. "It is all right, Yahwa. Habib will take you home. You are too sick to be here and we have work to do. We will check on you tomorrow."

Nazir and Ali stared helplessly as Habib dragged Yahwa from the apartment. Nazir found his voice and said, "I will go with him and help. I know where he lives."

Mohammed glared at him. "Be seated. Habib will be fine. We know where he lives as well. He doesn't need any help. You must tell us the security set up since Yahwa cannot. We must have the security plan in detail to carry on."

Nazir's heart almost stopped and his gut felt like it would explode. He sat down on the sofa and stared at the Jihad leaders. He was speechless, his face pale and drawn. He struggled for control. It was difficult not to cry, and he knew if he did, the leaders would regard him as a baby. He would lose all respect.

Ali looked at his brother with dread. He could taste Nazir's fear. Ali knew now that he hated Jihad. He seriously doubted that Habib was taking Yahwa home. Screw the idea of Holy War. He liked it in the United States. He always had. He liked the American way of life and was proud to be an American Muslim. After this was over, he would never entertain the thought of Jihad, and in fact, might work against it. But for now, he was scared and he knew he had to cooperate. He spoke softly to Nazir, "My brother, what is the matter? We must share the security plan with the leaders. Tell them what you know."

Nazir stared at his brother, his eyes big, his body slumped in defeat.

Once again, Mohammed voice was harsh with contempt though his face remained calm and serene, "What is wrong with you? Tell us the security plan. We need the electrical drawings for the hotels and the Convention Center. Tell us."

Nazir shook his head and looked at the Jihad leader "Brother, I do not know. Yahwa would not share the information. He said I had no need to know. He said you had instructed him not to include me. I have no information."

Mohammed gestured to Omar and said, "Contact Habib and have him return with the drawings. See what he can get from Yahwa." He turned his attention back to Nazir and demanded, "Did he say anything to you at all that could be helpful?" Omar walked outside to make his phone call.

"He only said there were undercover NOPD everywhere, snipers on the roofs and that the FBI and Secret Service were working with them. That is all."

Mohammed's gaze was intent as he growled at Nazir, "This information is useless. This same information was on CNN tonight." He tapped Omar on the shoulder and they disappeared into the bedroom.

Nazir, Ali, and Syed sat quietly in the living room. Ali suspected that Syed was there to guard them. Nazir knew Ali was anxious and terrified. He was scared as well. The gestures and eye contact between Ali and Nazir spoke volumes. Syed watched both men as he cleaned his nails with a file. Ali saw the file as a weapon.

After a few minutes, Ali stood and said, "I'm going back to the hospital. Perhaps I can learn more about the virus. I will call you, Nazir, with any information I learn."

Nazir embraced his little brother, his only friend and the only person in the world he loved and trusted and said, "Go with Allah, little brother." Ali nodded at Syed and left.

Nazir wondered if he would ever see Ali again. He also wondered if he would see nightfall.

Chapter 24

Alex sat up in her bed, wet with sweat and overcome with panic. *Is someone in my house? Did I hear something? Am I hearing things?* The terror in her heart rose to exponential levels as she listened intently for any unusual sounds. She thought she had heard the slight click of a lock as a door closed. The clock on her night table glowed three in the morning, and the ticking sounded like a time bomb as it reverberated through her ears. *There, I hear it again. Someone must be here.* Alex slid to the side of her bed and opened her night table drawer, and took out her small silver derringer .45. She smiled grimly as she remembered the last time she had used it. It had only been eight months before, but it seemed like eons ago. Thank God her grandfather had made her an excellent shot as a young girl. She groped for her cell phone and then remembered that she had left it in the kitchen, too tired from the evening before to retrieve it and plug into the charger by her bed. She silently rose from her bed, slipped on her robe and moved quietly from the bedroom area of her house into the hall where her house phone was located cursing herself for her stupidity all the way down the hall.

She picked up the house phone gently and muffled the sound of the dial tone with her hand, just in case someone was in the house and could hear it. As she placed the phone to her ear to dial 911, nothing happened. Her anxiety escalated when she realized the phone was dead. There was no dial tone. It was then she noticed the dogs down the street were barking furiously. Her heart was beating at panic levels and she was dizzy.

It's amazing how the most wonderful place in your life can become the most terrifying. How dare some SOB enter my home without my permission. Alex's fury overcame her judgment for several moments as she continued her trek silently toward the kitchen, searching for her cell phone. As she passed her living room, she felt a cool draft. One of the French doors leading to her terrace was open. Alex's fear climbed as she reached the kitchen and dialed 911. Then she dialed Jack Francoise. He answered on the first ring.

"Alex. What's the matter?" Jack's voice was alert, but tired. She heard a female voice murmur, "Is Alex OK?"

"Jack, someone's been in my house. My French door is open, the double one in my living room. They were locked and shuttered when everyone left last night." Alex stammered a little but her voice was clear. She could feel the panic eating at her flesh.

Jack could hear the fear and quiet desperation in her voice. He knew she was scared. "Get back into your bedroom, and lock the door. We'll be there soon, " Jack's voice was low and angry and insistent as he added, "It's OK, Alex, you'll be just fine."

"OK. Will do," Alex murmured as she clicked off.

As Alex returned to her room, she heard the sound of a distant siren. Within several minutes, floodlights brightened her house and yard and there was a loud, insistent knocking at her front door.

"Ms. Destephano, Ms. Destephano. Are you all right? It's Josh, Elizabeth's friend."

Alex immediately remembered Josh, the young policeman from Jack's station who had helped her several other times when she had experienced unwanted activity at home. She gratefully opened her front door and greeted him and his partner, a young Asian-American cop she hadn't met before.

"Thanks for coming, Josh," Alex said breathlessly. "I woke up, thought I heard something, like a door closing, sort of like the soft click of a lock. I came in here and the French door was open."

Josh moved over to the door. "Yes, it's been forced open. Look at the lock, Jimmy," Josh said as he motioned to his partner. "By the way, Ms. Destephano, this is Officer James Smith. He's my new partner."

Alex nodded her head and extended her hand. "Nice to meet you, Officer Smith. Thank you for coming."

"You bet. Thank you ma'am. I am happy to be of service," Jimmy said as he examined the door and nodded. "Yeah, for sure, man, it's been forced. Sorry for this ma'am," Jimmy said apologetically as he looked at Alex. Josh had told him that Alex was one of the Commander's favorite people. God forbid that he should piss off one of the Commander's friends. "Let me call in and see if we can get someone over here to dust for prints."

"Thanks, Officer Smith. I truly appreciate it." Alex's voice was emotional and she had tears in her eyes. She tried to wipe them away so the NOPD officers wouldn't notice but it was useless. Josh was pretty sharp and was about to say something when another NOPD officer entered the front door. It was Mac Mackenzie.

"What 'cha got, Mac? Did you find something out there?"

Officer Mackenzie, nodded at Josh and said, "Yeah man. We got fresh foot prints outside the French doors. Looks like a size 10 or so. Unusual tread in the tennis shoes. Not like anything I've ever seen before. Sure ain't one that looks like an Adidas or Nike shoe like I've ever seen."

"Can we get a plate?" Josh asked.

Mac nodded. "Yeah, man. No problem. He looked at Alex and said, "Your automatic sprinkler system was good to us tonight. The prints are fresh and deep in the soil. They should make a great plate for easy identification."

Alex smiled gratefully at the young officer and said, "Thank you, Officer, that's really good news. Maybe we will get lucky and figure out who my intruder was."

"Alex, Alex where are you?" Jack's voice was loud and demanding.

Alex and the NOPD officers looked toward the foyer just as Commander Françoise entered the living room. Both officers saluted as Jack waved them at ease. He gave Alex a gentle look and said, "What the hell is going on here? I just left here three hours ago and things were perfect. Can't you stay out of trouble for just one day?"

Alex walked toward Jack and gave him a big hug. "Thanks for coming, Jack, but you're a bit late. Your men have done all the work and they've done a good job."

"They damn well better, right guys? By the way, somebody give me a report," Jack demanded his voice now serious. The time for joking was over. He stared at Josh and asked, "What do you have?"

As Josh was reporting their findings to Jack he was interrupted by Jack's cell phone. Jack motioned for Josh to stop. Alex could tell by the look on Jack's face that the phone call was bad news. He turned his back on the three of them and talked softly into the phone as he moved toward the kitchen. As Alex and the NOPD officers stood quietly looking at each other, she heard the tell tale sound of her Keurig heating water. Jack did love her coffee maker. As the Commander re-entered the living room his face was subdued and his tone was solemn.

"Get dressed, Alex. That was Yvette on the phone. There's more trouble at the hospital."

"Oh my God, now what has happened? How could things get much worse?" Once again, Alex's heart sped up and her spirits plummeted.

Jack's voice was tired and he looked morose. "It could be worse, trust me. It's basically more of the same, a lot of bull shit. Grab a sweat suit for now. You may want to pack your clothes for the rest of the day in case you don't get back."

As Alex moved toward her bedroom her heart was once again racing. *What the hell is happening now. How could things get worse? I don't think I can take much more of this.* As she quickly donned jeans and a sweater, she was overcome by a feeling of panic and had to sit and gather her thoughts for several moments. She rose from her chair and went to her closet, she surveyed her clothes and wondered if she were picking the last outfit she would ever wear. *I've got to cut this negative thinking out. My grandparents need me and they're coming to New Orleans today. Besides, I have to provide support for Beth Blankenship.*

Alex stood in front of her mirror and looked at herself trying to figure out how she was going to face the worst and possibly last day of her life. She raised her shoulders until she stood at her full height of about 5'9". She thought back to when she was a little girl, about seven years old, when they had come to take her mother away, once again, to what Alex supposed, now, was a psychiatric hospital. She remembered crying her eyes out in her grandparents' living room as the rescue squad bandaged her mother's bleeding arms and put her in wrist and body restraints. She could still visualize drops of blood on the marble foyer at her grandparents' farm outside of Richmond.

She believed her mother was dying and that she would never see her again. She felt an enormous pain in her heart and she thought she would die. She remembered following the slow-moving ambulance from window to window as it took her mother away from her again. That had been the story of her life as a child. Her mother....always sick and always leaving.

After a few minutes her grandmother, Kathryn Lee, had come to her and said, "Come on, Alexandra. We must get ourselves together and face a new day. We will find the strength to do it. In the meantime let's put on your prettiest dress, and we'll go to Richmond for a wonderful lunch and an afternoon of shopping. Then we'll go over to Hermitage Manor, play the piano and sing with the older ladies and gentlemen." In retrospect, her grandmother was teaching how to care for and protect herself while she did things for other people. Self healing by helping others was the mantra of her grandmother's charitable nature. *I can do this. I have to do this. I'm going to be fine.* As Alex grabbed her cosmetics kit from her bathroom, she said a silent prayer for strength and peace. She also thanked God for her wonderful grandmother. By the time she rejoined Jack in the living room she felt energetic and ready to tackle the world.

Jack gave her strange look and said, "What the hell, Alex. You look like you just got home from the spa. What did you do in there?" Jack examined her carefully and looked amazed.

Alex flashed him a smile and said, "It's magic Jack, with a great deal of help from people that love me and from above."

Jack shrugged his shoulders and gestured toward his officers. He said, "Carry on men. Call me if you catch the intruder."

Chapter 25

Habib was desperate, tired, and hungry. He was lost in uptown New Orleans and there were cop cars everywhere. Why in the hell hadn't he just killed the lawyer woman? When Omar had given him her name and address as the hospital administrator he had suggested that Omar kill her. What was one less infidel? Habib could have murdered her, he'd had ample opportunity but had decided not to because, well, he just didn't like to kill people. He knew his Jihad leaders would consider this weak and unacceptable since a mission of Jihad was to kill the infidels. They would probably torture and destroy him for not disposing of the hospital lawyer. As a matter of fact, he didn't really think he wanted to be involved in Jihad. He'd been thinking that for a long time. He'd tried to deny the feelings but he just couldn't. Not anymore.

As he stopped to rest behind a small garage in between two garbage cans, Habib reviewed his evening in his mind. He had sensed desperation in Nazir and the silent, uncooperative feelings of Ali. He knew the young college student wasn't, like himself, a committed Jihadist. Habib wished he could escape from the Jihad but there was no way. He shook his head, anguished by the expectations and demands of the leaders.

By the time he had gotten Yahwa back to his apartment the man was almost dead. It took no effort at all to strangle him, particularly after Yahwa hadn't been able to produce the electrical drawings and security information that the leaders demanded. The man had been out of his mind due to his high fever. In some respects Habib considered the killing of Yahwa a killing of mercy. However, Habib knew he'd be dead as well if he didn't return with the security plan and building documents that Mohammed and Omar had demanded. Thank Allah he had been able to pirate the electrical drawings and security notes from yesterday's meeting from Alex's laptop. He reached for the USB device in his pocket. It was safe, and hopefully, his key to freedom. Habib wanted nothing more than to disappear into the New Orleans underground after the Jihad attacks today. He prayed to Allah that he would be successful. He loved his faith, he loved Allah but he hated Jihad and everything associated with it. *As-salaam'alaykim, peace be with you my brother,* Habib muttered as he had softly closed Yahwa's door. He didn't notice the dark figure loitering across the street.

Habib crouched lower behind the garage to escape the high beam of a police searchlight. He was now prone on the ground, his teeth clenched with silent desperation. As the police searchlight reflected off the metal trashcans, he could hear the voices of two New Orleans policemen. They knew he was hiding close by. As the beams of their searchlights traveled all around him, Habib continued to pray for freedom, freedom from the New Orleans police as well as the Jihadists. Finally the voices and the lights moved away and he felt relieved, and hopeful. He checked his watch and moved quickly in the shadows back to Nazir's small apartment, where he knew Mohammed was counting the minutes until he reappeared. Somehow he told himself, he would escape and become a free man with the help of Allah.

Chapter 26

Alex and Jack were quiet on their way to Crescent City Medical Center, each caught up in their own thoughts. Finally, the silence was ponderous and deafening. Alex broke the stillness in the car.

"OK, Jack. Speak up. What in heaven's name is going on at the hospital now?"

Jack hesitated for a few moments and replied, "Some SOB got his hands on some of the blood and serum from the viral victims. Whoever it was managed to contaminate a bunch of sterile instrument kits they use in OR."

Alex was shocked and speechless. She said nothing for a minute or so, her mind digesting this information and forming all sorts of horrific scenarios. "Oh my God, Jack. How did we discover this?"

The Commander shook his head and replied, "It was strictly by luck. One of the CCMC nurses was opening a sterile pack up in the OR and she noticed that one of the sterile sponges was wet. It was a off color so she sent it to the lab and had it tested. She put a rush on it so the results come back quickly. It was positive for the virus."

The implications were staggering. Alex ran the potential legal scenarios through her mind and knew the cost of liability was significant to CCMC. "What else," she asked, her voice curt.

"It's not any better. In fact, it gets worse. Yvette sent CDC staff to the sterile supply in the Operating Room and found that 100% of the sterile surgical kits, sterile dressings and equipment and, well, whatever you use to operate on people, were contaminated."

"Any idea how many surgeries were done today?"

Jack shook his head and said, "We're meeting Robert at the hospital. He's checking on those patients now, and Yvette has asked the CDC to develop an antidote or vaccine, or something, whatever you people do to try and stop the spread on the virus."

"How in the world do you develop an antiviral or vaccine when you can't identify the virus? I don't see that happening very soon." Alex's voice was sarcastic, all of the wind knocked out of her sails.

Jack continued, "Of course, it may be too late for some of those people."

"Yeah. What about the other floors, the other sterile supplies on the carts on the medical and surgical units?" Alex paused, not really wanting to know the answer.

"Don't know. They were checking. All I know is there was no tampering with sterile equipment on the medical floors or in the intensive care units."

"Humph. Interesting." Alex's eyebrows arched like they always did when she was putting information together

"Interesting how?"

"Don't know yet. It will be interesting to see where they, or if they, contaminated any other supplies. I mean, if there are other supplies contaminated, where are they are located in the hospital?"

Jack gave her a puzzled look. "We should know that soon," he said as he maneuvered his big silver Cadillac into the physician's parking lot and pulled into the space closest to the door.

Alex was daunted by the dozens of law enforcement vehicles surrounding the hospital. There were National Guard, Louisiana State police and NOPD officers, and vehicles everywhere. *How in the world could anyone break in here? This place is a fortress.* Over her shoulder, she noticed the dozens of press members and news media trucks. They were quiet. Probably resting up for the early morning attack. *Thank God for small things.* Alex guessed they didn't know about the viral leak or they'd be clamoring for information.

The pair were stopped at the entrance by the National Guard. Both presented credentials and were admitted into the ED entrance. Once again, they were stopped by an undercover officer as well as hospital security. After presenting their identification once again, they asked to see Dr. Charmaine.

After several very long minutes of watching Jack pace around the small ED reception area, Alex took a seat. The emergency department waiting room was closed since the ED was closed to the public. The area had recently been cleaned. Alex could smell the disinfectant and shampoo on the upholstered furniture. She opted for a plastic chair. As she was checking her phone for messages, she looked up at the sound of Jack's voice.

"Yo, Alex. We're going back. Hurry up." Alex, a bit piqued by his impatience hesitated for about 30 seconds at which time he growled, "Yo, get over here. We've got work to do."

Alex shot him a dirty look as they moved back toward the ED conference room, which was as cluttered now as it had been earlier in the day. Robert and Yvette were seated at the table talking quietly. As Robert noticed Alex, he rose and walked toward her. He gave her a big hug as Alex watched

Yvette's eyes roll. For what? Was it disgust, anger, or jealously? Whatever it was, Alex didn't care, but she smiled. *So, Yvette did have the hots, still, for the handsome surgeon.* Alex stuffed her thought about that for later.

"Are you OK, Alex? Jack said someone broke into your house again. Are you hurt?" Robert's concern was genuine and Alex allowed herself to stay in his arms just a bit longer than she would have normally. Besides, it felt good to have this close human contact with someone. Boy, she did have some of the bitchy in her as she glanced back into the disapproving face of Yvette Charmaine. She needed to calm it down and besides, jealously was not a part of her nature, at least not generally, and there was way too much going on to start.

"No, no. I'm OK. I'm fine. They got some footprints so hopefully they will be able to find whoever it was. So, what's happening here?" she asked dismissing her home invasion with the wave of her hand.

Yvette nodded to Alex and Jack and said, "You guys sit down. We can update you."

Alex grabbed a bottle of water from the credenza as Jack went for the coffee, which was so thick it gave Alex stomach pains just watching it drip from the stainless carafe. "Jack, that's going to kill you. It's nothing but sludge. Can't we get some fresh coffee?"

Yvette looked a bit miffed, "You're the one in power around here Alex. It's almost 4 a.m. so your guess is as good as mine about dietary services. Right now, I am more concerned about Central Services," Yvette finished, her voice a bit sarcastic.

Alex nodded, stung by Yvette's sarcasm and asked in a crisp voice, "What's up? Robert, can you and Yvette fill me in?"

Robert nodded as he picked up on the bad vibes between Alex and Yvette. "All of the sterile supplies in the OR were contaminated with the virus, as were all of the sterile supplies on the carts on the surgical floors. We'd have never figured it out if the nurse in OR hadn't noticed the dressing was damp." He shook his head thinking out loud, "Oh my God, can you imagine how horrible that would have been if we had contaminated all of our surgical patients with this virus we can't even identify?"

Alex shuddered at the thought but nodded and looked at Yvette and Robert. "Thank God for the vigilance of CCMC nurses, all nurses for that fact. What about the medicine floors, the intensive and cardiac care units? Have those supplies been contaminated?"

Yvette spoke, "We don't think so, although the supplies in interventional radiology have been contaminated. Basically, anywhere in this medical complex where you might change a wound dressing, start an IV or perform surgery have contaminated supplies."

Alex nodded and said, "Interesting, don't you think?"

"Interesting? What the hell is interesting? It's another crime in my mind. Something I'm missing here?" Jack roared impatiently.

Alex was having difficulty keeping her composure. She was angry and said quietly, "Calm down, big guy, I'm on your side. I think the pattern is interesting. That's all."

"Pattern? What pattern? Why, Alex, what are you thinking?" Robert asked, a confused look on his handsome face. Even with no sleep, Robert was drop-dead gorgeous.

Alex noticed she had the rapt attention of all three and said, "It seems interesting to me that whoever did this selected areas where the patients are fairly healthy. Most surgical patients are healthy as are most patients having diagnostic testing."

Jack was still perplexed. He didn't get it. "What the hell do you mean, healthy people? Ain't nobody here really healthy or they wouldn't be here." His voice was impatient, querulous.

Alex rolled her eyes and said, "Jack, what I mean is that I see a bit of a pattern. The perp who did this isn't messing with people in the ICUs who are critically ill or people on medicine units who often have terminal or chronic diseases. He or she just seems to want to infect healthy people with the virus, that's all. It's kind of like the patients in ICU and on the chronic disease units are going to die anyway so he's hitting the healthy group of patients and trying to infect them with the virus. He's setting priorities with whom he wanted to kill. He's going for a greater impact."

The conference door opened and Elizabeth Tippett entered. "Hello, everyone, or should I say a very early good morning to all of you?" Elizabeth was dressed for work in a dark navy blue suit, white cashmere sweater, low heeled navy shoes and conservative, but very real, jewelry. Alex called this her 'TV camera look.

"Liz, what's up?" Alex had a sinking feeling in her stomach. "I didn't expect you here. Somebody needs to get some sleep so they can be sharp enough to run this place," Alex wisecracked but knew her voice was strained because her vocal cords hurt from keeping her voice calm when indeed she really wanted to stand up, scream and then rip out everyone's vocal cords so they would shut up. She could barely speak her stress level was so high.

"The hospital operator called me. I guess she couldn't reach you or Robert. She got a telephone call that someone in the hospital had spread the virus all over the hospital in an attempt to make even more people sick. Then I got a call from my good friend at CNN. He said the same thing. Is any of this true?" As Liz's eyes searched the faces of her friends - it was evident that the story was true.

Alex's shoulders slumped as if in defeat. "Hell yes, someone had been contaminating the sterile supply carts on some of the floors. I guess you'll have to make a statement. How in the world did CNN know? Are the terrorists calling them directly?"

Liz shrugged her shoulders. "Somebody is. Anyway, we need to make a statement. Half the world already knows there's a bad virus here at CCMC and we've been totally mum about it. It's been on network TV and cable since yesterday afternoon. It's time for us to get out there and say we have this stuff under control," Liz implored her colleagues. "What'd'ya say?"

"You're right. I'll be a part of the news conference as well," Yvette offered. "I can speak from the viral, CDC aspect. I generally don't offer this, but there's a lot going on in this city and we've a lot riding on how we handle this."

Everyone nodded except for Jack who growled, "Screw that, I'm not saying anything to the liberal press. They're lying bastards and they twist everything. They have never quoted me correctly, never. They just screw it up anyway. Count me out," he said as his phone signaled a text message.

"Oh shit, what the hell..." Jack had a dark scowl on his face.

"What, Jack, what is it?" Alex asked, alarmed by the Commander's response.

Jack shook his head, "It just doesn't stop coming. We got a body downtown, stabbed in the chest with a syringe of something hanging out of the stab wound. Anybody want to guess what? What do you suppose that could be?"

An instant later, a Code Blue sounded in the ED and Yvette rushed to respond. "Well, there is another person with the virus who is unable to breathe. We've got to figure this out," she said as she dashed from the room with Robert following her.

In the silence that followed, Alex was barraged with actions she should take but clarity was slow in coming. The situation was convoluted at best and had to be handled delicately. Finally, she glanced at Elizabeth and said, "Liz, why not release a statement to the press and we'll plan a conference this afternoon after we find out more of what's happening. In the meantime, contact the head of Central Supply and have them collect every sterile supply in this hospital and destroy it, according to Yvette's directions. Cancel any surgeries until after we get new sterile supplies, or better yet, get on the horn to East Jefferson and see if they can lend us enough for the day or until we can resupply. Have the Central Supply people work on this. They have their own network."

"Sure. Anything else?" Elizabeth was frantically taking notes. Alex smiled. Liz was so capable, but sometimes she just didn't get it.

"Nope, I'm going home to clean up, do some thinking, and then I am picking up my grandparents at the airport at 10:00 so I should be back on campus around noon or so. If you need me, call, text, or email."

"Will do, thanks Alex. Get some rest."

Alex nodded, then turned to Jack and said, "OK, big guy, walk me out of here. Can you give me a ride or should I call Martin?"

"Nah, I'll take you. Dead is dead and there's no rush for me to get down there. "I'll get you home," Jack promised as the two friends left the hospital, walking through the police barricades, armed guards, and undercover cops. Alex marveled at how much easier it was to get out of the place than get in. Getting out was a piece of cake, but then, getting in probably wasn't that hard either. Not if someone was stealing body fluids and injecting them in other people and sterile dressing kits. *What a bitch*, she thought. The world was going to hell all around her. *It's a good thing he is giving me a ride home. If he had carted the CDC around and not the hospital attorney, I'd be mad.* She turned and said this to Jack and he gave her a dirty look and said, "Shut up, Alex. I drive you around all the time." She smiled at him as he continued to grumble.

Chapter 27

Habib felt out of place, a bit like a turncoat or defector, as he handed the thumb drive he had copied from Alex's computer to Mohammed. Perhaps he was the infidel now since he knew he wanted nothing more to do with Jihad. An interesting thought. As Habib considered his role as a infidel, Mohammed examined him carefully and asked, "Was there any trouble, brother?"

Habib shrugged his shoulders and felt guilty. He had never met anyone with eyes like Mohammed. Mohammed's eyes were blank and held thousands of secrets. They were unreadable. Habib's voice was strong as he replied, "No, not really. I had to break into the lawyer's house to get plans of the hospital's electrical and design systems. She also had these hard copies of the electrical and HVAC systems for the Convention Center on her desk in her home office. I don't have the plans for the Hilton. I was unable to get these but perhaps I could find them online," Habib offered, unsure of Mohammed's response. He knew his voice sounded convincing but he felt weak and unsure. He noticed that Syed looked at him strangely. Habib cringed under his careful scrutiny. Habib felt his gut turn over and looked away.

Omar grabbed the Convention Center plans from Habib and examined them. After several minutes he nodded at Mohammed and said, "Brother, this will work. The heating and cooling system is well designed and there are many vents to assist us. We will have no problem."

"What if the American leader does not go to the Convention Center? Then our plans will fail," Syed commented with an angry scowl. "We must have all of the plans," he said as he gave Habib a deprecating look and added, "You did not fulfill your mission, brother. What do you have to say for yourself?" He was glowering with impatience and anger.

Habib was silent for several moments and replied, "I did the best I could. There were New Orleans police everywhere, and I did not want to jeopardize our mission. I think I can find the hotel plans on the internet."

Syed continued to scowl at Habib as Mohammed and Omar watched the exchange in silence. Habib worked hard to control his non-verbal behavior and keep his breathing normal. He felt his heart rate quicken, and the pain in his gut was fierce. It took all the strength he could muster not to double over. He met Syed eye to eye and said, "I have done nothing wrong, I have not disappointed Allah, brother."

Mohammed gave Habib a half-smile and asked, "What of Yahwa? Was there trouble?"

Habib felt his face redden once again as he replied, "No. There was no trouble. Yahwa was almost dead when I strangled him. He wouldn't have lived another hour. By the time I got him home, he was bleeding from his mouth and nose." Habib shuddered as he remembered how hard he had scrubbed to get Yahwa's blood off of his hands and arms. He prayed he didn't catch the same sickness as his dead comrade.

"The body?" Omar continued to give him the same steady look. "Did you dispose of it?"

He shook his head. "No. I felt it better to leave it there, in his home. It will look as if he died from the virus. I doubt they ever do an autopsy. There are many bodies mounting up at the hospital. I saw an ambulance remove four bodies a little while ago. Besides, by the time they find him we will be a long way from New Orleans and he will just be considered a casualty of the virus."

Omar gave Habib a half smile and said, "Good work, brother," and then turned to Syed and asked, "Was your trip to the hospital eventful?"

"No, sir. Not eventful at all. I got my mission done and I can vouch that there are lots of dead people from the virus. It is very lethal. I hope we are safe from it," Syed added, looking uncertain. Unknown to the others, Syed had showered twice since returning from Crescent City Medical. He hated germs. He could stand a lot of heat and eat a lot of sand but he couldn't handle germs. They freaked out the hardened, committed Jihadist.

"We will be fine," Mohammed assured him. "We are working for Allah and will be kept safe."

"What of Vadim? Any word of him?" Mohammed asked.

Syed and Habib both shook their heads negatively.

"Where are Nazir and Ali?" Habib ventured.

"Nazir is sleeping in his room and Ali is back at the lab. We should all get some rest. Today and tomorrow will be great days for us. We will triumph! Death to the infidels," Omar said softly as he pulled his pallet from his bag.

As Syed and Habib lay face to face on the floor in Nazir's apartment, Habib asked, "What did you do at the hospital, Syed?"

"You have no need to know, Habib," Syed said as he turned away from his brother. "No need to know at all," Syed muttered as he closed his eyes.

Habib felt his gut constrict and he flexed his knees in pain. *He knows I want out. What am I to do*? Finally Habib thought of a plan and fell into a troubled sleep.

Chapter 28

It was a beautiful October day. The morning air was crisp and clean. As Alex backed her black, seldom-driven Mercedes out of her garage and headed toward Interstate 10 to Kenner, she felt invigorated by the cool air. She had managed a short nap and felt clear-headed and well-rested as she headed toward the airport. She had called Bridgett with a dozen 'chores', and had just gotten off the phone with Elizabeth who was doing an admirable job at holding the media at bay. Her last call was to Jack as she drove down the road.

"Yo, Alex, what's up?

Alex could hear the exhaustion in Jack's voice. She knew he hadn't had five hours of rest in the past 40 hours. She felt guilty and a little alarmed about Monique being alone for such long periods of time. Perhaps she and her grandmother could visit Monique later in the day if things were quiet. "Nothing, Jack. Just checking in. I'm on my way to the airport to pick up my grandparents."

"Oh, yeah, I forgot they were coming. Are they staying at your house?" Jack's voice sounded pleased. He was fond of Kathryn and Adam and saw them every time they were in New Orleans. He'd even visited them in Virginia several times. Congressman Adam Patrick Lee was Jack's kind of politician, a law and order man, tough on the Middle East policy and sanctions and a believer in kicking ass and kicking ass really well once you thought out the plan. In fact, he and the Congressmen had their own mutual admiration society. They were dedicated to each other. Jack smiled as he thought about their infrequent Jack Daniel's nights in Virginia.

"Granddad's going to be living between the Palm Court, Hotel Burgundy, and my house but Grand and Beth Blankenship are staying with me."

"I'll arrange for some additional police protection for you all."

"No, Jack, don't," Alex started to protest. "We'll be fine and I want this to be low key. Beth and Grand are stressed beyond belief."

"Yeah, Alex. That tennis shoe print they found in your yard has been traced to a brand of tennis shoes manufactured in either India or somewhere in the Middle East." Jack stopped for a few moments, allowing the implication to sink in.

Alex's stomach flip-flopped. "Huh, are you saying a terrorist broke into my house last night?" The thought of a terrorist in her home chilled her blood and her lungs were about to explode. There was no air in the car to breathe.

Jack sighed, exasperated, "No, not exactly. At least, I am not speaking legally. I am saying that someone with a tennis shoe made in that part of the world broke in to your home the day before you will be entertaining two Congressional wives. Considering what is going on these days, I suggest you have more police protection. After all, your grandfather isn't a favorite of the Muslim world with his views on what should happen in the Middle East."

"But we already have secret service agents who will be protecting Beth. I think we are OK. I really think we're fine."

Jack was insistent. "Make up the beds in your Carriage House, Alex. You're having more NOPD and Secret Service around your house than you ever wanted to see," Jack said as he clicked off the phone.

Damn, what the hell. I really wish my life were simpler. I suppose I'll have to feed these people, too, Alex thought although she knew she really didn't have to. It was just her way.

It was the way she'd been raised. In her grandparents' home in Virginia, everyone was fed, and they were well-fed. Once you entered the long driveway at Wyndley Farm in Hanover County, Virginia, you loosened your belt in anticipation of Grand's wonderful food and drink.

Alex picked up her phone once again and dialed her cleaning crew, and asked them to clean and freshen the Carriage House and give her main house a quick clean as well. She remembered the dark prints near the French door in the living room. She had neglected to clean them this morning. That dirt had to be gone by the time she got her grandparents back to her house. Thank goodness she had good connections and could get things done quickly. She also arranged for some great Cajun cooking via Martin's wife. As she was ticking through meal plans, the traffic on the notorious Interstate 10 came to a slow, halting stop at Causeway. She checked her watch. She was going to be late. Her grandparents were probably landing right about now. She could hear her grandfather growl when he didn't see her standing at ground transportation. She had texted them to let them know she'd be picking them up and not Martin as originally planned. She hoped this would defuse some of their angst.

Alex jumped when her phone rang again. It was Jack. Again.

"What's up, Commander?" Alex bantered. "I'm stuck in traffic at Causeway."

"We identified the body from the killing last night, you know, the one that was stabbed in the chest and had the syringe hanging from the stab wound?"

"Yes, I remember. Thought he was shot in the chest? He wasn't?" Alex drummed her fingers impatiently against her steering wheel. She rarely drove in the city because she hated New Orleans traffic.

"Yeah, turned out he wasn't. He was strangled and stabbed but even more important than that, he had been injected with the virus in his heart. The same virus that's all over the hospital. He had blood coming from his nose and mouth unrelated to the killings."

"Why would someone strangle him? It sounds as though he would have died anyway," Alex responded, her voice curious. "Right?"

"Yeah, it does look that way. I think they strangled him so they could stick the syringe into his chest. And yes, the syringe was full of live virus. Maddy identified it and compared it to the fluids from other patients she had gotten from Yvette. The lab matched them. It was an identical match."

Alex thought for a minute and said, "Wow, this is pretty heavy. Why would they strangle someone who was dying from the virus and then stick a syringe of it in a stab wound? There's gotta be a message here. Certainly sounds like overkill to me."

"You're right, Alex. There is. You don't know the worst part yet."

"Jack, they're all worst parts. There's no good parts in this drama. But, what's the worst part?" Alex probed.

"Guy was NOPD. As a matter of fact, he was part of the NOPD blue security team. He was at yesterday's meeting."

Alex mind flashed back to the young man of Middle Eastern descent who had seemed avidly interested in every detail of the meeting. Her heart rate quickened, "Jack, was he the uniformed officer standing at the door?"

"Yeah, why? We hired him a year ago or so. I think he may be from Iran."

"I noticed him yesterday at the security meeting. He was so attentive. It was like he was memorizing every word that anyone uttered. As a matter of fact, I was a bit suspicious of him. I meant to mention him to you. He looked to me like he had something up his sleeve." Alex stopped for moment and continued,

"Jack, what do you know about this guy?"

"Why do you ask?" Jack's voice was guarded.

"Because I think he either contaminated all of the sterile supplies in the hospital or knew who did. I think it's interesting that whoever did it was pretty smart and knew their way around hospitals. He's one of them."

"Yeah, probably was," Jack agreed.

"Your cop was a terrorist. What a well thought out plan! Why risk your life trying to infect people who are already most likely going to die." Alex shivered at the thought.

It made perfect sense to Jack. "You're good, Alex. However, the dead cop did not infect the hospital. He was long dead before that happened. Maddy thinks he died before midnight. If you ever want to give up the law, you can come investigate for me. I think you're on to something. Where'd you learn to think like such a sicko?' Jack half joked.

Alex continued, nonplussed. "At the very least he is, well, was, a big part of this plan. He was a plant in the NOPD from a terrorist organization. That's huge, Jack."

Jack sighed and said, "You're right, Alex. We checked him out via the FBI's facial recognition software. He was here under an assumed name. He has ties to several terrorist groups in the Middle East."

Alex groaned. "Oh my God, Jack. All of this is true and I was hoping they were exaggerating. Do you think he was tied to Ben Blankenship's murder? Why did they kill him? Kill the terrorist, not Ben? Is it because they're letting us know they are behind the virus? Do you think it's a show of power for them?"

Jack was thoughtful. "Yeah. For sure a show of power. I've no idea why they killed him and made such a public display, Alex. We're working on it. I've got to go. My phone is blowing up with texts and I've another call coming in. Be careful. The security will be at your house by noon," Jack promised and clicked off.

Chapter 29

Travis Stoner, Jeff Bodine and John Houser sat around the conference table in the Police Commissioner's office at One Police Plaza. The table was covered with half-full coffee cups and empty doughnut boxes. Each man sat quietly, mesmerized with his own thoughts until Bodine spoke up, his voice sounded loud in the large empty room. "Ted. Where's Jack? Does he know we're meeting?"

Bodine's voice jerked Commissioner Ted Scott back into a reality he didn't want to face. "Yeah, he does. He's running down some evidence on the murder of the Jihadist we found downtown last night, you know, the one with the virus and syringe hanging out of his chest." Ted stood and paced the room wondering if Jack was also taking his time in order to miss the meeting. Jack hated coming downtown, always afraid he would run into the Mayor. Certainly he wouldn't play that card today, would he? Just to be sure, the Commissioner pulled out his phone and texted Jack.

Stoner said, "Let's get started. Jeff, do you have anything new?"

"Just a little. We know that Mohammed Abdu and Omar Hassan arrived in New Orleans late last night. We know where they're staying. These two are Jihad leaders, have been for years, and are professors of Middle Eastern studies in New York. They are Chechen, from the North Caucasus region of Russia. As we said earlier, this is a Russian Red Jihad mission. The North Caucasus region is a Russian hot bed of insurgency and these insurgents are fighting the Russians as well as the West. Mohammed and Omar have been on our radar for years, actually since before 9/11. We've got nonstop eyes on the place where they're staying and are watching and recording every movement they make."

182

The FBI agent paused as Jack entered the room and dropped into the nearest seat.

"Hey Jack, I was just saying the two Jihad leaders, Mohammed Abdu and Omar Hassan, arrived in New Orleans via plane late last night. They are leaders in a terrorist cell in New York. They met with a member of the local cell Nazir and his younger brother Ali at their apartment in the Foubourg Marigny. We know nothing of Nazir. Neither he, nor his little brother, are of great importance to us. We're assuming they are minor players. We also know several other terrorists came in yesterday via car and are at the same location. We haven't identified them yet but will shortly. We're running them through the FBI facial recognition software now."

Jack nodded as he pulled a 8 x 10 glossy, black and white photo from a manila file. "I'm betting this is one of them."

Ted examined the picture of a bearded man in western clothing bending over a body. "Yeah, I'd say this is the guy who murdered the guy with the syringe. Right?"

Jack nodded and slid the picture across the table toward Houser.

"What else do you have, Jack?"

"The dead guy is, unfortunately, NOPD, a street cop. He's been working in the US under an assumed name for a number of years. We hired him from the Miami/Dade PD several years ago. His references were impeccable. He was clean as far as we were concerned. Unfortunately, we just learned he had an entirely new identity. His real name is Yawah Amir Abbudin. He has worked in the US for over 10 years infiltrating police systems for several terror organizations. He was at our meeting yesterday so we need to assume he passed on everything we talked about to Mohammed and Omar before he died."

Bodine slammed his fist into the conference table and several half-full coffee cups overturned. No one moved to sop up the coffee that was running everywhere. "Damn, I was afraid of something like this. We'll have to move to an alternate plan. Anything else, Jack?"

Jack thought for a minute and said, "Yahwa, had the virus. No question. He died from the same strain we're treating over at CCMC. He was strangled and then shot and the syringe shoved into his bullet wound."

"These terrorists are mean sons of bitches. They think nothing of killing their own. No matter what the skill level and degree of training," Bodine added.

Houser shook his head. "What the hell does this mean? Why strangle and shoot your own man, especially if he was almost dead anyway? This is screwed up." He looked around the room, "What do you guys think?"

Stoner shrugged his shoulders. "We'll probably never know. Jack, do you have a theory? But remember, gentlemen, these man don't have the respect for human life that we do. No question about that."

Jack was amazed at how calm Stoner was under stress. He didn't even appear tired and was totally calm and in control. His clothes were pressed and he looked impeccable. Jack looked like he still had on yesterday's shirt and pants, but he didn't. He had showered and shaved earlier in his office. The other men either looked tired or had stress lines all over their faces. And, the President hadn't even gotten to town yet. It was gonna be a long two days.

Jack paused for a moment and then nodded in agreement, "You got that right Stoner. These bastards are savages. Sicko mothers. But yeah, I'm working on a theory. I'm thinking that maybe the terrorists were afraid he would become incoherent and babble or that he'd check himself into the hospital and get better. At any rate, they didn't need him anymore. Whatever the deal, the bastards didn't trust him anymore so they killed him."

Jeff Bodine contemplated Jack's assessment and added, "Yeah, it could be that. At any rate, he was no longer useful to them and he was sick, so they offed him."

"OK, but what's the message with the syringe sticking out of his chest? That has to have some sort of meaning. What's the deal with that?" The question came from John Houser. "Why the hell would they stick a full syringe of the virus in a chest wound. That's pretty sick, wouldn't you agree?" Houser's face was angry and displayed his contempt for the actions of the terrorists.

"Yeah, as I said, a bunch of sick bastards. This is just another power play. I think they were showing us they were in charge, in charge of the virus and in charge of the city, and they would do anything, even kill their own to bring us down. At least, that's what Ms. Destephano and I believe." Jack reported and gave a tight half smile to the group.

Ted was reflective for a moment and added, "You're on to something, Jack. Have you reported what happened at the hospital early this morning, before we discovered the body downtown?"

"Thanks, Commissioner. I have not." Jack almost looked apologetic, or as apologetic as Jack ever looked, as he faced his colleagues around the table. "Sometime early this morning, most likely between 2 and 3 a.m., one of the terrorists managed to get through the police barricades, NOPD, National Guard and FBI agents, got his/her hands on the virus, and injected every sterile supply kit in the operating room, surgical floors and radiology with the virus. They were able to move through the hospital without detection or even raise any suspicion. These are the skill sets of the people we are working against. They are trained, and very smart."

Bodine shook his head. "What a bitch. They are relentless bastards. We've got some clever people here. Why do you suppose they didn't contaminate all of the supplies on all the floors? You think time was a factor?"

Jack shook his head. "Don't think it was time. Alex thinks it's because they only wanted to kill healthy people. Would make a bigger impact - killing healthy folks. Patients on medicine and in the ICU are generally critically or chronically ill. She thinks the perp only wanted to spend his time on people who are basically healthy."

Stoner shrugged his shoulders and spoke up. "I agree. I also think they want the killings and the virus to last as long as possible. Anything else, anyone?"

John Houser raised his hand. "Are you sure they got the virus from the hospital? Could they have brought it with them?"

"Dr. Charmaine reported the virus in the syringe and injected into the sterile supplies was an identical match to what she is treating in the emergency department," Stoner answered. At least, that's what we're assuming now."

"Either that or someone has broken into the City Morgue and raided the Medical Examiner's lab," suggested Commissioner Scott. "Is it possible that someone on the CDC team could have done this? They would have ready access."

Oh shit, I hadn't even thought of that, Jack thought, feeling like a moron. *Yvette will kill me when I ask her this question but I have to.* "Yeah, I suppose that could have happened but I haven't heard of anything missing or amiss in the ME's office. I'll check it out. I'll also check with Dr. Charmaine about her team's potential part in this." Jack wanted to crawl under the table. He wasn't thinking well. He needed to rest and take another shower. Hot water cleared his brain and made him think better. As soon as this meeting was over, he was disappearing to his office for a nap. It was proving to be a long day and he'd not recovered from yesterday.

Stoner stood and addressed the group, "Men, we'll meet this evening. We still need to determine where POTUS will speak and that location could change several times based on the intel we receive. Currently, we're planning for the Hyatt since we know the terrorists have the plans for the Convention Center. Actually, we're operating on the assumption they have the plans for all the local hotels. I do know the first lady will not be coming to New Orleans. Her husband believes the threat is too great. See you at five this evening. Stay safe."

As the men filed out of the conference room, Jack couldn't help but notice the desperation in their eyes. They weren't sure they were going to win this and neither was he.

Chapter 30

Alex was a half an hour late meeting her grandparents and she was frantic. Knowing her grandfather and his level of impatience, there was a high probability that he'd rented a car and was on his way to her house. She shook her head in exasperation. Damn the traffic in New Orleans. She had texted her grandmother but had gotten no answer. As she drove through the flight arrival area she saw no sign of her grandparents. Alex was surprised and circled back through the arrival area of the New Orleans International airport hoping they'd be sitting outside on the bench but they were not. Finally, she pulled into the garage adjacent to the airport, walked into the daylight and called her grandmother's cell phone.

"Alexandra, so sorry we are late. They held the flight on the ground in Dulles because they were concerned about terror activity or a terror threat or something. Finally, they let us leave but the plane was 45 minutes late getting here into New Orleans. We still have to pick up our luggage but we'll be right out as soon as we can."

Alex breathed a sigh of relief. "That's fine, Grand. I was afraid I'd missed you. I am right outside. Do you need me to come in and help you with luggage?"

"Oh no, your Grandfather will arrange for a Skycap. We'll be fine. Just give us a few minutes."

"I will. I'll go and get the car out of the garage and then circle around the flight arrival area. I am so excited to see you! I was getting worried," Alex could feel the relief pulsate through her body. She'd really been freaked out when they hadn't been there. *I need to get control of myself. I've got several long days ahead and I don't want to upset my grandmother,* she thought as she backed her black Mercedes out of the parking space. She failed to see the tall bearded form of Syed in the corner and she also missed Habib peering at her as she slowly exited the parking ramp.

Her grandmother was seated on a bench in the passenger pickup zone, and her grandfather, whom she had once thought larger than life itself, was talking with an enormous Sky Cap who looked like Magic Johnson. The skycap was guarding their two Pullman suitcases. *Oh my goodness, they look so old. When did this happen? How long has it been since I've seen them?* Alex could feel tears spring into her eyes as she looked at her aging grandparents. Her Grand looked frail on the bench surrounded by her omnipresent books and knitting bag. Alex had tried for several years to get Kathryn to use her Kindle eBook reader but Kathryn declared she would only read books where she could feel the paper and touch the cover. Upon further inspection of her grandmother's seated figure, Alex wondered if she had lost weight. She'd been in Virginia visiting her grandparents with Robert and Jack a little less than six months ago but she could swear her grandmother looked 20 pounds lighter. Besides, Alex did not think her grandmother's color looked good. Kathryn's usually beautiful complexion was pale and wan and her vibrant blue eyes were dull and tired. *I really need to get Robert to check her out while they're here. I don't like the way that she looks. Could she be sick and not telling me?*

Alex's eyes traveled to her grandfather's face. She could tell he was upset. The lines around his eyes were accentuated and deeper than usual. His body spoke of exhaustion to her. He also appeared older and unwell and that was upsetting to her. She had never considered the likelihood that her powerful, opinionated, and passionate grandfather could grow old or weak. As the possibility occurred to Alex that she could or would soon lose two people that meant the most to her in the world, she had to wipe away hot, blistering tears. In order to pull herself together and regain her composure she circled the arrival loop at the airport one more time before pulling over to gather her grandparents.

As Alex slid her Mercedes right in front of her grandparents, her granddad jumped up in anticipation. Her grandmother rose as well and had wrapped Alex in a huge hug the moment she exited her vehicle.

"Alexandra, you look lovely but I must say I've seen you looking better," her grandmother noted as she scrutinized Alex's rust colored suit and all white silk blouse. "Of course, that russet colored suit is spectacular for this time a year and it sets off your auburn hair beautifully."

"Hell, Kathryn leave the girl alone. We just got here and I think she looks good as ever." Congressman Adam Patrick Lee retorted as he gave his granddaughter an enormous bear hug, held her at arm's length and then commented, "You do look a little tired. What the hell has been going on here in Satan's city? Should your grandmother and I believe everything CNN, Fox and network news are reporting?"

Alex laughed and said, "I have no idea. What are they reporting? Wait, before you answer. Let's get our luggage loaded before the NOPD throw us in the slammer for loitering with airport security as their witness," Alex suggested as she motioned for the skycap to load their bags.

Once the three were comfortably settled in Alex's car and on their way to uptown New Orleans, Adam began his news report.

"CNN has reported more than 10 deaths from an unknown virus that for some reason the best minds at the CDC cannot identify. They have also suggested that the virus may be part of a terrorist plot against the city and our country. Fox news is reporting that the terrorists plot is aimed at destroying as many American politicians as possible as well as many of the citizens of New Orleans. Both networks say that security is tight. What do you think?"

Alex watched her grandfather's eyes in the rearview mirror and replied, "I'd say that's pretty accurate, for once. Humph, pretty impressive actually. I wish I could say it was different, but unfortunately it's not. Actually, it's a little worse."

"Oh, no, my God, Alex! What else is going on? Isn't this enough?" her grandmother lamented. "When this is over would you please consider moving somewhere else, hopefully closer to Virginia? I do worry about your living here," her grandmother bemoaned, touching her beloved granddaughter's knee tenderly.

That sentence said a million things to Alex about the state of her grandmother's mind. Never had Kathryn interfered in her personal or professional life. Kathryn had always encouraged her to take control of her destiny. Alex knew that her grandmother had given up her professional life as a Washington, DC lawyer to be a congressional wife to Adam. Oftentimes, Alex believed her grandmother wondered about the life she had given up and possibly had regretted her decision. The fact that she was asking Alex to move closer to Virginia reinforced that worry and the same gut feeling that Alex experienced earlier, and she knew she would need to explore these issues with her grandmother over the coming days. She made a mental note to mention it to Robert who knew her grandmother and her grandmother's support for 'all things Alex'.

"Come on Alex, tell us what's going on. What the hell else has happened in this heathen city?" Her grandfather questioned impatiently from the back seat. "Spit it out so we can figure it out."

"Keep your pants on, granddad. I'm gonna tell you. But you've got to promise to pipe down." Alex saw a bright smile cross her grandmother's face. That lightened her spirits a bit.

She continued, "First of all, someone crossed through the NOPD barricades, the National Guard and the Louisiana State Police defenses at CCMC last night and managed to inject all of our sterile supplies with the virus throughout most of the hospital. Secondly, sometime last night someone burglarized my house looking for God's knows what, and escaped out the French door in the living room."

Alex thought Adam was going to jump through the seat. She heard his quick intake of breath and could feel the heat of his rage in the front seat. She wished she hadn't told him. It was only an instant before the barrage of words assaulted her. She could feel her grandmother stiffen beside her in anticipation of the angry volley of words.

"What the fuck, did you just say someone broke into your house? What the hell for? What do you have that a terrorist might want?" Her grandfather's voice was angry, and his face was suffused with blood.

"I'm clueless. Jack thinks they were looking for a diagram of the hospital or something. This was before they broke into CCMC. Anyway, it was fine and nothing happened. Nobody was hurt or anything. I wish I hadn't told you now. You've got to stop getting so upset," Alex chided her grandfather.

After a moment of silence, her grandfather began again, "What the devil is happening? What does Jack think?"

Alex shook her head. "What we think changes minute by minute. That's most of it, at least, that's all I know now. I've met Travis Stoner from the Secret Service and he seemed to have everything under control. They are bringing in multiple resources. The FBI is bringing in specially trained hazard teams. Secret Service hasn't decided where the President will speak for security reasons. Guess we will know tomorrow. I did hear the first lady isn't coming."

"I would hope not," Adam growled. "Damn city is under siege and you got the leader of the free world and half of the politicians in the same place. This is perfect for a terror attack, and plus, you have a ruthless killer running all over town killing good people: good people and good politicians. This is a match in heaven for Red Jihad."

Alex almost ran the car off the interstate. "You know about Red Jihad? That is who they think is behind this. The Red Jihad!"

"Red Jihad? Of course I know about Red Jihad," her grandfather scoffed at her. "I have been watching mother fuckers like them grow their organizations for 40 years. Yeah, I know all about them. Most of the activity is coming out of Chechnya and those bastards, the Chechen insurgents hate Mother Russia as much as the West." Adam was silent for a moment and added, "These SOBs kill people over there all the time. Defenseless women and children, on the trains, on the subways. They're a bunch of ruthless bastards." *I probably know as much about them as anyone else in the United States."*

As Alex drove her car into the double garage, she wondered what else her grandfather knew. She knew that he had grave concerns over the Middle East and had worked for years to pass sanctions against rogue countries. He had been all over the Clinton Administration prior to 9/11 for disregarding critical intelligence. Of course, he was also well connected with the NSA and the National Security Council, and he was a member of the Congressional Committees on Intelligence, Homeland Security, and Governmental Affairs. She'd never really put all of this together before. In addition, he was a darling of the military. *Well, there you have it. My grandfather is a major player in our national defense and I never even thought about it. I wonder what else he does that I don't know about.*

As Alex pulled into her driveway and opened her garage door, she was still thinking about the national security intelligence power wielded by her grandfather. She helped her grandmother out of the front seat and said, "OK you two, let's go in for some sweet tea." She turned to her grandfather and said, "Martin is picking you up in about 30 minutes and taking you to the Hotel Burgundy to pick up Beth. I'll have him bring in your luggage. After I get Grand settled, I am going into the hospital for a few hours and I will be home late this afternoon"

Her grandparents nodded in understanding as they entered Alex's house through the breezeway that connected the garage to the house. As planned, Martin arrived and whisked her grandfather downtown, leaving Alex to settle in with her grandmother.

Chapter 31

Adam Patrick Lee was pissed, and when Congressman Lee was pissed, he didn't always use the best judgment. When thinking clearly, one of Adam's Lee best bits of wisdom was to think 10 times before speaking, particularly with the press, but now, he was way past good judgment. He'd been concerned when he had seen the strain and fatigue on Alex's face as she told them about what been happening at the hospital. His concern had turned to fury when he learned from Commander Francoise that someone, most likely someone who was instrumental in the attack against the city, had broken into Alex's home. How dare these Jihad sons of bitches come to America and assume they could destroy our nation, way of life and take over our civilization. He'd show those bastards. He would use every smidgeon of power he had to lobby for and pass tougher and tougher sanctions against the problematic Middle Eastern countries. Besides, this whole thing with the Red Jihad had really gotten him to thinking. He'd not been surprised when he learned the Red Jihad was responsible for the Boston Bombings. *Damn Russians.* In his mind, the KGB had never gone away. It had merely gone into hiding until once again they would emerge with a force far greater than their resources during the Cold War. *What was it the Jihadists said? Why have 10,000 men when you could recruit 10 million foot soldiers to do your killing, secretly and all over the world and never leave home?* Once again, Adam Lee cursed the internet. Besides, the Russians had been a boil on America's ass since before the Cold War. He had warned all of his colleagues in the Senate and the House that Russia would once again raise her nasty head against the West. In Congress, Adam Patrick Lee was known as a law and order politician and the leading Congressional advocate for sanctions against terrorist countries. His thoughts were interrupted when Martin spoke. Adam had forgotten that he was in a cab en route to Hotel Burgundy. He was on his way to see Beth Blankenship.

He turned toward Martin and said, "Martin, I am so sorry. I was caught up in my thoughts. I didn't hear a word you said. Could you repeat it for me?"

"Sorry if I'm botherin' you, Mr. Congressman. I jus said I was sorry about your friend getting' hurt from Washington and I am really sorry that Miss Alex is so upset 'bout how things are the hospital. Things is bad here in Naw'lins for your visit."

Martin's New Orleans dialect grated on Congressman's Lee nerves but he stiffened his back and said nothing, a major feat for Adam Lee since he hated New Orleans and everything about it. He considered it a hellhole and the city of Satan and he had often voiced his opinion.

His voice was quiet as he replied. "Thanks, Martin. It could be better but it is certainly none of your doing. It'll get better soon. We'll nail the bastards who are making this virus and doing all of this killing. Francoise will get 'em." Adam's soft, Southern Virginia accent was melodious and he spoke with more bravado than he felt. He hoped he'd been convincing.

Martin nodded at the wheel and continued, "Yes suh, Commander Jack is the best we got here. He'll get 'em, trust me, whoever is doing all of this with all the help we have here from de Feds." Martin gestured with his finger and said, "There's de Hotel Burgundy ahead. Looks like a lot of the press are there. Been like that the whole day. Talking to all those politicians staying there who are comin' and goin'. They are just pumping them for information. Want to go around back?"

"That'd be great. I am picking up Mrs. Blankenship and I would like to usher her out, away from the press. Can you give us about 15 minutes and then circle back and get us?"

"Sure, no problems. I'll be back in fifteen."

Adam nodded and extended his hand, "Thanks, man. Appreciate the ride."

Martin high-fived the Congressman as he skillfully maneuvered his white Lincoln Town Car out into the French Quarter traffic.

Chapter 32

Ali was tired and his heart was torn. His easy fun-loving spirit had been reduced to nothing and his ability to think clearly and make decisions was decidedly absent. Last night, after the meeting with the Jihad leaders, he had returned to his lab to continue to work on the virus. He had worked until the wee hours of the morning and then returned to his apartment where he could barely pass by the sleeping bodies on the way to his small bedroom. His heart had almost stopped beating when Syed had tripped him up with an AK47 and then laughed at his fear. Ali hated Syed. In fact, he hated all of them and he hated what they were doing. He wished more than anything there was something he could do to put the world right again. Two days ago, his life had been perfect. School was great, he was happy, Nazir was less stressed, and life seemed good. Now, Nazir was becoming a big wacko in Ali's opinion and he was terrified for him. In fact, he didn't trust any of the men sleeping on his living room floor. For all he knew, they would kill all of them. He was pretty sure they had killed Yahwa, but of course, he wasn't certain. Nazir had denied it repeatedly. Ali wasn't sure that Nazir even knew what was going on, or had any idea what would happen to them. The way he read the situation, Nazir was clueless about a lot of things, naïve and filled with fear. He just wanted the Jihad out of their apartment.

After several fitful hours, Ali had given up on sleep and by 8:00 a.m., he had returned to work. He was examining several samples of mutating viral fluids under an electron microscope when a light bulb went off in his head. His heart raced with excitement and as he ran the assays again, he was convinced that his conclusions were correct. He knew exactly what was causing the virus and more than that, he knew what the viruses were. He had identified the virus that was causing all of the deaths. In the world of virology, that was practically a win and Ali, with a sense of renewed energy and strength, continued working rapidly. Perhaps he could help after all. He made a decision not to tell Dr. Smith until he was positive he was correct, and if he had just a few more hours, he could be sure. He checked the large clock on the wall in the lab. It was a little after noon. Perhaps by five o'clock he would have some real answers and they could start treating the people.

Chapter 33

Kathryn Rosseau Lee, sat in Alex's sunroom with a glass of lemonade and watched her beloved granddaughter as she talked on her cell phone to the CDC doctor. She saw Alex put her hand to her mouth, most likely in dismay, as she listened to the physician's report. Alex saw her grandmother watching her and walked with her cell phone to the kitchen, supposedly to make lunch, in an effort to keep her grandmother from listening to her side of the conversation.

Kathryn was apprehensive, tortured in fact, that the two most important people in her life were involved in what was potentially becoming the worst days of her life, possibly even the final days of all of their lives. She bowed her head and said a silent prayer for Beth Blankenship and for her small family. Her beliefs and her faith were her strength and she needed a lot of strength right now, for herself, Alex, Adam, and Beth. She supposed she'd be on her knees a lot in the next 24 hours. As she continued to wait, her eyes perused the beautiful silk orchid painting in the sunroom, and she wondered how there could be so much beauty and so much evil in the world at the same time. Kathryn felt as though the two forces were colliding right there in Alex's lovely solarium. She tried to shrug off a feeling of free-floating anxiety but she was unsuccessful. For some reason, she was besieged by feelings of discomfort and uneasiness. In truth, she was afraid and she didn't know why. That startled her and in common day speak, she guessed she was freaked out.

Alex returned from the kitchen, a bright smile on her face and a tuna fish sandwich, potato chips and sweet iced tea. Her grandmother accepted her lunch gratefully. She felt a bit weak and dizzy. As Alex bent down to kiss her grandmother on the cheek, she noticed her grandmother's pale face and anxious look.

"Grand, what's the matter? Do you feel OK? Was the flight from Virginia too much for you?" The concern in Alex's voice was obvious and when Alex reached for her wrist to check her pulse, her grandmother protested.

"Stop it, I'm fine. Just hungry. It's just old lady diabetes." Kathryn's voice was sharp as she slapped her granddaughter's hand away. "What's new at the hospital. It didn't sound good." Grand gave Alex "the look" which let Alex know that she was aware that Kathryn knew she hadn't gone into the kitchen for just a sandwich.

Alex smiled and patted her grandmother's hand. "I can't get anything by you, can I?"

Kathryn gave her a doleful look. "No, probably not and you never will. I've been on to you since you were less than two years old. I don't see that changing now unless I become totally senile or demented."

"I truly don't see that in your future," Alex opined as she gave her grandmother a sideways look. "Anyway, that was Dr. Yvette Charmaine. She is the chief CDC doctor at CCMC and she told me there are now 33 cases of the virus with 13 people dead. They are all dying from some mysterious lung ailment. It doesn't seem the virus is directly killing them."

Kathryn shook her head. "That seems like a lot of sick people in just a short period of time. This only began yesterday, correct?"

Alex was taken back. "Wow, was it only yesterday? It seems like this has been going on for over a week, "Yes, I guess so, although it seems like it's been a lot longer. The past 24 hours have been hell."

"I'm sure. Tomorrow it will all be over and we can go to Commander's Palace for dinner."

"Yes, that'd be great. Cannot wait. Keep holding on to that thought." Alex knew that Commander's was her grandmother's favorite restaurant and Alex was determined to get her there before her grandparents left the city.

Kathryn nodded as Alex continued, "I'm going to have to go to the hospital. Martin's wife is bringing over Gumbo and Shrimp Remoulade for dinner. You've met her, right?"

Kathryn smiled, "Oh yes, indeed. A really colorful lady. Her name is Carla, right? Always so bright and happy."

Alex shook her head and smiled, "Grand, you are just the best. You say things so well. Yes, Carla is bright and colorful with a heart of gold and more importantly, she is a fantastic Cajun cook. Since we are feeding God and Country, she's the best. Also, Jack is sending over additional NOPD offers for security and they will be staying in the Carriage House with the Secret Service who are here to protect Beth and granddad."

Kathryn laughed, "Well, we certainly should be safe enough. When do you think your grandfather will be back with Beth. I would like a quick nap."

Alex checked her watch, "I'd say about an hour. Go for it. I'm out of here. I really need to get over to the medical center to check on things. It seems like forever since I saw Bridget. Call me if you need me. I'll probably be back around four."

Kathryn smiled as she thought of Bridgett, Alex's wonderful, delightful, funny, and always-happy secretary. "Please ask Bridgett to stop by, would you? I enjoy her so much."

"I will. She wants to see you. She told me yesterday. Oh Grand," Alex paused, "you should have seen her yesterday. She was dressed all in pink and orange and she looked sensational. Even her toes were pink with orange stars on them. It was unbelievable! She literally sparkled. Oh, and by the way, she wants to take me shopping."

Kathryn laughed and said, "That's Bridgett, for sure! Go with her Alex. It would be fun. Maybe I could go as well. We could both use a little color in our lives."

"It's a date. I'll set it up with Bridgett today. She will love it."

Kathryn hugged Alex goodbye and immediately headed for Alex's beautifully appointed grey and silver guest room. It was her room away from home and she was dying for a brief rest. She felt sad and despondent and she didn't know why. These were not feelings she was accustomed to feeling and she didn't like them at all. *Perhaps a nap will take these feelings away.*

Chapter 34

Ali smiled broadly at one of his graduate school buddies who called out to him as he exited the double doors of The Department of Tropical Medicine at Tulane University Medical Center. All in all, it had been a great day and Ali was pleased with his work on identifying the virus. He'd left several messages for Dr. Smith to report his progress but they had not yet connected.

"Anthony, how goes it? Where have you been keeping yourself? Haven't seen you for weeks!" Ali was never more American than when he was at school. He loved his graduate school friends and relished the time he spent with them. They made him feel welcomed and accepted. He had never felt that way among his Muslim friends. Perhaps he was more American than Muslim, an accusation Nazir had been making for several years. Right now, this second, he really didn't hate his life. He was just glad to see the friendly face.

"Ali my friend! Where have you been? Do you have time for cup of coffee so we can catch up?"

"Sure, dude. I sure do. I've been working almost nonstop trying to help identify the virus that's over at Crescent City Medical. Let's head back to the campus coffee bar and we can talk a while. What do you say?"

"I'm there," said Anthony happily as the two young men turned and begin the journey to the campus coffee bar. "Catch me up on this virus. I know very little about it. Is this the one I heard about on the local news?"

Ali nodded excitedly. "Yeah, that's the one. It's been all over the local and national news and the virus has killed a bunch of people. I've been helping Dr. Smith isolate and to identify it."

Anthony was interested. "Have you identified it?"

Ali shrugged his shoulders. "I think so but I have to check my findings with Dr. Smith   before I can say for sure. I worked almost all night long last night in the lab, but boy did I learn a lot. I think I might have most of the data I need for my thesis." Ali was excited. This was the best break he'd had in days. He loved sitting around shooting the breeze with his school buddies.

Anthony was impressed and said, "Cool dude, that's awesome. Not to change the subject or anything, but do you want to play basketball on Sunday afternoon?"

Ali hesitated for a moment and said, "Sure. I need a break. Same place?"

"Yep," Anthony said as he chugged his coffee and checked his watch. "I got to get my skinny ass out of here. Tonight's my second anniversary and if I don't get Linda some flowers and a gift, I can guarantee you I won't be celebrating a third year of marriage. I've been so busy studying and working at the library the two of us seem to pass like ships in the night. Between her schedule and mine we've barely spoken for days."

"Aw, dude, you know Linda loves you. You just need to make it up to her tonight."

"I intend to. I can't believe she married an ugly old grunt like me."

"Me neither, it must have been an off day for her," Ali said as he clapped his buddy on the back, "Have a great time. She's a great catch. You're a lucky guy."

"Yeah, for sure. Will do. See you Sunday," Anthony flashed him a smile and departed.

Chapter 35

Nazir's small apartment had become the epicenter for New Orleans Jihad activity. As Ali tried to sneak past the men sprawled all over the living room, Syed grabbed him roughly by his collar.

"Sit down, boy genius," Syed hissed in his ear, the stench of his breath overcoming Ali's senses. "The leaders have a special job for you." Ali fell onto the sofa, weak with nausea from the stench of Syed's breath. He smelled like day-old hummus, olives and tooth decay and the combination made him queasy. The entire apartment stunk of sweat, bad food, and foul odors. His eyes searched Nazir who was in a corner. Nazir's fear and uncertainty was obvious.

"Ali, I am glad you are here," said Omar, his dark, unreadable eyes penetrating the young scientist. "I have a special task for you. Our mission in New Orleans has changed a bit. We have received orders from above to destroy as many of the infidels as we possibly can. Your brother," Omar said, as he gestured toward Nazir "has volunteered to wear explosives into the, what do you call it here, the French Quarter?"

Ali's heart sank and he was overcome by feelings of helplessness. Tears jumped into his eyes. "No, no, please no. Do not make my brother take his own life. Please do not make him a suicide bomber. He is all I have."

Omar laughed and said, "Do not worry, Ali, he will not die. He will simply be a diversion, a decoy so to speak. We want to frighten the infidels with explosives so they will run inside buildings."

Ali was confused. "But why, Omar? Why would we want to frighten them? I thought you wanted the American

President and the politicians. Why frighten the locals and the tourists?"

Mohammed's face was dark with impatience. His control was much less obvious than Omar's careful observations. His voice was clipped and precise. "Ali, listen. You are smart and we are only saying this one time. If your brother dies as a suicide bomber, he will die honorably. He will die for Allah. He will be a warrior. But, that is not the plan. Your brother will be a decoy. Our plan is to kill the American people."

"How will you do that?" Ali could feel the tension and fear pressing into his brain. His voice was weak and timid. He asked again louder, "How will you kill the Americans?"

Mohammed gave Ali a tight half smile. His voice was quiet. "You will do that for us, Ali."

"Me? But how? I am one person." Ali's voice was incredulous, uncertain. He was practically shouting at the esteemed leader. He was paralyzed with anxiety and apprehension.

"You, my young brain, will turn the virus into a gas and it will be released all over New Orleans. It's just that simple. We will kill thousands. It will make 9/11 look like child's play."

Ali was stunned, speechless. He stood there waiting for more and indeed, the leaders were not finished with him.

Chapter 36

Adam Lee entered the Hotel Burgundy through the kitchen. As he walked past the executive kitchen chefs, sous chefs, and short order cooks, he noticed they were all wearing facemasks. Adam's senses were heightened by the smell of good food. The good, heady smell of Cajun spices seemed to awaken his senses and energize him. *New Orleans is the devil's city, but it does have some of the best damn food in the world.* For the first time in several days, he realized he was hungry and that was a good feeling. He was feeling in control again. He was even starting to feel normal. He stopped for a second to watch a guy quickly chop enormous gulf shrimp into tiny pieces. He watched another cook dump huge crab claws into a enormous cauldron of gumbo simmering on an eight burner stove. The smells were invigorating and pungent, and Adam would have paid a hundred dollars for a bowl of the spicy Naw'lins gumbo. Suddenly, as if reading the Congressman's mind, a chef dipped a ladle into the steaming liquid added rice and handed the bowl to Adam.

"Welcome to Naw'lins," the Executive Chef said in greeting. "We have the best Gumbo in the Vieux Carre and I would like for you to be a taste tester." Adam eyes lit with pleasure and he smiled and pumped his hand in thanks and retired to a small table to relish the hot liquid. It certainly beat the tuna salad sandwich that Alex had fixed for him. But, then, he smiled, his lovely redheaded granddaughter really wasn't much of a cook. But of course, she was a nurse and a lawyer and he was mighty proud of her. He wished she would return to Virginia. He was worried about his beloved Kathryn and the amount of time she spent alone at their farm in Virginia while he was in DC trying to work with a gridlocked Congress. He'd have to investigate an opportunity for her, maybe even get a position created for her....*You know, all of this health reform crap. Surely, Alex could manage that. Yeah, he'd get right on that when all of this bull shit in New Orleans was over.* Adam finished his gumbo, waved at the kitchen staff, and exited the kitchen into the back hall of the Hotel. He nodded to a secret service agent who approached and called him by name. The agent clapped Adam on the back and walked with him to a bank of elevators in the main lobby. As Adam assured the agent that things were "gonna be OK," the agent shook his hand and returned to his station in the back lobby of the hotel.

Adam admired the antique brass elevator and held his breath as it groaned to the fourth floor. The elevator was brightly polished and he couldn't see any fingerprints or smudges anywhere. The kitchen had been impeccably clean as well. It was hard to believe that a kitchen worker and a political guest had contacted the virus here. Humph. The entire virus thing reeked of terrorism and he was sure that Ben's death was associated. Too coincidental. As far as Adam was concerned, where there was smoke, there was fire and the death of Louisiana Senator Beau Lamont and Hayes Hanley solidified a conspiracy in Adam's mind. Adam had been briefed early in the morning by the Secret Service. He was up to date on everything, even the things his granddaughter didn't want him to know.

Finally, the elevator creaked to a halt and the door opened. The hotel was beautifully appointed. The walls were a pale shade of peach and the carpet was beautifully designed. Even though Adam Patrick Lee was an old farm boy from Virginia, his wife had taught him the importance of having beauty in his world, and over the years he had acquired a taste for beautiful things. Adam had never told anyone, but he actually collected art glass. Whenever anyone at the farm commented on the art glass collection at Wyndley, he gave all of the credit to Kathryn. He also turned wood as well, but no one knew that either. That was Adam's plan for retirement. He planned to spend days in his wood working shop which he'd had constructed in one of the barns at Wyndley. Finally he located Beth's suite at the end of the hall and knocked softly on her door. Beth immediately opened the heavy mahogany door, her dark luxurious hair in disarray and fell sobbing into Adam's arms. She was broken with pain and heartache and as Adam talked to her softly, her weeping finally abated. As Beth began to settle down, Adam felt his anger sweep his body and his gut twisted in pain. He hated the sons of bitches who had killed his adopted son and protégé. Adam had been grooming Ben to take his place in Congress, to work on foreign policy and intelligence and campaign for law enforcement and security all over the planet.

But some sick bastard had ended that yesterday morning. He checked his watch. He'd told Martin 15 minutes but of course, that was before he stopped for Gumbo.

"Beth," he said softly, "can you go tidy up a bit and we can go to Alex's house? She and Kathryn are waiting for you and I think a change of scenery will do you good. I'll have someone retrieve your luggage later. I have a cab waiting downstairs."

Beth gave Adam a small, tight smile and said, "Sure. I'll be ready in five minutes and I've already packed my overnight bag."

As Beth readied herself for the short drive to Alex's house, anger gnawed at Adam's gut. He become more and more angry about the death of Ben, and his heart broke for Ben's bereaved wife and fatherless children. He could feel his blood pressure skyrocketing and heard Kathryn telling him to calm down in her "don't give me any more crap" voice. As Adam tried to settle down, Beth reappeared, looking wanly beautiful in black pants and a white blouse with a gold necklace. She looked the epitome of a congressional wife. She'd have been a great first lady.

"Ready?" Adam asked as he reached for her arm.

Beth nodded and they left the room. They were quiet on the way to the lobby and Adam was dismayed when Martin's cab wasn't out back. He checked his watch. It had been almost 45 minutes since he's been dropped off. Adam reached for his cell phone to call Martin when the Secret Service agent gestured for him to come forward and said, "Congressman Lee, your cabby is at the front. The back entry is blocked by a delivery truck. I'll walk out with you. We'll get both of you in the car. There's a ton of press."

Adam nodded. He wished he was leaving by the back door so he wouldn't have to talk to them. He was furious about the death of Ben Blankenship and the break in at Alex's house last night. Who in the hell do these bastard turban-heads think they are?

Chapter 37

"Oh my gosh, Alex! You've got to come here and see your granddad on CNN. He's really mad!" Bridgett stood in Alex's doorway, resplendent in a bright emerald green two-piece dress with matching green shoes. She had the remote in hand, her enormous eyes wide with amazement. "I hope he doesn't stroke out or anything, 'cuz he's so mad."

Alex said nothing, but her mouth formed an O. *Oh no, I hope Adam didn't lose it on national TV.*

Bridgett continued waving the remote excitedly in the air. "He just got interviewed and he called the terrorists and people who made this virus a bunch of rag heads who hid behind something. I'm not sure what. I'd say he was mighty pissed."

Alex stood up from her desk, grabbed the remote from Bridgett, and clicked on CNN. Sure enough there was her grandfather along with Beth Blankenship standing outside the Hotel Burgundy. One look at her grandfather validated his look of rage and she cringed as she heard his words. *Oh my God! How are we going to do damage control on this?* She couldn't believe that Adam had called the terrorists rag heads and chicken shits unworthy of life. He had also disrespected the Quran, probably the worst part of the interview. Adam had accused terrorists of twisting the words of the Quran to meet their needs, and had called them cowards for hiding their faces. She felt as though she were in a trance as she watched CNN rerun the news bite over and over and over again.

"Alex, Alex what do you want me to do? Should I call someone? Say something! You're making me very nervous. Say something!" Bridgett pleaded as she roughly grabbed Alex's shoulder. "You're not gonna die on me, are you?" Bridgett's voice was loud and her tone was tragic.

Alex returned to reality and saw Bridgett's anguished blue eyes. "Bridge, call Elizabeth and asked her to come here. I need her advice on how to handle this. Oh my God, I can't believe my grandfather did this. This behavior violates every press related rule I've ever heard him mention." Alex rolled her eyes in disbelief. *What the hell. What could they do now? She couldn't believe he'd broken bad on the terrorists in front of the press.*

Bridgett glanced over her shoulder on her way out of Alex's office and said, "I love your grandfather. Don't be hard on him. After all, he's just telling the truth. Someone needs to say it the way it is and at least he was brave enough to do it."

Alex gave Bridgett a thumbs up as she waved her out of her office just as her phone rang. Jack's number was digitally displayed. Alex answered, her voice strained, "Jack, what's up?"

Jack was laughing so hard he couldn't speak and for some reason that made Alex angry. Finally Jack stopped laughing enough to say, "I got to tell you, Alex. Your grandfather is some man. I guess you saw his news conference?"

Alex replied tersely, "Yes, I saw it. It's a disaster. I can hardly believe he stood up and said what he did. Even if it is true, and even if we all believe it, it was something that should never have been said by a ranking, senior United States Congressman to a major news network or any network for that manner. I don't know what happened to him. I'm worried about him. It is just not like him to lose control."

Jack responded with a snort and guffaw, "Well, you gotta hand it to him. Probably wasn't the most politically correct thing to do, but at least he has balls and he's honest. He told it like it is and I think he'll get a lot of respect for it. No other politician would be so honest or truthful. He's a great man who loves his country and as far as I am concerned, he's paid his dues and he can say whatever the hell he wants. They'll send some pansy ass political aide out to clean it up."

Alex was silent. Perhaps it wasn't as bad as she thought. She needed to call and make sure he was OK.

"Al, are you there?"

"Yeah, Jack. What's up? I'm just thinking."

"Can I get your attention for a minute? I am worried about one possibility based on Adam's remarks." Jack's voice was serious.

"What?" Alex could identify a free-floating anxiety. She repeated, her voice demanding, "What, Jack?"

"Retaliation. Pure and simple. Retaliation."

"Against who, my grandfather?"

"Yeah, your grandfather and/or his family."

Terror seized Alex and she could hardly breathe. "My grandmother," she gasped, "She's home alone. Is the NOPD there yet?"

"Yeah, she's OK. I checked and I am sending another office as well. I talked to Stoner who thinks there could be trouble as well. He's trying to get consent from Treasury to offer protection to your grandparents as well. In the meantime, they are scanning the airwaves and internet for any threats of retaliation. So are Bodine's people. It'll work out. Gotta go. " Jack hoped he sounded convincing to Alex, when in fact, he was worried shitless about the Congressman and his family.

Jack clicked off just as Liz entered Alex's office. Liz was laughing, and once again Alex found herself second-guessing her concern. *Perhaps I should lighten up and listen to his news conference again. Maybe it'll make me laugh. And to think I was scared to death last night. This time the threat was to her grandparents and that scared Alex a million times more.*

Elizabeth Tippett gave Alex a huge grin and said, "Would you like me to give your grandfather some pointers on meeting with the press, perhaps some press etiquette?" Elizabeth joked.

Alex gave a short laugh and said, "I think it's a little late for that. Seriously, Liz how do you think this will go down?"

Liz thought for a minute and said, "I'm no Washington insider, but I would suspect the opposite party will grill him for lunch and dinner for the next two years. He'll be on every late night TV show, but I doubt he ever has to run a re-election campaign, ever. They will use him in Saturday Night Live skits for the next six months, but I suspect he'll become a folk hero, Alex, mark my words. He only told the truth and that's all most Americans want to hear."

Alex knew Liz was only trying to make her feel better but she did believe there was some truth in what she was saying. She gave her a big hug. "Thanks, Liz, hope you are right. But he did break every rule there is and set back diplomatic relations 50 years."

"Probably did, but I think I am right. As disgusted as Americans are with Congress, they will actually love a politician that is as honest as your grandfather. They can identify with a little humanity and honesty."

Alex nodded and said, "Sure hope so. I also hope my grandmother doesn't kill him. She'll be furious about this."

"One more thing," Liz added. "By the time the pundits, talks shows and Sunday news reviews have discussed this ad nauseum, Adam will be given grace because Ben Blankenship was his protégé, his adopted son. Wait and see, it will be OK. He will be a hero."

"Thanks! You've made me feel much better. Let's focus on getting through the next few days." Alex didn't share her concerns about retaliation with Elizabeth. She couldn't bring herself to talk about it. At least, not yet.

Chapter 38

Kathryn Rosseau Lee was troubled and heavy of heart. She hadn't been able to fall asleep in the guest room and had returned to the solarium to sit in the sun. As she rocked slowly in Alex's antique oak rocking chair and viewed her lovely courtyard, she appreciated many of her beloved granddaughter's talents. In addition to being smart and educated, Alex was kind, compassionate, and gentle. She cared about those less fortunate than herself. She had always worked with her grandmother in her charity and church work. Most of all, Alexandra was an extraordinary artist. From an early age, Kathryn had expected Alex to study art. She smiled fondly as she remembered their early days at the Richmond Children's Museum where Alex insisted they go every Saturday on their 'trip to town.' At the museum she donned one of her grandfather's old shirts, stood at an easel and spent several hours merrily creating colorful pictures with tempera paint, all of which Kathryn had kept, most of them framed in colored paper frames. In additional to painting, Alex had loved to play dress up and write plays. She had loved the Children's Theatre in Richmond and in Hanover where she had won small parts in many plays. Kathryn had been stunned when Alex had turned down admission to the coveted School of the Arts at Virginia Commonwealth University in Richmond, Virginia and decided to study nursing instead. And then, law school? This decision had really shocked Kathryn, even to this day. Kathryn often wondered if Alex's tenacity to complete law school had been the final straw in the demise of her marriage to Robert. Was it her fault? Had Alex moved into law because her grandmother was a lawyer? In her heart, Kathryn knew Robert was the best man in the world for Alexandra. He loved her more than life itself, but Robert, with his affluent Creole upbringing, had wanted Alex to be a stay at home wife and mother. At that point, his arrogance hadn't allowed him to appreciate a professional wife. Oh well, couldn't fix that one.

Kathryn was tired. She closed her eyes and confronted her deep uncertainties. She knew Alex was unhappy and that the practice of law didn't fit her outgoing personality and creative personality. Oh, how she hoped Alex and Robert would reunite. Then she could rest in peace.

Her thoughts turned to her husband. Adam Lee was a stubborn, dogmatic, dictatorial, and hard-headed pain in the ass and had been no treat to live with for 50-plus years, but she knew he was dedicated to his family, home, and country. She also knew he loved her and Alex more than life. She shook her head sadly as she remembered the events of recent weeks. Lately, he'd seemed to be absentminded, a bit off his mark, forgetful and that worried her. Her husband had a steel-trap mind and the memory of an elephant. He could smell a rat better than most cats and he rarely missed anything. His sixth sense was extraordinary. But lately... well, he'd been absentminded, a bit scattered and that was an enormous change. The differences chilled her and she feared for his future, their future. Adam was a wily, perspicacious politician and it had stunned her when a couple of things had slipped by him. He had been devastated that he'd forgotten. One slip had been his attendance at a national security committee meeting. His aide had called Kathryn looking for him but Kathryn had been no help. They couldn't reach him at his Washington apartment or by cell phone. He was flat missing, not around, and clearly not available. And of course, the death of Ben Blankenship had totally devastated him. He hadn't slept and his distress was palpable. As Kathryn closed her eyes to contemplate, she began to feel sleepy. She checked her watch. It was only about 2:00 p.m. so she could catch a quick nap before Adam returned with Beth. She needed it. She was exhausted. The trip had been long and getting up at 4 a.m. always messed her up. The sunshine coming in Alex's windows and Handel's Water Music lulled her into a deep sleep.

Chapter 39

Ali walked down Canal on his way home from Tulane, his eyes staring at the sidewalk, not wanting to see the people he'd probably kill the next day. The young scientist was scruffy and disheveled. Dr. Smith had expressed alarm at Ali's appearance, and thinking he was overworked and stressed, had literally ordered him out of the virology lab. Ali was deeply depressed and he felt powerless and physically immobilized by the demands of the Jihadists. He could hardly believe his work on identifying the virus had turned into a murder weapon that would kill thousands of New Orleanians in just a few hours. As the young man brushed tears from his eyes, he sat down at a Starbucks and ordered coffee. He turned the situation over and over in his mind trying to think of a way to thwart the terrorists' plan. He honestly didn't think he could live on this earth if his love for science resulted in the death of thousands.

A tap on the shoulder startled him. He looked up from the wrought iron table and was surprised to see Habib. *Oh no, are these bastards following me? I will never live through this. Perhaps I shouldn't.*

"May I sit down?" Habib asked.

Ali shrugged his shoulder and replied, "Yeah, I guess. You guys are following me anyway. Why not?" Ali's voice was sarcastic and he hoped he sounded diffident and non-committal to the young Jihadist.

The two young Muslims sat in silence, each deep in thought when Habib finally broke the silence, his voice gentle, almost kind. Ali looked at him with surprise.

"They've asked you to do a lot, my brother. They have revised the plan based on your ability to create the airborne weaponized virus."

Ali said nothing. He stared at Habib, his eyes dark and angry. He had no obligation to tell this guy anything, and he wasn't planning to. Ali wasn't prone to violence at all, but he really wanted to cold cock Habib.

Habib continued softly, "Did you do it. Did you turn the virus into a gas?"

Ali stood to leave, "Why would I tell you? It's not your business. Get out of my way," he added as Habib stood to block his access to the door.

"Sit down, Ali," Habib pleaded. "Maybe you and I are on the same side."

"I don't think so, asshole," Ali spat the words at him. "I'm a Muslim and I love Allah but I am not a Jihadist and I hate everything about it. The secrecy, the killing, the terror. I absolutely abhors it. Now, get out of my way."

Habib put his hand on his arm. "Shhhh. Be quiet, everyone is looking at you. Let us go somewhere where we can talk privately."

Ali looked around and noted several couples staring at them strangely. *Oh shit, now they'll call the police and Omar will kill Nazir for sure. Especially if they know the leak came from me.* Once again, terror gripped Ali's chest and he thought his head would explode from anxiety.

Habib grabbed Ali by his collar and said loudly, "If I hear anything about you calling, texting, touching or communicating with my sister again, I will kill you. Do you get it? LEAVE MY SISTER ALONE!"

Ali nodded, firmly removed Habib's hand from his collar, and said, "Yeah, got it, asshole."

Habib gave Ali an intense look and cut his eyes to the left.

Ali stormed out of the coffee shop and turned left, walking briskly toward the French Quarter. *What the hell was up with Habib? Was he saving his ass or mine with the talk about his sister?* As he passed Harrah's Casino, he thought sadly about all of the people who would die there tomorrow. All because of him. The stress squeezed his heart and he could hardly breathe. He, a young Muslim man, a graduate student in virology, would be responsible for the deaths of thousands of people and he wasn't even a believer in Jihad. As he wiped the tears from his eyes, he felt someone walking beside him. It was Habib.

Ali's devastation turned to anger. "Now what?" he asked accusingly.

Habib whispered, "My brother, I think we are on the same side. Let us talk."

Ali gave Habib a shrewd look and said, "Why the hell would I talk to you? You're one of them. For all I know, you are a spy. You're a Jihadist bastard. You're just trying to pump me, see what I am going to do. Get out of my way."

"No, brother I'm not. I really have changed my beliefs about Jihad. I want to help you stop this. I don't think I can do this anymore. I really don't." Habib looked directly into Ali's eyes and said again, "Please, Ali. Let's go and talk. I want to help you. I want to help us."

Ali's glared at Habib, his voice accusingly, "Talk? Why would I talk to you? You killed Yahwa. You murdered him, you bastard. He was going to die anyway. Why would I talk to you?"

Tears were streaming down Habib's face as he uttered softly, "Yes, I killed Yahwa. That's why I know I can never kill again. I cannot do these things. Please, let's go talk somewhere quiet. I think we can figure a way to stop this."

Habib's words impressed Ali. He shrugged his shoulders and started walking, "What the hell. I don't trust you at all, but we're probably all gonna die anyway, so why not?"

Chapter 40

Jack, Stoner, Ted Scott, Bodine and John Houser huddled together in front of the St. Louis Cathedral in the French Quarter. The Quarter was vibrant, animated, and alive with activity. The law enforcement officials were surrounded by laughing tourists bejeweled in Mardi Gras beads. Sidewalk artists engaged in creating and selling their art. Mimes colored gold and silver struck poses as statues. Street musicians played on brass instruments and worn flattop guitars. Dozens of people sipped Hurricanes from Pat O'Briens, Pimms from the Napoleon, or a Gin Fizz from just about anywhere. Others were eating crawfish pie and alligator on a stick. All around them, life was good and people were laughing. The world was a safe place that day in New Orleans.

Jack and Ted had gone to Mass at St. Louis' as they frequently did each week. Today had been different. They had gone to pray for the safety of the city and its people. During Mass, Stoner had sent them a 911 text. As the group briefly chatted outside the Cathedral, Jack's attention was drawn to a mime dressed in silver with red tears running down his painted silver face. The mime had a huge red hole in his heart and carried a torn American flag in one silver hand and a child's gun in the other. Overall, the mime was threatening and sinister in appearance and Jack was overcome with a disturbing and ominous feeling. The symbolism was eerie and Jack shook off a feeling of foreboding. The symbolism struck a chord ...red tears... a torn American flag. He wondered if it was a prediction of things to come. He pushed the mime from his mind and turned his attention to Agent Stoner.

Stoner's voice was terse, his face solemn. "Let's walk. I've got new info." He paused for a moment and continued, his voice incredulous, "What the hell is that? Is it a parade or something. What I mean is, what are they?" The generally articulate Stoner stumbled over his words as he pointed to a line of beautiful, gaudily dressed, and bejeweled women walking with great difficulty in five-inch heels on the cobblestones of Jackson Square. "What are they? Are they hookers?" The group sported blonde wigs, huge hair, false eyelashes, purple and blue eye shadow, and airbrushed, nine-inch nails.

As Jack turned to look, he broke out into a huge grin. "That's a Drag Parade, Stoner. Where you been, man?"

"Huh?" Stoner mumbled as he searched his brain for meaning.

"A Drag Parade. We have 'em all the time. They're men dressed as women. We have everything here in the Big Easy. You gotta come for Mardi Gras if this is flippin' you out." At that moment, one of the Drag Queens jumped out of the Parade line and ran over and gave Jack an enormous, wet, sloppy kiss.

Jack laughed, "Janine, how the hell are you. You got some new threads, he observed."

Janine wobbled precariously on her five-inch heels and hollered, "CO MAN DUH, come and march with us. We need a little bit of diversity. In fact, you gents can come too. You'll make us look better."

Jack thought Travis Stoner was going to pass out as Janine continued, "We Queens want to be appreciated, and when there's so few of us, it's hard to be noticed. You all will make us stand out. She peered out of her heavily made up eyes and false eyelashes and asked, "Is that you, Commish?"

Ted laughed and said, "Yeah, it's me, girl. How goes it."

As Janine moved forward to wrap New Orleans Police Commissioner Ted Scott in an enormous hug, Stoner looked as though he could pass out. Police work was definitely different in New Orleans. He couldn't imagine being recognized or pulled over by people who looked like this. *Oh, my god. I would just die. They'd kick me out of the Secret Service for subversive group activity,* he thought. Much less being kissed or hugged. For once, he remained in a disbelieving silence. John Houser punched him and said, "Hey, Stoner, it's OK. We have them in Baton Rouge too. It's just part of life here." Bodine just grinned at the men.

As Stoner began to recover, Jack and Ted were bidding goodbye to Janine and the group of law enforcement officers darted into Jax's Brewery, took the elevator to the second floor, and secured a table overlooking the Mississippi River. The afternoon was beautiful, the sky sunny and for once, the mighty Mississippi didn't look like an enormous mud puddle. Jack took that as a good sign.

Stoner cleared his throat and said, "Well, men, that was pretty interesting. Never seen much like that, certainly not in the Midwest where I grew up. There are a few in DC, but this group," he stammered and continued, "this group is much more memorable."

Jack laughed uproariously and said, "Seriously, Stoner, you gotta come back during Mardi Gras or just for fun so me, Bodine and Ted can show you some stuff. I'm sure you need the info to do a better job in guarding POTUS."

Stoner laughed but shook his head, "Not sure about that one, Jack. But it would be fun to come back and see the sights. Kick back, have a few beers, maybe a Hurricane...." Stoner seemed to be invigorated by the idea of partying with the guys. Or perhaps, it was just the idea of getting through the next few days.

Ted intervened, "Believe it or not Stoner, several of that group, Janine being one, are our best snitches. Janine's helped us bring down quite a few perps in the city. Also, we have a great snitch network among our prostitutes. We've really impacted crime perpetuated by the Dixie Mafia in New Orleans. These parade folks have helped."

Bodine chimed in. "Yeah, Ted's correct. The Queens are great about sharing info for a little bit of money. They are all over the city, particularly the Quarter, and trust me, they know lots of stuff. They are a tremendous resource for the FBI here in NOLA.

"Humph. Interesting. Wouldn't have thought that," Stoner added, still a bit unsure of his colleagues. But, it was their city, their state, so they would know.

Major John Houser added, glancing at the Commissioner, "That's for sure, Ted. One of those snitches helped us bring down that sniper shooting randomly on Route 10 several years ago. Remember that one, you all?"

"Hell, yeah," Jack added. "That was one bad dude." He turned to Stoner and Houser and continued, "I have four of them helping me look for St. Germaine, but we'll talk about that another day. Stoner, what new info do you have that you pulled Ted and me out of Mass? Two heathens like us need to be in church, pretty much 24/7," Jack snorted.

Stoner's face lost all traces of gaiety and happiness in an instant as the stress and strain lines of the past several days returned. He said, "Well, two things. Neither one good. The first is that we believe Congressman Adam Patrick Lee's news conference comments have elevated our threat. There's new intel that the Jihadists are increasing the targets."

"How's that?" asked Houser.

"Internet chatter suggests they plan to widen the target."

"Huh, don't follow," said Houser.

"They plan to kill the President, politicians and as many of the citizens of New Orleans as they can."

Ted interrupted, "How are they planning to kill masses? Any ideas?" His voice was troubled. He felt fear quiver up his spine.

"Who knows, it could be explosives, contamination of water supply, gas, who the hell knows. It's wide open. These Jihadists are creative and deadly, " Stoner sighed.

"Is the threat contained to New Orleans?" asked Houser, wondering if he should activate the State Police in Baton Rouge.

"Far as we know. We've increased the numbers of snipers, undercover officers, etc., but as you know, this city is tough to defend," Stoner ended on a low note.

"I'll call the Governor for more National Guard, " Ted offered.

"Good. Anything else we can do?" Jack asked.

"Not yet, at least not that I know of. I'll keep you informed."

Jack was over the edge. "Those fucking sons of bitches," he roared, jumping to his feet. "Never will that happen to my town. Somehow we're gonna beat these bastards, I'm convinced. We're gonna get them, the murdering fuckers. What else do you have?" Jack paced around the table impatiently, his face dark with fury.

"Sit down, Jack and save your energy. You're going to need it. There's a direct threat against the Congressman's family and I understand Alex's grandmother is in New Orleans as well, correct Jack?"

"Yeah, we've covered there. I've got two NOPD over there now at her house and frequent patrols. I know you're planning to send an agent as well, Stoner, to protect Beth Blankenship. Has that changed?"

"No. I am working on the authorization. Meanwhile, we have an agent with Congressman Lee and Mrs. Blankenship now. Once his news conference went viral, we knew there'd be repercussions."

Houser was angry as well. "I gotta give it to Congressman Lee. I agree with everything he said and he's an incredible politician but I'm sorry it happened. It just complicates an already bad situation."

Stoner nodded in agreement and grunted. "Yeah. No question there, John. Congressmen Lee is one of the best, but his lack of discretion has made things worse." Stoner hunched his shoulders and glanced into the angry, beet red face of Jack Francoise. "Jack, just so you understand.... It's not a threat to hurt them. It's a threat to kill them, all of them, and that includes Alexandra Destephano, and I know you are close to her."

As Jack processed the information, he felt his phone vibrate. He had a message from Jason Aldridge. "Call me, Jack. Trouble over at the Destephano house."

Jack looked at the group. "I'm on my way to Alex's house. There's trouble already. Ted, can you ride with me."

"Absolutely. Stoner, keep us in the loop. We're available at all times."

"I'll send over a back up FBI agent," offered Bodine. "Let me know if you need anything else."

"Thanks, man," Jack nodded gratefully, his heart pounding in his chest.

Stoner nodded and Houser added, "Good luck guys, this sucks. It's just really sick and I am pretty worried. Ted, I'll call the Governor for you and ask for more National Guard."

Ted nodded his thanks and rushed after Jack who was already way ahead of him. *Shit, this really wasn't good,* the NOPD Commissioner thought. For the first time in his life, Ted Scott was really scared.

Chapter 41

Kathryn Lee woke up suddenly to a popping noise. *Oh, good, Alexandra is cooking popcorn. I hope she has the kind with the cinnamon and sea salt. Surely, she would have. That was her favorite too. What time is it? Where are Adam and Beth?* As Kathryn rose from the rocking chair, she noticed the prone body of a NOPD patrolman lying behind a cluster of palm trees in Alex's courtyard. As she moved closer to the French doors to look out, she noticed blood spreading around in a dark circle covering the paving blocks around the palm trees in the courtyard. *Oh my God, oh my God, someone has shot the policeman. I've got to call for help.*

As Kathryn turned to reach for her cell phone next to the oak rocker, she heard breaking glass and the French door opened and a man dressed in black entered. He was tall, dark, and bearded. In an instant, he lunged forward, grabbed her by her snow-white hair, and threw her to the floor, cracking her shoulder in the process. Then he banged her head over and over again against Alex's marble floor. Her last conscious thought was her prayer that Adam and Alex would be spared. As she lapsed into unconsciousness, she felt herself facing a brisk wind as she cantered on her favorite mare through the sunlit fields of Wyndley as Alex's horse, Dundee watched her sadly from the pasture. And then, there was nothing.

Chapter 42

"Alex, Alex, oh no, Alex, I just don't know how to tell you this," Bridgett gasped, tears streaming from her eyes as she burst into Alex's office the second time in that many hours. "It's just awful, but I have to let you know."

"What Bridgett? You have to calm down. What do I need to know," Alex asked, her heart pounding in her chest. When Bridgett didn't respond in several seconds, she asked again, this time her voice impatient, "Dammit, what is going on? Tell me for God's sake." Alex was beside herself with fear and unease. She could barely breathe. Within seconds, Elizabeth entered Alex's office and placed her arm around Alex's shoulders. Alex pushed Liz's arm away in annoyance. For some reason, Liz's touch irritated her.

Bridgett raised her tear streaked face, her blue eyes filled with pain and concern toward her boss and said in a heaving, but small voice. "It's your grandmother. Someone has beaten her up. She's hurt pretty bad."

"Oh, no. Nooooooo." Alex could hardly speak as the air whooshed out of her lungs. As she gasped for breath, she demanded, "When, where is she? Where is she? Where is my grandmother?" Her voice was frantic and her eyes terrified.

Bridgett took a deep breath and continued, "Commander Francoise called and said she's in an ambulance on her way to Tulane. They didn't want to bring her to CCMC because of the virus. They thought Tulane would be safer," Bridgett added, bursting into fresh tears. Tears streamed down her face.

Alex collapsed on the silk sofa in her office stunned and quiet. She was unable to speak. Elizabeth sat opposite her in a Queen Anne chair and added, "The Commander asked me to let you know that Robert is headed over to Tulane to see her when she arrives." Liz's voice was controlled and calm. "What can I do for you? What can Bridgett and I do for you?" Elizabeth's eyes were gentle as she probed Alex's face for ways she could help.

Alex gave them a bewildered, confused look and replied, "Do for me? I have no idea? What *can* you do for me?"

Elizabeth nodded and continued, "Jack is coming to pick you up and take you to Tulane. You'll meet Robert there."

Alex nodded her understanding and asked suddenly, her voice terrified, "What of my grandfather. Does he know?"

"Yes, he and Mrs. Blankenship arrived with Martin just as the ambulance was taking your grandmother away. Martin had apparently taken the Congressman to the liquor store for some whiskey and Mrs. Blankenship had wanted some wine. Fortunately, he didn't see her. Jack is having Dr. Desmonde come and stay with the Congressman and Mrs. Blankenship for a few hours."

Alex shook her head incredulous at that bit of information. "Monique, how can she do that? She's ill herself. I don't think she's well enough to go. It'll cause a setback for her."

"Well," Elizabeth intoned, "From what I heard, she insisted and as you know, the Commander is no match for the bewitching and stubborn psychiatrist once she makes up her mind. He said he'd take her so she'd leave him alone. Anyway, Josh is taking her over there now."

Alex smiled thinly, as she imagined Monique badgering Jack in any way she could to get her way. The tiny, dark-haired psychiatrist was a force to be reckoned with, no question and there was no way the bullish, tough, gnarly police Commander was going to ever win an argument with the elegant Dr. D. Alex's eyes implored Bridgett and she asked, "Bridge, can you go over there as well and keep your eyes on my granddad and Mrs. Blankenship? I also want you to keep your eyes on Monique."

"Absolutely! Of course I will. I can stay as long as you need me to. My mother would just *love* to run my house and my family for a while. She's always itching to get over there and clean and rearrange my furniture anyway. She'll probably cook up enough food for the next month."

Elizabeth interrupted and said, "I think they'll be in your grandfather's suite at the Palm Court. I don't think Jack thought it a good idea for your grandfather to see your house."

Alex's tears burned her eyes as the realization settled in. "What do you mean? What's wrong with my house?"

Liz hesitated and added, "The perp killed two police officers before he hurt your grandmother. I think that as soon as forensics cleans up over there, you'll be able to go back, but not tonight or tomorrow. For now, I've secured a connecting suite at the Palm for you."

"Two NOPD are dead? Oh my God, this is awful, devastating. Jack must be beside himself," Alex added, feeling breathless.

Liz nodded in agreement. "Yes, for sure, I think everyone is upset. Apparently, the Secret Service agent, who had just arrived, chased the guy but lost him. It is pretty bad over there. The perp was a tall bearded fellow dressed in black. They think he is Muslim, maybe even the same guy that broke in several days ago."

"Thank goodness for Josh! He'll keep us informed, " Alex added, thinking of Elizabeth's handsome NOPD boyfriend. She smiled gratefully, turned to Bridgett, and asked, "Are you still willing to babysit my granddad and Dr. D?"

"Absolutely," Bridget declared as she gave Alex a swift hug. "I love you and I'll take care of everything. I'm leaving now," she assured them as she left the office in a blur of vivid color.

"She's pretty amazing, isn't she?" Liz commented as they watched Bridget depart, her tall, voluptuous figure a mass of blonde curls and bright colors, her high heels clicking on the outer office floor as she gathered her things. They could hear her footsteps as they clicked down the hall until she stepped onto the elevator.

"Yeah, she is," Alex, admitted absently. "What else is there? Is there other news?"

"Jack thinks the attack on your grandmother was in retaliation to your grandfather's comments on the news. Apparently, Agent Stoner and FBI Special Agent Bodine are in agreement."

Alex covered her face with her hands, tears streaming from her eyes. "Oh no! This is going to kill my grandfather. He is going to feel responsible. What am I going to do?" Elizabeth patted her arm and said, "You're going to have a good cry, think about how life sucks and then you're calling your grandfather and after that conversation, you'll meet Robert over at Tulane to check on your grandmother." Liz's voice was forceful and her advice pragmatic.

Chapter 43

Ali and Habib sat across from each other on the floor in Ali's apartment, avoiding all eye contact or body language that could cause speculation about their new-found friendship. Nazir was sitting quietly in a chair by the window examining a set of plans. Ali doubted he was even looking at the plans.

"What are you reading?" Ali asked, as he attempted to engage his brother in conversation. Nazir's body language was shut down and he avoided contact with everyone. He didn't answer, so Ali moved toward him and shook his shoulder, "Brother, what are you doing?"

Nazir gave Ali a blank stare but said nothing. His eyes moved toward the kitchen where Omar and Mohammed talked quietly. Ali strained, trying to eavesdrop on their conversation but the voices were too soft, the words too unclear for even his young ears to pick up. Suddenly, the door burst open and slammed against the wall. Ali jumped in surprise as the tall dark figure of Syed entered, carrying a long, stainless steel projectile in his hands. Ali had no idea what it was or how they planned to use the projectile.

Syed deliberately kicked Habib's leg, wagged his finger purposefully in his face and glared at Ali as he quickly moved toward the kitchen.

"What's up, boy genius?" Syed snarled as he shoved Ali against the wall as he passed him. Ali was scared of Syed and knew he was mean, malicious, and cruel. Ali closed his eyes to cut out the image of the Jihadist rushing toward the kitchen. Within seconds, the conversation began but Ali couldn't understand a word. He gave a quick look to Habib who was attempting to listen as well. A short time later, Mohammed, Omar and Syed returned to the living room. Mohammed pulled a syringe from his pocket along with a large vial of medicine.

"This," Mohammed declared, raising the vial into the light, "This will make sure that no one anywhere close to our path of destruction survives tomorrow. I promise you all, just as I promised Allah, that all will die!" Mohammed looked into the eyes of everyone in the apartment as Ali realized the enormity of what the Jihad leader had promised.

Oh no, Ali thought as his heart sank deeper into his chest. That just squelched my idea to use a weak strain of the virus as an aerosol. I wonder what they are adding to the mix? As the thoughts of what the terrorists could do to assure death to masses of people ran through Ali's mind, he again found tears creeping into his eyes. These were vile and wicked men who would never stop killing and maiming innocent people. Ali wanted his graduate student life back and he wanted these horrors to go away.

Nazir raised his eyes to a soft tapping on the windows. All of a sudden, he sprang from his chair and shouted, "Look, look. Look at the window. It's Vadim."

Ali's eyes darted to the window, just as Vadim waved a vial of fluid, gave them a deprecating smile and disappeared. Ali knew Vadim was taunting the Jihadists with the vial of virus that had been stored for decades. He knew it contained the original virus. As he ran to the door he was knocked roughly aside by Syed as he and Omar pursued the Russian down the street. It was not quite dark but somehow, someway, Ali knew they would never catch the nefarious Russian. He was playing cat and mouse with them and Vadim would win. Ali hoped Vadim would ambush the two terrorists and kill them. Then it would be over. That would put an end to his nightmare and life could return to normal. Ali closed his eyes and remembered the life he'd had only three short days ago. He prayed to his God, "Please Allah, let this be over."

Chapter 44

Alex was beside herself with anxiety as she watched the traffic move at a snail's pace up and down Tulane Avenue. The ED waiting room at Tulane University Hospital was unfriendly and foreign. The pearl gray walls of the ED, designed to comfort and ease anxiety did nothing to mitigate Alex's fear and apprehension at all. She had convinced her grandfather who was paralyzed with guilt and grief, to stay at the Palm Court with Beth. She promised him that as soon as she had a report on her grandmother she would call him. Adam, his personality dulled and temperament unusually docile, had grudgingly agreed. In the meantime, Beth Blankenship's condition had worsened and she had become severely agitated after learning about the attack on Kathryn. Monique had sedated her so she could get some rest. Finally, her impatience negated her judgment and she walked once again to the clerk working the emergency department desk.

The clerk watched her approach and waved her back to her seat. "I'm sorry, ma'am. You'll just have to be seated. I have no information for you, " the uncaring, uninvolved emergency department clerk repeated to Alex for the third time in an hour as she pulled another stick of gum out of the pack and stuck it between her obviously plumped up bright red lips.

Alex was paralyzed with grief and anger. She ticked off all of the things she could do to get the clerk fired, she realized it would not help to make a scene.

"All right, would you please call back there and see if Dr. Bonnet can come out and speak with me."

"Sure, in a few minutes," the clerk quipped eyeing Alex from head to toe. "They're pretty busy back there now and I have strict instructions not to interrupt them, not for anyone, *not even you.*"

Alex doubted this was true but decided to retreat to her seat. "Thank you," she said softly as she left the ED window and returned to her seat. The emergency department at Tulane was quiet. Alex stared at her handbag. The straps of Alex's leather handbag had been twisted in so many different directions in an effort to allay her anxiety, it was questionable whether the straps could ever be straightened again. For the twenty-fifth time in that many minutes Alex checked the large boldface clock in the emergency room waiting area- t was a little after 6 p.m.. She had been there for less than two hours but it seems much longer. Unfortunately Jack, who had kept her company for about a half an hour had to leave after receiving a text from Stoner asking him to attend a security briefing downtown. He promised to return when he could but Alex had made him promise to check on Monique first. She was deeply concerned about her good friend who was still recovering from a brain injury. The last thing any of them needed was for Monique to relapse and lose the miraculous gains she had made in her therapy. Finally the emergency department double doors swung open and Robert emerged. Alex ran to him and fell into his arms, tears covering her face.

"Robert, Robert, please, tell me how my grandmother is," Alex cried out. She knew her voice was hysterical and as much as she tried to control her tears she could not.

Robert put his arms around Alex and patted her back as he had done so many times before. "Let's go and grab some coffee and I'll tell you what's going on," he said his voice grave.

Alex broke the hug and searched his face. Her former husband's visage was grim, his eyes serious. The lines on his face were deepened and accentuated as they often were when he was tired or stressed. Alex felt panic seize her heart. She was breathless.

"Oh no, Robert, please, tell me she is OK," Alex wailed.

Robert's look was sad and his voice was wistful. "I don't know if I can."

A primal moan escaped Alex's lips and her weeping was uncontrolled as Robert led her out of the emergency department to a quiet place in the rear of the cafeteria. He quickly returned with hot tea for her and a strong coffee for himself while Alex remained numb and silent.

As she reached for her tea cup, Alex was awash again with fresh tears as she was reminded of the hundreds of cups of tea she had shared with her grandmother in the kitchen and by the fireplace at Wyndley. Oh, if she could just go back to those days and leave this troubled city and these troubling times. Get away from these horrible people. She craved the scent of the freshly cut pastures, the smell of fresh manure on the fields, the crisp smell of the evergreen woods where she and Dundee rode every day she was home. She yearned for a glass of Virginia wine in the Gazebo overlooking the river. *Please, God, let her go home to Virginia once again for tea with me. There are so many things I want to tell her that I never have. There are so many things that I need to know from her. Things about my mother, my father. Things about me. I need her wisdom. Please, let me attend Fork Church once again with my grandparents and pray with them. I need that in my life and it has been sadly remiss. I am not ready for her to leave me.* As Alex sent up her prayers, she also prayed for strength so she could know.

Robert watched the emotions flicker across Alex's face, and felt her pain and panic. He loved Kathryn Rosseau Lee as much as she did. He knew that Kathryn, more than anyone else, wanted the two of them to reunite their marriage. He loved Kathryn for that and he loved her because she had raised his beloved Alex. She had taught Alex to embrace her values and become her own person. Alex was a strong woman, just like her grandmother. Robert considered Kathryn Lee one of the kindest, most intelligent women he had ever known. That's why telling Alex the specifics of her grandmother's current state was going to be so hard for both of them.

Alex's clear blue eye looked directly into Robert's grey eyes, her heart pounding, "How is she?"

The sadness and distress on Robert's face make Alex's heart scream in her chest. Her pain was unbearable and she could hardly breathe. For a moment, Robert seemed unable to speak.

Oh my God, he's going to tell me my grandmother is dead. Please, please Robert. Don't tell me that. Alex thought her heart would burst. What would she do without her grandmother. This was just not the right time to lose her. There were so many things she still wanted to tell her.

Finally, Alex ventured a few words, "Is... is she alive? Please, Robert tell me she is."

After a brief instant Robert nodded. "Yes, she's alive."

Alex's heart flooded with relief.

"But her injuries are very serious. She is beyond critical. I don't know if she will make it. The man who attacked her left her for dead. I am sure he thought she was, " Robert added sadly. "I'm sorry, but I must be honest with you."

Alex suddenly changed from a distraught granddaughter to an objective clinical nurse. "What are her injuries? What part of them are critical," she asked crisply.

"All of them at her age. She's unconscious. She has a head injury. She has numerous cuts and bruises. Her right shoulder is broken but I'm most concerned about her head injury and her broken ribs. She had at least three broken ribs and another is cracked. I'm worried about her breathing based on that."

Alex was shaken but contemplative. *What kind of bastard animal could beat up an elderly lady.*

"My grandmother will be OK. She will make it. We must be sure she doesn't get pneumonia. That worries me as does the head injury. She is breathing on her own, right?" Alex smiled brightly, her voice filled with false reassurance.

Robert nodded and added, "She is breathing on her own now, but that could change. We cannot be sure. The injuries that she sustained are grave, placing her in a precarious state." Robert had held nothing back and felt now that Alex knew the extent of Kathryn's injuries. "I hope she will, but we can't be sure. She is 76 years old."

Alex was defiant, "Yes, she is, but have you ever seen a more vibrant, healthier, 76 year old? Grand rides horses almost every day. She hikes miles every week and she goes to the gym three times a week and works out with weights. She also swims and does water aerobics. She had a great set of lungs and if anyone can make it, she can and she *will.*"

"Your grandmother is in excellent health for someone her age. I believe that if anyone can survive this it is Kathryn," Robert agreed hopefully but added, "She's still very ill and very critical."

"When can I see her? I'll plan to spend the night. Will you be sure there's an order to that effect?"

Robert started to object and then didn't. "Let's talk about that. We can share staying with her. You and I are also running a hospital that is currently harboring an unknown virus and is surrounded by NOPD, National Guard and FBI agents."

Alex considered this and added, "OK, you're about the only person I would trust with her. I need to call granddad and let him know. Then can we see her?" Alex was considerably more cheerful now that she had the facts and could work with them.

Robert checked his watch. "She's probably in ICU by now. Sure, let's go," he said as he put his arm around Alex and they left the cafeteria talking quietly as they made their way to the large, modern Tulane intensive care unit.

Chapter 45

Mohammed Abdu arose just before dawn, had a brief conversation with Syed in the kitchen and joined comrade Omar Hassan in the living room of Nazir's apartment. It was mission day and he felt good. A refreshing night's sleep had cleared his head and all concerns about the work for the day. *This will be the best and the most lethal activity ever noted in the West. Down with the infidels! Praise Allah.* Mohammed Abdu had joy in his heart as he joined his friends for morning prayers. The friends retrieved their prayer rugs from the corner of Nazir's apartment and knelt together in prayer. The leaders prayed for success and victory against the American leaders and infidels in New Orleans. The mission had taken years of planning and Mohammed was certain it would be a success.

Refreshed after a simple breakfast of fruit and eggs, the two Jihad leaders walked downtown toward the pier of New Orleans where they stopped in a bar close to the convention center for coffee. Omar surveyed his long-time friend critically and questioned him, "Did you speak with Syed this morning? Are there any details you need for me to handle?"

Mohammed Abdu shook his head. "Syed left to begin his deliveries. All of the canisters are loaded with both the virus and the syringes filled with Novichok. We will be successful, my brother. It will be a victory for Allah."

Omar smiled broadly and asked, "Do you have any concerns about Syed getting the job done?"

Once again, Mohammed shook his head. "Not at all. I trust Syed. He is well-trained, faithful and dedicated. I am not so sure about Habib so I would like for you to watch him carefully today. I am not sure of his allegiance to our cause. I think he is faltering in his commitment. If you see anything alarming or suspicious, he must be neutralized. He will not be a great loss to us. While he has been radicalized and trained, I am not sure of his fidelity. He is young and we have not invested considerable time in his development or progression in the organization."

"I will, brother, but I hope it does not come to that. If it does, I will handle it. What of Nazir?"

Mohammed thought for a moment and said, "He is weak, dedicated but expendable. I will decide in several hours. Do you believe he can be trained to be a brave Jihad warrior?"

Omar shrugged his shoulders, "I don't know. I think you are right, he is weak and he gets rattled much too easily. In some ways, I believe he is prone to hysterics. I don't believe he can be trained. Perhaps he can be useful in the recruitment and radicalizing part of our cause."

Mohammed was non-committal. "Perhaps. Let us see how well he does with explosives strapped to his torso and a detonator switch in his hand. That will give us some idea of his limits." Mohammed thought for a moment and added, "You know, my brother, I think I may load up Habib with explosives as well. It is not part of the plan, but it will help us get more people inside where they will inhale the virus and poison. We can drop him off near the Casino which will most likely be our main killing field."

Omar nodded in agreement as they watched a battered, unmarked delivery van slow to a stop in a loading zone close to the convention center. They continued to watch carefully as a young man with dark hair and a beard exited the delivery van, loaded six stainless steel canisters on a dolly system, and entered the Convention Center. Twenty minutes later, he reemerged and delivered six more canisters into the huge Convention Center. Satisfied, he stopped for a cigarette against the side of the building and then drove off in his van to make additional deliveries.

Omar smiled and said, "He is doing well. No one would suspect him."

Mohammed was silent about Syed's work. "Come, let us move," suggested Mohammed, "the sun is shining directly into my eyes."

After a five-minute walk, the two sat on a bench and watched as the same delivery van stopped near Harrah's Casino and delivered an additional six canisters inside the Casino and an additional four canisters inside of Harrah's New Orleans Hotel. Omar gave Mohammed a slight smile and murmured, "Ah, our delivery boy continues to do well."

Mohammed nodded in agreement as Syed returned to his van for more canisters, which he delivered to the Hilton and Hyatt Hotels. Omar checked his watch and said, "We are right on schedule. We timed this well."

As Syed returned once again to his van, Mohammed made a suggestion.

"Brother," he said lazily, stretching his arms over his head, "Let us walk up to the upper French Quarter. I think I would like to see the famous Cafe du Monde that all the tourists talk about in New Orleans. Perhaps I may try, what is it, a beignet?" Mohammed gave Omar a slight smile, his voice sarcastic. "Who knows, it may be one of the last beignets ever prepared there."

Omar nodded gleefully, "I hope so, brother. We will triumph." The two Jihad leaders had just settled down with their cafe au lait and beignets in the green-stripped canopied Cafe du Monde when they spotted Syed walking up the street, whistling happily and stopping to talk with several locals and tourists. He had four canisters loaded on his worker's dolly. He delivered two canisters to the server behind the counter in the outside cafe who scribbled his name on the sheet in acceptance. He then continued to Jax Brewery where he deposited the remaining canisters in the food court that was part of the refurbished brewery shopping mall. Omar and Mohammed drank their coffee silently, their spirits soaring with each canister delivered. He returned and distributed an additional six canisters to six food carts along the route.

Mohammed was drinking his coffee and dreaming about victory when the vibration of his burn phone startled him. He'd received a text message, which he promptly shared with Omar. His voice was hushed.

"The American President will speak at 1 p.m. He will be at the Convention Center. Our timing is perfect, brother. We will move forward as we planned." Omar could see the spark of anticipation in Mohammed's eyes. He felt gleeful but cautioned himself against feeling successful. He never, *what is it the infidels say, 'counted his chickens before they are hatched'* or something like that? Omar was way too smart for that. He'd been around the block many times, just as Mohammed had, and both knew the best of planning could be ruined in an instant. Anyway, both were eagerly anticipating the deaths of most of America's political leaders as well as thousands of American infidels. That made Omar the happiest man in the world. *Praise to Allah and death to the infidels.*

Chapter 46

Alex was tired and worn to a frazzle but optimistic. It was a little after 9 a.m. and she had stayed with her Grand until two in the morning when Robert had returned to the Tulane ICU to sit with her. Alex looked great for someone who'd had a hellish two days. Heeding the advice of her grandmother to 'look your best when you felt your worst' Alex had done her best to dress well for the day. Carla, Martin's wife, had brought over a suitcase full of clothes, and Alex had selected a teal suit with a white silk blouse, gold jewelry and a pair of three-inch high heels, which made her incredible long legs appear even longer. Her highlighted auburn hair was in a casual chignon and she had replaced her purse with a matching silk teal bag. Jack had given her a long, low whistle earlier when she had seen him outside the hospital. Somehow, her grandmother was right. Looking good certainly made you feel good. *I will make it through this day and we will prevail. My family will be good.*

Alex and Robert were heartened and encouraged by her grandmother's progress. Kathryn's vital signs were stable and her breathing, though labored, was steady and her lungs remained clear thanks to the excellence of the nursing and respiratory care at Tulane. It had made her cry when the nurses turned her grandmother because the pain of her broken shoulder and fractured ribs was excruciating. She cringed when Kathryn, still unconscious for the most part, cried out in pain. Alex had never known her strong, no-nonsense grandmother to show any emotion but kindness. She had never heard her complain of pain or complain about anything. It tore her to pieces to see her black and blue from the beating. At any rate, she was hopeful her grandmother would regain consciousness during the day. She knew her grandmother had squeezed her fingers several times during the night when Alex had asked her questions. As she sat at her desk at the hospital and pondered these questions, Robert entered her office.

"Hey, who's with my grandmother?"

"I left her for a while when your granddad came in to visit. Don't worry, Alex," he reassured her as he saw her face fall, "there's a great nurse taking care of her that I have known forever. Besides, Bridgett called and Angela is off today and has volunteered to go over and stay today with Kathryn as well. She's in the best of hands."

Alex was overjoyed. Angela Richelieu was a top-notch ICU nurse and Bridgett's twin sister. "Oh, wow, that's great. Thanks, Robert. I will have to do something great for Bridgett and Angela when things are calmer. They are both the best. If Grand wakes up, she'll be excited to see Angela."

Robert nodded and Alex continued, "I am so lucky to have such wonderful friends here in New Orleans. They're just the best."

"I've just come from the ED and talked with Yvette. There are currently 33 active cases of the virus at CCMC and 17 people had died since yesterday morning. Yvette reports that most of the victims have died from the virulent lung disease or pneumonia that we still haven't isolated. They're growing new cultures from the most recent victims, so we will hopefully know something this evening."

Alex shook her head. "Yes, I know. I talked with Yvette several hours ago. She believes the number of cases and deaths are staggering for such a short period of time, particularly in an industrialized area. She also said they were close to an actual identification of the virus and the most recent testing suggested it was a mutating virus."

Robert nodded, "Yeah. That's why it's been so hard to narrow the virus down. Ted Smith and his lab assistant, a grad student named Ali Nassir, are developing an anti-viral antidote that may assist us in treating the current patients. Hopefully, they will test it over the weekend on any new cases."

"That's great news." Alex was so thankful for Robert. *Thank God for Robert. He was a wonderful man, friend, and physician. Besides, he was the only person in the world, other than the Congressman, that loved her grandmother as much as she did. Grand had always been a staunch supporter of the handsome surgeon. Kathryn had first known Robert's family, the aristocratic Bonnets of Louisiana, when Robert's father had been the Governor of Louisiana. Now Robert's dad was a United States Senator from Louisiana and her grandmother saw both his parents fairly often. Robert's mother and Kathryn Rosseau Lee had worked on several Congressional wives committees and events over the years and Kathryn had been delighted when Alex and Robert had married at the University of Virginia Chapel in Charlottesville a little less than 10 years ago.*

Robert gave her a quizzical look. "What are you thinking about? You look like you're in another world. Come back to reality."

Alex grinned at him and said, "I'm thinking about you and our families. How lucky we are to have known each other for so many years!"

"No argument here," Robert agreed. "But I have to rush off. I got a ton of people to see and I want to get back over to Tulane. You OK here?"

"Yeah, I promised Jack I'd meet him in the Quarter after lunch if I could. I think I can since Angela's with Grand, so I'll go by the hospital before I go meet him. I'll have to change clothes, though. Can't wear this get up."

Robert appraised her beautiful outfit and said, "I agree. You look far too good to be bumming around the Quarter with

Jack and his police. As a matter of fact, you look great. You're always so beautiful." Robert's voice was wistful.

"Stop it, I'm a mess! I haven't slept in what seems like days. Pretty soon I'm gonna look like Francoise." Alex objected. "Thanks for everything with Grand." Alex trusted Robert with her life and that of her family. She knew he would make the very best decisions for her grandmother and keep her in the loop. She loved him in so many ways. Perhaps they could have dinner again when all of this was over and they could pursue their, well, what would you call it, courtship? She smiled at the thought of a courtship with Robert. After all, they had been married for over five years. She stood and said, "Gotta go. Martin's picking me up out front and taking me to the Palm and to see Granddad."

Robert blew her a kiss on the way out. She blew one back. *Oh, hell, what am I doing? Is this a big mistake?*

As Alex waited for Martin in front of hospital, she reflected on her conversation with her grandfather. She'd meant to discuss it with Robert but time had run out. Adam was devastated and blamed himself for Kathryn's injuries. His depression and self-blame were over-powering and Alex was worried about him. She'd spent at least an hour prevailing upon him to straighten up since they had many challenges in front of them and had reminded him he needed to stay strong for Kathryn. Her heart had broken when her strong, stubborn, famous, and politically powerful grandfather had dissolved into tears. It had been a difficult phone call.

Martin was quiet as he picked up Alex. Martin was generally quiet when bad things were happening and he didn't ask any questions other than how her grandparents were. After Alex gave him a report he looked over at her and said, "Ms. Alex, you shore do look gud today. I don't know how you does it."

Alex flashed him a brilliant smile as he continued, "I's so sorry my city has treated you so rough this year. I just don't understand why things are so hard for you. I promise you, though, that a new year is a comin' and things will be better. You ain't had nuthin' but bad luck this year."

Alex nodded and said, "Yeah, Martin, I could go for a change in luck. Have you got time to take me a couple of places?"

"Sure. As long as the Congressman don't need me."

Alex groaned inwardly. She was chopped meat when it came to her grandfather. Martin loved the Congressman. "He won't. He's with my grandmother. Can you drop me at Hotel Burgundy for a couple of minutes? I have to pick up some items for Mrs. Blankenship and then I need to go see my grandmother for a little bit and then change clothes and go to the Quarter."

Martin was surprised. "You goin' to the Quarter with all them bad men and poleeze down there? Why?" Catching Alex's look in the mirror he continued, "Shore things, Ms. Alex. We'll be there in five."

The city was eerily quiet and traffic was almost non-existent. It was Saturday morning but generally there was considerable traffic in New Orleans all of the time. This made Alex a bit uneasy. As the big white cab entered the Quarter and drove up to the Hotel Burgundy, Alex was astounded at the numbers of NOPD, National Guard, and other law officials in the Quarter.

"I'll be back in a second, Martin. Wait for me, will you?"

"Of course Ms. Alex. I'll be right here. Them poleeze are too tied up to be messin' with me in a no parking zone today. The President comin' has sure changed this city, ain't it?"

Alex laughed outright and said, "You got that right. Things are totally different since all the politicians and the President got here. Just give me a couple of minutes." *If you only knew, if you even had a clue you wouldn't believe it, I don't want to believe it,* Alex thought as she walked toward the heavy brass doors and opened them. Glancing over her shoulder, she smiled at Martin and continued holding the door open to help a dark-headed, bearded young man wheel a dolly filled with metal canisters into the hotel lobby. *Wonder where the doorman is,* she thought. Glancing at her watch, she figured he must be on break. It was almost mid-morning. Coffee-break time. As she stood waiting for the elevator, she absently watched as the young man wheeled two canisters into the hotel coffee shop and left the other three in the lobby.

Alex was surprised to see Stoner emerge when the elevator opened in the lobby. He was equally surprised to see her. He gave her an appreciative glance.

"Ms. Destephano, you look wonderful today. How is your grandmother?"

"Agent Stoner, thank you." Alex quipped, "I figured that if this is the last day of my life, I may as well dress up for it."

Stoner didn't smile but said, "Now, it's not that bad. You know the good guys always win, right?"

Alex gave him a dazzling smile and displayed her beautiful white teeth. "Yes, you're right. We do. My grandmother is doing pretty well. My grandfather is with her now but I am going over in a few minutes. I'm picking up a few things for Beth Blankenship. How are things going here?" Over Stoner's shoulder, Alex could see the deliveryman exiting the hotel with his dolly. Was it her imagination or was he rushing out. She turned her full attention back to Stoner.

"OK, so far. We've set up a central command post over at One Shell Square, and there's a second one at Harrah's Hotel on Poydras. We picked the tallest buildings in town. The hotel is over 327 feet tall, and it will give us good surveillance over most of the lower Quarter. Most of our internet surveillance and computer visioning equipment, video surveillance, camera feeds, data analysts and technical personnel will be over at One Shell but Houser, Bodine and I will be over at Harrah's. Jack and Ted will be on the ground."

Alex threw her head back and laughed, "Yeah, for sure. If I know Jack Francoise, he's going to be on the street along with three of his best cops. Don't think you'll see much of him up at Harrah's."

Stoner nodded, "Yeah, you're probably right. Francoise is still a street cop at heart."

"No question, Agent, now you all just get through this day and we'll have a great dinner at my house and you can drink all the wine you want! How's that for inspiration," Alex questioned, giving the tough secret service agent a hug.

"Best offer I've had since the last time you invited me, Alex. I absolutely plan to take you up on it." As Alex gave the straight-laced Stoner a final hug and watched him leave the hotel, she saw the dark blue delivery van ease down the street, the dark haired guy driving carefully, dark sunglasses covering most of his face.

As she exited the elevator, Alex raced for Beth's suite to gather her things. The day was getting away from her. She had to check on her grandmother and meet Jack in the French Quarter by 12:30.

Chapter 47

Syed grinned as he rolled his cart down the cobbled streets of the French Quarter toward his parked van. Now he understood why they called New Orleans 'The Big Easy'. He was astounded by the stupidity of the Americans who worked in the hotels, bars, and places of business he'd visited on his three and on-half hour trek through the city. No one had questioned him as a new delivery guy. No one had asked about the metal canisters and no one had even balked at signing the delivery invoices. All in all it had been, what was it they called it, oh yes, *a piece of cake,* he remembered, proud of his ability to remember colloquial English.

As he reached his van, Syed dug his cell phone out of his pocket and texted Mohammed.

"Done. Instructions?"

Mohammed retrieved his phone, smiled at the text and punched in the word, "Trouble?" with his powerful fingers.

"No, a piece of cake. Now I know why they call this place the Big Easy." Syed wondered if Mohammed understood colloquial English. He figured he did since he'd lived in the United States for many years.

Mohammed raised his eyebrows, showed the text to Omar who grinned and replied, his long beard bobbing up and down as he spoke.

"Well, Syed is a bit more American than we thought, huh, brother?"

Mohammed nodded in appreciation, his thick brows arching in delight. "Syed is a good student of Jihad. He understands that he must *know* his enemies. He will go far. His genius with electronics is invaluable to us. His idea for detonating the canisters was brilliant," Mohammed said as he texted "Return to Nazir's house."

Syed tossed the burn phone into a trash bin and proceeded to Nazir's place. He ditched the blue van on the side of the road and decided to walk. He was close and it only took him about 20 minutes to walk. It would have been much longer by car with all the police presence. He did his best to spot all the regular and added security cameras, kept his hood up and his sun glasses on the entire time he walked.

Omar and Mohammed met him outside Nazir's apartment. "Well done, my brother," Omar said, congratulating the dark- haired Jihadist on his delivery adventure. "We watched you. You gave no questionable behavioral cues. We saw no evidence of any reason for anomaly detection. Your behavior did nothing to raise suspicions. The computers should not pick you up. I am positive you were undetected. Well done."

Mohammed nodded in agreement and continued, "I too must compliment you, Syed. I admire the way you Americanized yourself while performing your tasks. Lighting the cigarette and smoking in the van before delivering the canisters into the Harrah's Casino and the casino hotel was brilliant as was loitering around the French Market. Smoking at the Convention Center was smart too. You looked just like an American deliveryman. You studied well for your part. You are to be commended and I will make sure that you are."

Syed's dark skin flushed briefly with pleasure. He was happy to have pleased the leaders. He would do anything to win the Holy War and kill the infidels. He simply replied, "It was easy. The Americans are stupid. They are ignorant."

Omar and Mohammed laughed aloud and Syed smiled and flushed again with pleasure.

As they entered the shotgun style apartment, Habib, and Ali sat in the living room. They looked at the three laughing Jihadists with a sense of unease and foreboding. Syed gave them a dirty look and asked, "What have you been doing this morning, boys? Nothing, I would guess?" Syed's voice dripped in sarcasm.

Ali responded, "I went to my lab and worked until a few minutes ago." Habib remained silent. Mohammed stared at the two men and asked, "Where is Nazir?"

"In his room," Habib answered. "He's been in there praying all morning."

"Get him," Mohammed gestured to Syed. "Bring him out here for instructions."

Syed immediately disappeared and returned with a disheveled Nazir in tow. Ali was alarmed as he looked at his brother. Nazir seemed to have experienced a nervous breakdown. His face was pale and he could hardly speak. His eyes seemed to jump around in their sockets and he was incoherent. Ali couldn't understand his speech. It was garbled. He wondered if Syed have given him drugs. He rose to go to him.

"Sit, Ali. Now," Omar growled at the young man. "Leave your brother alone. He is on his mission now. He cannot be interrupted."

Mohammed returned from the kitchen, his sleeves rolled up exposing his thick, strong arms with powerful muscles. Ali suspected the rest of him was just as powerful but didn't want to find out. He was built like a tree trunk. Strong and thick. Mohammed had a bottle of water in one hand and stood, towering over the men seated on the couch, an obvious dominance gesture. The power play was undeniable and it was working on Ali. He was terrified beyond belief. Habib expressed no outward signs of fear but Ali could swear he could smell fear emanating from his body.

The Jihad leader smiled at Habib and Nazir and said, "There has been a change in plans. You will both enter the French Quarter as suicide bombers. Nazir, you will enter from the French Market and proceed to the Cafe DuMonde and Habib, you will enter a block up from Harrah's Casino. Syed will strap both of you with vests loaded with explosives. You'll be carrying approximately 60 pounds of explosives and iron shrapnel. The shrapnel will increase the lethal aspects of the bomb. In addition to the vest, you will carry a backpack with more shrapnel and explosives, mainly TNT. The explosives will be wired through a couple of batteries and up the pants leg to a simple trigger device. This device will be located in your pocket. You will have control over the detonator. Do you understand what I am saying?"

Habib nodded slowly while Nazir's blank look persisted.

Mohammed looked at his watch and asked again, this time loudly, "Nazir, do you understand? You will be a suicide bomber."

Nazir nodded slightly and continued to listen to Mohammed. He was unable to speak.

"As I said last night, the purpose of this ruse is to scare people into buildings where we have located the weaponized, aerosol virus and Novichok."

Ali was numb with disbelief. *Oh my God, Novichok! Ali was stunned. How could they do this? Novichok was a chemical nerve agent more deadly that VX. VX was another nerve agent that was similar to sarin gas but was in liquid form. Many referred to VX as liquid sarin but it was much, much worse. But, Novichok was a liquid. It wouldn't work.* Ali felt a sense of relief for an instant and then remembered. *Of course,*

Novichok would work. It would vaporize in a canister. The canisters were nothing but CO2 tanks. In combination with the weaponized virus, it would be absolutely lethal. There was no possibility that Ali's secret anti-viral agent he had added to the aerosol virus would help anyone who inhaled Novichok.

As Ali continued to think, his skin pricked in fear. The Jihadists were smart. Novichok was a lethal killer. Ali was terrified as he reviewed Novichok in his mind. *Some forms of Novichok were thought to be 10 times more lethal than VX, which was similar to sarin. These people were monsters, absolutely monsters. And they were doing this for his God? Ali wasn't so sure. He knew these people would die a horrific death.* He paled and his stomach soured as he considered the agony the Red Jihad planned to thrust against the defenseless people of New Orleans in just a matter of a few hours.

Mohammed continued, "It is not our plan for you to detonate your trigger. That will be your choice."

Ali saw Syed smile. *He's going to detonate the triggers remotely. I just know he is. What can I do? I wonder if the leaders know he is planning to kill his comrades?*

"If you fulfill this suicide mission, you will be hailed and remembered as a Warrior Martyr. Your pictures will grace our internet sites and web pages, and your martyrdom will be memorialized on our blogs. You will be revered in our chat rooms and you will be heroes for eternity among the faithful. Even your bones will become sacred as they too become killing tools to destroy the infidels. Remember what our Quran says,

"And kill them wherever you find them, and drive them out from where they drove you out....and fight not with them at the Sacred Mosque until they fight with you in it, so if they fight you in it, slay them." and, "Such is the recompenses of the disbelievers."
(Surah 2:191, the Quran)

Ali glanced at Nazir and saw he seemed peaceful. He had a tranquil look on his face. Ali thought he would vomit. He knew his brother would take his own life and a quick look at Habib suggested that Habib also was calmed by the words. Habib appeared relaxed and serene. What a bunch of bullshit. Ali was sickened by all of it. He wanted to run.

Chapter 48

Jack and Ted stood in Command Center at Harrah's Hotel and looked down at the enormous crowd in the French Quarter. There was no way they could identify anyone from the high distance. All around them technicians constantly analyzed data feeds from multiple security cameras and used gesture recognition and behavioral clue analysis to trail and data mine any questionable or suspect behaviors.

Stoner and Bodine approached them and Bodine said, "We've got a hit on some gesture recognition. Come here and take a look."

"What the hell? Why is the President still coming?" Ted questioned.

Stoner shrugged his shoulders, "Don't know, the man is defiant and hardheaded. That's what got him elected and he's not changing now."

Oh my God, oh my God, what's going to happen to us? Jack's enormous body was paralyzed with fear. *Holy Mother, have mercy on all of us.*

Chapter 49

It was a little past noon on a beautiful Saturday afternoon. The sky was azure, the Mississippi River looked clean, and the mood in the Vieux Carre was jubilant. New Orleans, always ready for a party, was proudly celebrating the visit of the President of the United States. Signs stating "Fix America" popped up all over the Vieux Carre and American flags hung boldly from French Quarter balconies. Mimes, some on stilts, wore Uncle Sam outfits and strode around the Quarter. Hundreds of Americans sported red, white, and blue beads along with the traditional Mardi Gras beads of gold, purple, and green. Several locals were dressed as the Stature of Liberty and many, many revelers had on masks depicting the President and Vice President and other key political figures. The tempo was upbeat and thousands of partiers had no idea of the imminent danger.

It was always an instant party in the Big Easy and The Quarter was celebrating in full regalia. French Market vendors hawked American flags and patriotic trivia of all types and sizes throughout the Quarter and hundreds of tourists waved flags as they listened to jazzed up versions of The Star Spangled Banner and John Phillip Sousa. Citizens and tourists alike were celebrating Patriotism and the alcohol was flowing. The narrow streets were packed with activity and teeming with locals enjoying a day off. Tourists drinking Hurricanes from Pat O'Briens and Mimosas and Sazuracs, the quintessential New Orleans cocktails purchased from sidewalk cafes were dancing in the Streets, hoping for a glimpse of the President as he moved toward the Convention Center. Red, white, and blue colors filled the city. The day was picturesque, the weather perfect and the patriotism reminiscent of a Fourth of July parade. The crowd craned their necks and hoped for a glimpse of the most powerful man in the free world. It had been rumored that the President's motorcade would travel down Decatur Street to the River, but Alex knew that would not happen. The crowds and extraordinary security precautions would prevent that. She figured no one would see the President on the streets. It just wasn't happening that day in New Orleans.

Jackson Square was even more alive with activity. Alex, Jack, and Ted watched the crowds from a shaded bench practically out of sight of the crowd. All three were dressed as tourists and John was sipping cafe au lait from Cafe du Monde. Looking around, Alex couldn't help but admire and appreciate the spirit of the city. The boundless energy of New Orleans was addicting and the mood of the crowd happy and optimistic. *If only they knew what was happening. They'd be stampeding out of here.* While there was no question that New Orleans had the deep, dark problems and sinister underbelly of most large cities, the city seemed to possess its own life force and the essence of the city was deeply rooted in the customs, culture, and hearts of New Orleanians and their guests. Life was always good here-usually. Alex felt her heart lighten for a moment but the feeling was only temporary. She glanced upward. No one in the crowd knew about the dozen or so highly trained FBI snipers crouching on the roofs all over the Quarter, prepared to shoot in an instant. The crowd was oblivious to the constant vigilance of the Secret Service and FBI. They were unaware that facial recognition scanners using biometric technology had been implanted in security scanners at multiple locations throughout the French Quarter. NOPD police vehicles were parked at strategic intersections throughout the downtown area constantly scanning the license plates of passing vehicles. The license plates of Nazir and Habib were programmed into the scanner and an alarm would sound if they were spotted nearby. Locals and tourists didn't know about the Command Posts at One Shell Square and Harrah's Hotel where data analyst technicians sat in front of multiple computers constantly scanning video surveillance equipment and social media sites. Alex supposed the crowd assumed the National Guard and exaggerated police presence was just routine security for POTUS. Most of the crowd was preoccupied with having a great time and enjoying a beautiful day in New Orleans. Who could blame them? She wished she were part of the crowd who had no idea what could possibly happen in the next few hours.

Jack's bluetooth cracked as she continued to daydream. She knew no one would catch a glimpse of the President. Even the press and media, relentless in their pursuit, were confused. The Secret Service kept changing his route to the Convention Center. Security was much too tight and the Secret Service was moving him slowly and surreptitiously downtown toward the Convention Center, scrambling their signals to prevent any breaches in security.

Alex checked her watch. It was a little after one. She glanced upward, and couldn't see anything out of the ordinary, but she knew the snipers were there. She closed her eyes and continued to daydream. She was exhausted. The warm sun on her face encouraged her to close her eyes as she relived the last few days in her mind. The ordeal with her grandparents had depleted the little bit of reserve energy she had. She felt her Grand would be OK but Alex's clinical mind knew she could experience significant complications from her injuries. Kathryn could easily contract pneumonia with her cracked ribs or an infection from her numerous wounds based on the severity of her beatings. She could even have a stroke when she became fully alert and remembered the trauma of being beaten. Then, there were all the normal concerns you could expect from any elderly woman admitted to intensive care. Besides, Kathryn still had to have her broken shoulder repaired through surgery and that carried all kinds of risks. A negative thought creeped into Alex's brain as she finally allowed herself to admit the severity of the head injuries her grandmother had sustained could result in permanent brain injury. Robert had just said that to her several hours ago as he reminded her that her grandmother wasn't out of the woods yet.

A sick feeling came over her as she confronted other realities concerning her grandparents. At their age and frail health, recovering from the psychological trauma could take months and in her heart, she knew her grandmother would recover but didn't believe her grandfather would. As he considered the dangers he had placed on his family, he seemed to become more and more sullen and non-communicative as each hour passed. He was depressed and remorseful and Alex was fearful for his mental health. She had mentioned this to Robert who'd promised to talk with him. Adam was currently with her grandmother at Tulane University Hospital where he intended to stay until Kathryn was awake, alert and out of danger. He would not be participating in Operation Fix America, putting the health of his wife and family first. Monique continued to stay with Beth Blankenship over at the Palm Court and she seemed to be holding up well. Alex knew Monique was grateful for the opportunity to be useful. Besides, as one of the most prominent psychiatrists in the United States, she, more than anyone, could assist Beth with her grief. Alex only hoped her eminent psychiatrist friend didn't become overtired or jeopardize her own recovery. She'd been through so much. Alex opened her eyes, looked into the beautiful blue sky covering the city and sent up a prayer for Monique's continued recovery. Perhaps Monique could help her grandfather. This thought occurred to Alex like a thundering epiphany. As the medical director of The Pavilion, CCMCs psychiatric hospital, Monique Desmonde was well known for her work with depressed patients. *Please, please, please Lord. Let Monique continue to get better every day. I need her more than ever, and so does Jack.* Alex loved the beautiful Monique Desmonde, who had been so brutally targeted in a heinous crime just a few short months ago.

Alex continued to muse as she pushed bad thoughts from her mind and enjoyed the first moments of peace she'd experienced in days. She listened to the jazz and her muscles relaxed as her foot kept time with the music. Her eyes grew heavy with sleep. She dozed off for several moments, dreaming that she was once again at Wyndley Farm riding her mare Dundee through the woods and meadowlands. As her heart rate decreased and her breathing slowed, Alex dreamed about happier days. She loved her home in Virginia and missed it terribly. Perhaps, when this year was over she would return. She knew she could find a job in Charlottesville, probably at the University of Virginia or Martha Washington Hospital, part of the Sentara hospital chain. She might even consider a position in Richmond at Virginia Commonwealth University. VCU was a huge health sciences center with a medical and nursing school, with a premier reputation as one of the best hospitals in the world. It had a long, prestigious history and had pioneered the first heart transplant in the world. She had many friends working at VCU and several years ago, there was talk of adding another legal advisor. Of course, she mused, there were always opportunities in the beautiful Shenandoah Valley of Virginia, or maybe she could investigate the Medical Centers in Washington, DC and Northern Virginia, all within several hours of Wyndley Farm. She could get an apartment in Richmond or DC and be at Wyndley for long weekends, every weekend. Maybe she would do something in health policy. After all, before she switched to law, she was working on a PhD in nursing in health care policy. Hmmm. Thinking about this was inspiring. And, there would be no Don Montgomery, her incompetent, egotistical, ineffectual CEO. No Bette Farve, the devious, unconcerned, uncaring nurse executive.

Her thoughts turned to Robert and her love for him. He was always there for her and he always had been, *except of course, when he'd broken her heart and divorced her.* She shuddered when she considered life without him. The fact that she'd admitted to herself that she loved him stunned her. *I've spent years trying to convince myself that I don't love him. What is different today? Is it because this could be our last day on earth?* Tears stung Alex's eyes for a moment as she continued to think. *I wish I had told Robert how much I love him. I never even thought about that.* As Alex berated herself, she thought about all the love Robert had shown her over the past year. He loved her grandparents, at least her grandmother, as much as she did. Alex smiled as she remembered the difficult moments he'd experienced with Adam, her stubborn, dogmatic irascible grandfather, over the years. They were as different as black and white, but she knew Robert respected her grandfather greatly. Robert had handled some difficult moments with refinement and dignity.

Suddenly, Alex woke, startled and jumped up. Jack looked at her alarmed.

"What the hell, what's wrong, Alex," Jack demanded, seeing the wild-eyed look in Alex's beautiful blue eyes.

"Something is going to happen now. I think it's over there and..." Alex pointed as a high-pitched scream quickly shattered the peaceful solitude of the day and silenced her voice. The screaming quickly escalated to a fervent ear-piercing pitch. Alex saw a dusty blue van drive off onto Decatur.

"Oh my God, Jack, Ted. That's the terrorists! I saw that same van this morning at the Hotel Burgundy and at CCMC."

Jack grabbed his radio and began talking rapidly into his Bluetooth headset.

Pandemonium broke loose. People were running into Jackson Square from every direction. Parents were dragging their small children and several young mothers had abandoned strollers and were running with their babies. The chaos was frightening and the screams were deafening, the fear palpable.

Alex searched the crowd in vain for the cause of the fear. At that moment, a suicide bomber walked into the opposite end of Jackson Square from the direction of Cafe du Monde. Alex grabbed Jack and pointed as his Bluetooth wireless set squawked loudly. The bomber was a tall, dark-haired man with longish hair and a heavy beard. Even from the distance, Alex could see that he was speaking. In fact, he appeared to be chanting, and his eyes were flowing with tears. He looked unstable and hysterical. She could lip read the word "Allah." The man had a bomber jacket in his right hand and held either a cell phone, with a cord connecting it to a switch of some kind or electronic gadget, high in the air. He wore a vest with multiple pockets filled with explosives. In the distance, Alex noted the brightly dressed organ grinder, the one usually parked near Jackson Square with his monkey on a leash watching from the distance, standing next to his Calliope. *What the hell was going on? All of this was bizarre and surreal.*

Jack approached the bomber, his gun drawn. Alex noticed that Ted had circled behind the man. She screamed desperately to Jack, "Come back, come back! Run! Run! He's going to blow us up!" Alex knew her screams were fruitless and she fixed her eyes on the bomber. *So this is the last day of my life,* she thought sadly, as she stood mesmerized and waited for the inevitable. Jack continued to fight his way through the panicked crowd in an attempt to neutralize the situation. John had taken aim at the man's back but hadn't shot him. *Why haven't the snipers killed him? Why hasn't someone taken a shot? Is it because that would set off the bomb?*

In an instant, the man blew up before her eyes but Alex never saw his finger touch the trigger. She saw red as she hit the concrete of Jackson Square, deafened and stunned by the noise and hysteria of the crowd. *Was it fear or was it blood. I don't know.* As she lay on the concrete, Alex was confused and bewildered. Directly in front of her she saw a blond headed woman crying, attempting to crawl to her baby who was in a mangled stroller 30 feet away. Alex turned her head away from the sight of the toddler. The baby had to be dead. Blood streamed from the woman's head, and Alex was paralyzed in place, unable to speak or stand. All around her were mangled bodies and a cacophony of noise, tears, and moans. As she looked to her left, Alex cringed as she saw a young man she recognized. He was one of the pen and graphite artists, a regular artist on the Square. She'd purchased several of his originals. She thought his name was Phillip. He was unconscious, but

Alex could see that he'd lost his right leg, and she quickly spotted the missing limb in the bushes to the right of the benches behind the trashcans. The leg was bent grotesquely with the ankle and foot wrapped around the bottom of the trash container. Alex checked the tennis shoe on the limb wrapped around the trash can, and it matched the one on Phillip's still attached left leg. The shoes matched. She felt sick. She was so terrified, she knew she could pass out. She wanted to. As she processed the information, she looked down and saw she had both of her legs and arms. She fought for control and began to get up to help others but there was another deafening sound as one of the snipers fired from a rooftop near Jax's Brewery. She briefly saw a man with an automatic weapon fall to the ground, blood spurting from his chest. Suddenly, she was terrified. She couldn't find Jack or Ted. She looked around frantically for them.

"Jack, Jack," she cried. "Are we in Hell." Jack didn't respond and Alex's eyes searched frantically but she couldn't find him anywhere in the crowd. She felt her cell phone vibrate in the pocket of her jeans jacket. It was Robert.

She answered slowly and said, "Hello," in a garbled voice but she couldn't hear anything on the other end. The noise of the crowd was deafening. Blood, debris, and body parts surrounded her. The stampeding, terrified masses almost trampled her.

Am I in Hell? Am I in Hell? Is this really happening? This must be Hell. Maybe I am dead and none of this is happening. As Alex struggled to stand only to stagger and fall, she felt strong arms pick her up and support her. She opened her eyes and peered into the anguished face of Jack Francoise. *Oh my God, this man has saved my life again! What can I ever do to pay him back? Of course, that would only be a worry if I live through today,* she chuckled.

Jack was tense. "Gotta get you outta here, Alex! All Hell's breaking loose. These fuckers are killing us!" Jack's face was white with fury, his anger blatant and obvious.

Alex was confused and unable to speak. She looked at Jack and spotted Ted behind him. Ted shook his head and said, "He's right. These bastards are kicking our asses from all sides. When I started down here, people were passing out and getting sick in the Cafe DuMonde. Looks like they're being poisoned."

Jack's face was red. He was enraged and beside himself with anger. "We're gonna kill the bastards. Let's get out of here, get her safe, and get a gas mask."

Alex protested and said, "No, Jack. I want to stay and help. These people are dying all around us. I know I can help some of them. I'm a nurse, and a pretty good one at that."

"Get a grip, Alex. You can't even walk. Gotta get you to safety. These people are sick and dying and Adam Lee will beat my ass if something happens to you. Now, let's go." Jack was emphatic and Alex succumbed.

"OK. But I'm working over by the French Market."

"Bull shit," Jack grumbled as he helped her out of Jackson Square. "People are dropping like flies over there. You're not going any damn place but outta here until I check it out."

Alex glared at him. She hated it when he tried to boss her around. *I hate it when any man tries to boss me around.* She'd go over and work with the rescue squads once she got a gas mask. Jack was right. She could see the ambulances through the trees and the French Market, damaged in the explosion but still standing where the far end had quickly become a make shift MASH unit. Rescue workers had thrown paintings and trinkets on the ground, and treated the injured on tables where French Market vendors used to sell art, bric a brac and souvenirs. *Thank God, I'm a nurse and can help. There's no way I'm leaving the French Quarter until every injured person is out of* here. *I can start IVs, treat wounds, and do everything I've been educated to do over the years.* Ted stopped a moment as SAC Jeff Bodine came on radio.

She gave Jack a placating look and murmured, "Sure, Jack. I'm coming. Just get me over to the Market." *There ain't no way I'm leaving, but he doesn't need to know that now.*

Bodine's voice, strident with dread, blasted on the Bluetooth. "Got another bomber! Outside of Harrah's Hotel, right below us. Crowd's enormous, running down from your location. Bomber dropped off by a blue van. Got the plates. Got bodies dropping in Harrah's Casino, particularly in smoking section. They are dying and/or having seizures. Sending in bomb people and CDC. POTUS delivered safe to Convention Center but problems there too. Secret Service is moving him again."

Bodine's voice was lost as the second bomb detonated.

"Shit, shit, shit. Those mother fucking bastards. Ted, we've got to get over there." Jack hollered as he stared wild-eyed at Houser. By the way, where the hell is John? Where's John Houser ? I haven't seen him since the first bomb." Jack looked frantically for his friend, but didn't see him anywhere.

Alex scanned the area but there was no sign of Major Houser. "I'm sure he's OK. He probably is with Stoner and Bodine."

"Bullshit, Alex. He was on the other side of the square from us. He was closer to the fuckin' bomber." The tortured look in Jack's eyes constricted Alex's chest.

She said gently, "We'll find him, but for now, let's get out of here. You and Ted have to get down to Harrah's and I want to get over to the market. I'll look for John on the way. I see some state police up there. I'll see if he's with them. If not, I'll send them out to look for him." For a brief moment, Alex closed her eyes in dread of the sight, as she imagined hundreds of people lying in the streets between Harrah's Hotel and Harrah's Casino missing arms, legs, and other body parts. She shuddered. She couldn't get the sight of the mangled baby carriage out of her mind. She knew the blood and gore was horrific. Just like it was here. The anguished cries and moans from the injured and dying had not subsided. She didn't want to imagine it, but the scenes kept running through her brain and she couldn't force them out. She heard the screams and wails all around. Suddenly, another explosion rocked them and Jack hustled them out of the Jackson Square to a location in the old Pontalba Apartments.

"Jack, Jack, where are the other explosions coming from? Are there other bombs?"

"Don't know, Alex. Just stay here until we hear from Bodine or Stoner." Alex nodded but her heart was hammering out of her chest. She looked around. The Pontalba Apartments were now a yuppie French Quarter shopping center. She saw the blown-out front windows of Aunt Sally's Praline store and remembered better days. She sniffed the air for the sweet, sugary smell of maple syrup, sugar and walnuts but all she could smell was burning flesh and smoke. Nausea overcame her as she spied another body part, this time an arm with brightly painted pink nails with air brushed flamingos. She looked around frantically, expecting to find the owner, but saw no one with pink nails. *Oh my God, I don't know if I can survive this! I must be in hell or I must be dreaming! Certainly, this isn't really happening to me.*

"Can we go, Jack? I want to go help in the rescue," Alex persisted.

"No! We need to hear what is going on in places out of our visual scope."

"But..." Alex began.

Ted took her hand. "He's right. It's not safe to leave yet. I'm trying to get Stoner or Bodine, but I am sure Stoner is trying to get POTUS moved and Bodine is lost in the second explosion. Stay patient, Alex. We'll go soon."

"But, we have to find John..." she began but Jack barked at her. "That's enough, Alex. Stand down."

Alex knew she'd lost and as her eyes searched the Square for John Houser, she saw a young man bravely attempting to wheel his elderly mother, confined to a wheelchair, to safety. As Alex looked closer, she noticed the man was bleeding profusely, in his chest area, most likely from shrapnel injuries. Her eyes were drawn to his mother's beautiful white hair, matted and covered in blood and she was finally jolted into action. She immediately ran across the Square to help. The young man gave her a grateful smile as she quickly pushed his mother, manipulating the wheelchair around bodies and debris until they reached relative safety under the roof of the Pontalba apartments. Jack glared at her but amazed at her rescue, signaled for a NOPD officer to load the young man and his mother into an ambulance.

Alex again looked around for someone she could help and noticed the NOPD was powerless at crowd control although barricades were up. Jack had directed his men to assist in rescue efforts and most NOPD were assisting the National Guard in removing bodies from Jackson Square. *Oh my God, the local emergency rooms must be going crazy. I hope they have enough help.*

Once again, Bodine's voice pierced the static on the radio. His voice was calm but strained. "Jack, John, can you get down here? We've got bodies piling up at the Convention Center, the hotel, and Harrah's Casino. Can you spare some men?"

"On our way," the Commander barked, once again back in the race. "Have you seen John Houser?"

"Negative." Bodine said as he continued, "Several meeting rooms are filled with the same kind of poison nerve gas, we think. We're getting POTUS out and as many politicians as we can, but some are already down. Don't know where the gas is coming from. The HVAC systems are clean. No infiltration. CDC is looking everywhere. The water systems are OK and I don't think the suicide bombers released the gas because it wouldn't have diffused this quickly and in such a wide area."

Bodine paused for a minute and continued, "Stoner's back, POTUS is OK."

Suddenly, the clarity of what was happening smacked Alex in the face. She almost passed out as realization set in. *Oh, my God. Oh my God. It's the canisters. It's the canisters.* As the certainty of the situation sank into Alex's befuddled brain, she grabbed the radio from Jack and hollered into the speaker.

"Jeff, Jeff, Travis, it's the canisters. They're stainless steel. They're about two feet tall. Look in each room for them. They have to be in the casino as well. I saw a young man delivering them today."

There was silence on the other end of the phone.

Finally Stoner spoke, his voice slow and steady. "Canisters? Alex, what do you mean, canisters?"

Another epiphany slapped Alex in the face. Her gut doubled in pain and fear. She must make herself understood. She spoke slowly and distinctly, "Jeff, oh my God, please check the Hotel Burgundy. He delivered five of them there today. Stoner and I were talking at the elevator as he brought them in. They're stainless steel canisters with a knob valve on the end." Bodine snapped his fingers and 10 officers left the command center with gas masks. Travis continued to question Alex carefully, "Who is *he*?"

"He's a tall bearded guy with dark hair, who drove a dusty blue unmarked van."

Stoner was silent as he continued to listen.

Her voice was breathless as she continued. "He's the same guy who dropped off the suicide bombers. He's one of the terrorists. He's medium size, dark hair, no beard and looks very American. He'll be hard to find. Has on western clothes." Suddenly another realization set in. "Oh no, Travis, please send people to CCMC. I saw him there this morning as well. He was delivering to the hotel Cantina and the Cajun Cafe."

"Done. What else?" Stoner's voice was crisp. "What else do you know?"

Alex blurted out as it suddenly hit her, "They're soft drink canisters. That's what they are. Those stainless steel canisters are what they use for soft drinks. Those bastards have filled soft drink CO_2 containers with poison gas and are somehow remotely releasing the valve and killing people."

Alex stopped for a moment as her phone vibrated again signaling a text. She read the digital display:

The nerve gas is
Novichok and the virus is in the

container. There is an antidote
that should deactivate it but it
has not been tested. I am so
sorry my countrymen have
done this. We are not all bad.

Alex held her phone up to Jack and said, "Oh my God, Stoner. I just got a message from a terrorist on my cell phone. Jack, would you read it to him?" Alex asked as she offered up her phone.

Jack read the Secret Service the text and Stoner's voice was clipped as he responded. "Believe you've got it, Alex. The message is correct. We know about the Novichok. Actually, it couldn't be much worse."

"Oh no. What could be worse?" Alex's stomach sank. They were in Hell. There was no question about it.

"This is worse. We got the same tip on our hot line as well. It reports the tanks contain a combination of the weaponized aerosol virus and Novichok."

"I don't know what Novichok is."

Jack was livid with anger. His face bright red and splotchy as he spoke, "Those fucking bastards. Novichok is a nerve agent developed by the Russians that is thought to be at least 10 times more lethal than VX. VX is just a more potent version of Sarin. In other words, Novichok is the most deadly nerve chemical on the planet."

Terror encapsulated Alex's face. She could hardly breathe. She looked beseechingly to Jack and asked Stoner and Bodine, "What can we do?"

Stoner's voice was terse and Alex thought she detected fear in it. "We find the canisters, neutralize them, get POTUS and the politicians out of New Orleans, and hope for the best."

Jack grunted in anger, cursing savagely under his breath. "Yeah, and I'll help you after I kill the sons of bitches who have tried to destroy my city and kill my friends. Fuck them. They're dead." Jack threw his radio to the ground, grabbed Alex's arm and quickly moved out of the Quarter but not until Alex retrieved the radio.

"Stoner, Bodine," she asked in a small voice. "How many will die?"

Bodine replied honestly, "I've have no idea. Maybe thousands, maybe only several hundred. It depends on the penetration of the gas. Stay with us Jack; don't start a one- man vigilante committee."

Thousands could die. This probably was the last day for many of them. Alex, Jack, and Ted left the Quarter, as they tried to block out the woeful, depressing, anguished, and heartbreaking sounds of the wounded and dying. The sights and sounds of the injured etched themselves in Alex's brain forever. She knew she would never be the same again. She was irretrievably damaged and sobbed hopelessly as she watched the National Guard unload pallets of body bags. *I've got to find John Houser. That's what I'm doing next.*

Chapter 50

Mohammed Abdu, Omar Hassan, and Syed sat on the second floor of the Riverwalk, passing a hookah pipe and watching the gory scene below. They delighted in every minute of it. Every scream, every cry of pain and agony, and every sound of torture or distress heightened their joy and ecstasy.

"Death to the infidels," Mohammed declared, his thick fingers grasping the pipe as he watched Syed remotely activating the valves of the final CO_2 canisters located at CCMC and the Hotel Burgundy. As Syed pushed the numbers on his cell phone, Mohammed clapped him on the back, American-style, and said,

"Brother, you are a genius. Your electronic skills are invaluable to us. I thank Allah for you. I am sure we will enjoy many other celebrations together."

Syed's face was suffused with delight. His happiness spread in a smile from car to ear. He was so delighted he thought his chest would pop. He tried to appear humble but his eyes betrayed his humility – they were victorious! He said, "All my life I have wanted to work for Allah and destroy the infidels. Allah has blessed me with these skills."

Mohammed nodded in satisfaction, but Syed was watching Omar out of the side of his eye.

Omar was not as ebullient as Mohammed was and said little as the men continued to pass the Hookah. As the city began to recover, the screams became less noticeable and the ambulances moved out. Omar turned to Syed and asked, "Brother, did you activate the triggers on the explosives strapped to Nazir and Habib?"

Syed inhaled his tobacco, and was silent, a tightening feeling permeating his belly. Finally, his eyes flashing with fear and indignation replied. "Yes, I did. They were not dedicated. They were not Holy Jihadists. They would have double-crossed us. If not today, then another day."

The silence was deafening. Mohammed raised his eyebrow at Omar and said nothing. The three men continued to smoke and stare at the Mississippi River and the scene below. Somehow, the feelings of a great victory had dissipated and Syed was feeling stressed. He pushed away a twinge of fear in his chest. He knew Omar, even though he had said nothing, was displeased with him for killing his brothers. He guessed he would be upbraided for not following orders. He hoped that would be the extent of it.

Finally, Omar spoke and said quietly but with conviction, "It troubles me greatly that you disobeyed Mohammed's order and killed Habib and Nazir. It makes me believe that you will not be obedient."

Syed was defiant, "I did what I needed to do for Allah." He looked to Mohammed for support but Mohammed remained silent as he listened to the conversation. Finally, Mohammed said quietly, "Holy War is not the work of one soldier. It is the work and plans of many of us."

Syed said nothing and the silence ensued.

None of the men was aware of the presence behind them until a voice spoke in Russian, in the dialect of North Caucasus.

"Ah, my friends. Are you congratulating yourself on a hard-won victory?" Vadim asked, his tone sarcastic, his manner disrespectful. Vadim was dressed as a tourist and had taken off the brightly colored clothing he wore every day as the organ grinder. His monkey stood beside him, his leash attached to Vadim's wrist. The monkey's baleful, malevolent eyes glared at the three men. As Syed stared into the monkey's eyes, he could swear the monkey was planning a vindictive attack.

Mohammed rose from his seat, his thick body tense, ready to fight.

"You must be the traitor, Vadim. Why did you betray us? Mohammed accused the Russian. "Where is the real virus, the one you smuggled out of New Orleans in 1964?" Mohammed spat the words at the man, his manner deprecating and insulting. He hated the Russian.

Vadim, equally strong and well muscled, replied in a similar, derogatory tone, "Certainly you don't think I stole the virus, do you? I am not that old. However, it is our virus. It was developed by Russians just as the Novichok was developed as a Russian nerve agent. Have you idiots no imagination or the ability to develop your own weapons of mass destruction?"

As the men continued to stare at each other, Syed's autonomic nervous system kicked in. He wanted to run as far as he could away from the terrible fight he knew would soon ensue between the two men.

"Just a little history here for you," Vadim continued. "We helped the Americans make the virus years ago and planned to use it against them. Of course, our ruse was to use the virus to kill Castro when indeed we planned to kill the Americans." Vadim laughed aloud as he remembered the story from his childhood. He loved the story that depicted the stupidity of the American government. "The virus was mutated in order to kill Kennedy and countless other Americans. As a matter of fact, we can inject the virus directly into someone and they will die within hours of a lethal lung cancer."

Mohammed continued to stare at him and said nothing, waiting for the first chance to strike the Russian.

Vadim continued gleefully, "But don't worry, you are somewhat correct. The virus is the same virus and we have copious quantities of it in safekeeping. As a matter of fact, we'll probably use it against you bastard Muslim insurgents who send in suicide bombers and kill our citizens every day and denigrate the Russian way of life."

Mohammed was furious but continued to hold on to his patience.

"The virus was created by Dr. Mary Sherman and Dr. Ochsner in a secret lab in New Orleans and we grew it on diseased monkey kidneys. Later the American government helped us. My favorite part of the story is how the Americans accidentally contaminated the virus with a monkey virus, the Simian Virus, and then grew the polio vaccine on it and administered it to three million American children. The Americans *knew it would cause cancer in their children.* And to think, they call all us savages." Vadim stopped for a moment to examine the eyes of the three men. All were listening intently but the Russian knew it was only a matter of time before they attempted to attack him.

Vadim smiled and continued, "Now there is a huge increase in soft tissue cancers in Americans. The dumb Americans have weakened their infrastructure with their stupidity, causing an exponential increase in cancer all over the country *and they did it on purpose. Now, who is the monster?"* Vadim was smug, as he added, "Never fear, we *will* move against them again with this same, but much improved, cancer causing virus. They will die but this time, we *used you* to learn how they would react to a viral outbreak. And you Jihadists think you are so smart - blah! You are ignorant guinea pigs!" Vadim said as he spat at Mohammed's feet.

Mohammed was incensed with rage but held on to his temper. "You double crossed us, Vadim. You were to work with us. We cannot have that. You are a traitor to our cause and to Allah."

Vadim threw back his head and laughed hard. "A traitor? It is you and your pack of roving, thieving Jihadists who are the traitors. You are traitors to Mother Russia. You thieve in the night, and use your ignorant suicide bombers to kill innocent, hardworking Russians. You are traitors and sons of bitches and this is what I think of your Quran."

Panic boiled into outrage as Syed watched Vadim throw the Quran to the wooden floor of the Riverwalk deck then stomp and spit on it.

Omar lunged at Vadim but Vadim was prepared. He released his monkey and the beast attacked Omar, biting him repeatedly on his face and chest. The monkey then raked its paws across Omar's eyes until they streamed blood. Omar fell to the ground, bleeding profusely and clutching his eyes, moaning that he had been blinded.

Mohammed was furious and pulled his gun. He aimed at Vadim's head, but Vadim was quicker and wrenched the gun from Mohammed's hand. He cursed in English and watched helplessly as Vadim kicked his gun away from his reach, and with one hand, threw him to the deck.

Mohammed, resigned to death, looked at the writhing, bloody body of Omar. He reached out his hand to comfort his old friend, and said, "My brother, we have fought the Holy War long and hard. Allah will reward us." Omar nodded in understanding as he awaited death, always the strong, enduring Muslim warrior. Several seconds later, Mohammed watched helplessly as Vadim withdrew a syringe.

Mohammed, furious at the death of his friend, attempted to rise but Vadim kicked him hard in the chest and he fell back to the floor.

"You Jihad bastards have stolen our technology, our virus, our nuclear technology, and now our chemical weapons. I will give you a taste of your own medicine. You loaded the canisters with Novichok to kill the Americans. I will return the favor and use the nerve agent to prolong your death."

Mohammed did not resist as Vadim pinched his nostrils, forcing him to open his mouth in a few seconds to breathe. Mohammed's eyes grew wide as Vadim inserted the syringe into the Muslim leader's mouth. Syed watched in horrified silence as Mohammed began to twitch and seize violently until he finally convulsed in death. Syed was so fixated on the process that he failed to notice that Vadim was coming for him with another syringe in his hand.

"I watched you, you little Muslim bastard, as you blew your friends up today. Now it is your turn," Vadim said as he turned toward the young Muslim warrior.

As Syed stood his ground and spoke defiantly, the enormous Russian moved toward him. Syed replied, "Yes, I've killed them. Both of them. They were weak and not fitting to serve Allah."

Vadim thrust out an enormous hairy hand to grab Syed, but the Muslim was quick and twisted away from the Russian. In a second, he scaled the balcony and jumped from the second floor of the Riverwalk. Landing on his feet, he quickly disappeared into the crowd. Vadim spat a curse and reached for his weapon, but he knew it was too late. *If I shoot into the crowd, it will only be a matter of time before the FBI snipers pinpoint my position and come for me. I'll get the little bastard later. There is plenty of time for killing, especially the ignorant Jihad insurgents that spend their lives fighting President Putin and his men.* There was nothing more pleasurable for Vadim than killing Jihadists from the Cadesus. After all, those bastards had killed both of his sons. And besides, he'd liked Nazir. Nazir reminded him of his younger son, and he was filled with fury that these Jihadist bastards had killed him. He wondered where Ali was. Perhaps he'd try to find him and offer him protection.

Vadim did not know that Ali crouched behind a table in the bar down from them and had watched every movement of Vadim, Omar, and Mohammed. He'd watched Vadim kill the leaders and watched Syed escape.

What should I do? Ali was fraught with indecision. He'd wanted Syed to die, especially after he'd admitted killing Nazir. Now he wasn't so sure. He just wanted to hurt him, torture him for a long time before he killed him. But he would destroy him, if not today, then another day soon. After all, Syed had taken his only family from him. He was a vile, ignorant Jihad bastard.

Ali reached in his pocket and pulled out his phone. He sent a text to Syed.

Meet me at the apartment. I will help you. Ali

Ali waited in his hiding place until Vadim left with his monkey. He watched the city smolder below him as he carefully planned the death of Syed. Finally, he left and walked over to Decatur Street where he assisted the nice lawyer lady named Alex from the hospital help the injured people at the French Market. He liked her. He hoped they'd become friends but, in the meantime, he knew what he had to do.

Chapter 51

Alex hid in her bed under the covers. She had watched the sun rise through her bedroom window and had seen the shadows deepen as the heavens darkened and night descended onto New Orleans and into her room. She hadn't eaten or slept since before the attack, and she didn't want to. Ever. She had spoken only with Robert, and then, only about her grandparents. She wouldn't allow any other conversation. She knew he'd been trying to see her, but she hadn't answered her door bell or phone. Alex was powerless to move from her bed. In truth, she was emotionally and physically crippled. *I'm done, I will never get over this.* Each time she closed her eyes, all she could see were mangled bodies, limbs without torsos, pink painted fingernails without a hand, and blood. Blood was everywhere. She saw blood, body pieces, and human carnage on the walls of her bedroom and even on the floor . She didn't move. She could not. The memory of the twisted and bent baby carriage never left her mind, and the mangled steel pierced her heart as she remembered the desperation in the young mother's voice crying for her baby. The sounds of the dying, injured and tortured obsessed her brain, and she couldn't wipe the sights from her eyes nor the sounds from her ears. *Please, God, when will I get better? Will I ever?*

Finally, after a long time, several days, Alex really didn't know, she felt a presence in her room. It was a woman. Alex recognized the perfume, but she couldn't place it. As the woman pulled the covers from around her face, Alex stared up into the dark, intense eyes of Monique Desmonde, who simply said, "Come on, Alex. It is time to get up. We have things we must do."

Alex arose slowly from her bed, but fell helplessly onto the floor, unable to walk. She was startled at her weakened and debilitated state. As she lay on the floor, fear pumping though her heart, she could hear her blood racing through her veins.

She stared wordlessly at Monique, unable to speak and frantic with fear. Finally, she felt herself tenderly lifted by strong arms and carried into her sun room. She was placed on her chaise lounge where the sun was streaming through the French windows and she could smell fresh flowers. Hot tea was steeping on the coffee table.

Alex stared at Monique and Jack, her best friends in the world, but she was still wordless.

"Come, drink, Alex. Your grandparents need you. I need you, and so do Jack and Robert.

Alex nodded and said, "Thank you. I will." She smiled as she heard Jack heave an enormous sigh of relief. *Life would begin again. Thank you, God.*

AFTERMATH

Commander Jack Francoise stood to toast his most favorite people in the world. Alex nudged Robert and whispered, "This ought to be good. The big guy can certainly screw up a toast. We've both witnessed it before."

Robert chided her gently, admiring his beautiful date. She was serene in a beautiful emerald green gown with a lovely emerald and pearl encrusted necklace. Robert was pleased Alex had worn the necklace. It was a Bonnet family heirloom and his mother had presented it to Alex on their wedding day. "Shhh," he admonished. "Give him a chance. He may pull it off."

Alex rolled her eyes and muttered, "Yeah. Right. Sure he will," and squeezed Robert's hand under the table. Alex gazed around the restaurant aware that people were watching them. For a moment, a shadow of fear overcame her and she looked around for a Jihadist intent on killing her grandparents. Immediately, she chided herself. *I cannot live with this fear. It will kill me.*

It had been a little over a month since the terrorist attacks on the Crescent City and while the recovery was slow, the gang had gathered at Commander's Palace for the long awaited dinner. Thanksgiving had been only a week ago, and Alex had decided this would be her last big meal before the Christmas Holidays. She didn't want to add to the pounds she gained every year.

She gazed fondly at her grandmother. Kathryn looked beautiful in a pale rose gown, her arm in a sling as the Congressman hovered close by. Her bruises had faded, her white hair was growing back, and her blue eyes, so much like those of her granddaughter, sparkled in the candlelight. She had refused her wheelchair for the evening and had made sure the walker was placed well out of everyone's sight. Kathryn was doing great.

Jack stood and smiled happily at the people he loved best in the world. Monique sat to his right, demure in navy-blue silk, and Alex and Robert were seated along with the elder Lees and Yvette Charmaine who had flown to New Orleans from Atlanta for the celebration. Even John Houser from the state police had journeyed to NOLA for the celebration and was seated across from Jack. His wounds had healed well and he hoped to be back to work by the first of the year.

"Jack, get to it. I want some champagne," Monique hissed loudly. Jack gazed at his beautiful fiancée, dressed in silk, and once again wondered why she loved him.

"OK, Monique. I want to do this right. Give me a moment." Jack took a deep breath.

Alex had to admit that Jack cut a handsome figure in his tuxedo. His silver grey hair gleamed in the low light of the chandelier and she could swear he was thinner. She touched Monique and nodded toward Jack with approval. Monique flashed her a swift smile and mouthed, "I put him on a diet." Alex laughed out loud as Jack began his toast. Immediately he was overcome with emotion and tears streamed down his cheeks.

"I love you all and that's all I have to say," the burly commander said as he flopped back into his chair. "I just can't do this without blubbering all over myself and I'm a Police Commander and we can't do this in public."

Monique patted his leg as Alex shot Robert a triumphant smile and turned her attention toward the maitre de as he appeared with trays of Bananas Foster and Cherries Jubilee. Her grandmother had ordered her favorite bread pudding and light-hearted conversation continued through champagne and dessert. The evening ended with Adam and Kathryn inviting the group to Wyndley for Christmas. Alex was delighted and everyone, even Yvette, promised to come. Life was good after all. A short time later, Alex noticed how tired her grandmother was becoming and suggested the party continue at her home. She knew her grandparents needed to retire and she and Robert dropped them off at The Palm Court on their way home. Besides, she was dying to hear Jack and Yvette's final reports about the attack.

Alex sat impatiently in her solarium as Jack and Yvette talked endlessly in the kitchen. Monique and Robert sat quietly by her side.

Monique arched her eyebrows and said, "Really, Alex. Who's the impatient one now? They're just comparing their facts. We'll know in a few minutes."

Robert nodded in agreement. "It won't be long now. We've been waiting over a month."

Nevertheless, Alex was impatient as she moved toward the bar and poured herself her second snifter of Amarula. She loved the fruit flavored African liqueur even though it had a zillion calories an ounce. *What the hell! It's almost the Holidays.*

Several minutes later, Jack and Yvette emerged from the kitchen laughing, each with a cup of coffee. Yvette had a bottle of Bailey's Irish Cream in one hand and offered some to Robert and Monique. Robert declined, sticking to his brandy, and Monique consumed very little alcohol.

"OK, you all. What's the scoop? I want to know everything," Alex demanded as she turned an intense gaze toward the Commander and the CDC physician.

Jack laughed at her and said, "Geez, Alex. Keep your pants on. We're going to tell you everything we know. Take a break."

Alex gave Jack a withering look and he began, "The final death toll was 536 people, much less than we initially anticipated. All in all, that's not bad considering the thousands of people in the Quarter that day."

"It's still 536 too many," Alex blurted out. "Those people didn't deserve to die like that."

Robert placed his arm around Alex's shoulders and said calmly, "That's for sure, but there could have been many, many more, especially with the nerve gas and the aerosol virus."

Alex, her rage in check, nodded as Jack continued, "No politicians were killed which was amazing because the levels of the Novichok and virus were much higher in the canisters at the Convention Center and the Hotel Casino than other locations. Some of that is because the gas stayed in a confined place, while the canisters outside dissipated more quickly in the air. The President escaped unharmed, as you know, and the two U.S. Senators who were ill recovered and are doing well. No residual effects."

"What about the dead Jihadists? Were the FBI and Secret Service able to conclude they were totally responsible for the attacks?" asked Robert.

"Yeah." Jack nodded. "They were Russian Red, just as Stoner thought. The same group that attacked Boston. His intel was remarkably accurate, as was Bodine's, throughout the entire attack. Gotta hand it to those guys, they have the technology stuff going on. They are American heroes, both of them."

"Who killed them?" Alex changed the subject, not so sure Jack was right. She remained indignant about the attack and somewhere in her mind believed that the government should have totally prevented it. Of course she knew she was being unreasonable and dreaming, but she was still pissed. She guessed it was because they hadn't treated the sick and dying quickly enough. The smell of explosives and burning flesh, the cries of the wounded and the attack on her grandmother would be with her forever.

"We're pretty sure it was a Russian named Vadim. He's been around the Quarter for a few years with a Calliope and a pet monkey. We think his monkey carried the virus - at least the virus that killed Yahwa, Omar, and Mohammed. All three were covered with monkey bites and an analysis of their wounds detected a monkey Simian virus. We also think the Russian had access to the same virus created in the secret laboratory in New Orleans that Dr. Mary Sherman developed in the 1960s."

Jack looked closely at Alex, anticipating an irate outburst. Instead, Alex was calm, thoughtful.

"I saw the organ grinder. The man with the monkey. I saw him just before the first suicide bomber blew up and I'm sure the bomber didn't pull the trigger himself. I think someone else did," Alex added. "Anyway, the organ grinder was standing behind where the Commissioner was stationed on the outskirts of Jackson Square. The organ grinder was quiet. He just stood there as the bomber exploded in front of me, his finger in the air."

"Humph, interesting," Jack, said. "I'll have to check the video footage. Of course we have about 100,000 hours of video footage of that day. I may not get to it anytime soon."

Monique, who had been silent, asked, "What about the terrorist who delivered the canisters. Where is he? Is the government tracking him?"

Jack grinned happily. "This is the newest and best part. We think we found him just a few days ago - dead. At least we have a body that fits the description of Syed, the fourth Jihadist who came to New Orleans with Habib the day before the attack."

"So, he's dead?" asked Alex hopefully.

Jack nodded. "We think so. We had enough left of his face to run an image through facial recognition software and it matched with images taken in the Quarter. He was also matched on the CCMC cameras so we're pretty sure he's the one that infected all of the sterile supplies at the hospital. We also saw him on footage at the Hotel Burgundy. We're confident it's him, but are waiting for the final ID from Bodine and Stoner."

"Enough of his face? What do you mean?" Robert questioned.

"He's been dead for awhile. Several weeks at least. He was tortured and thrown in Bayou Savage in New Orleans East. He washed up, but the fish had feasted on him. We did have enough of him left to convince us he was killed slowly with Novichok and Simian Virus 40, the same virus we're sure is carried by Vadim's monkey. It appeared he had been tortured over a long while. There was evidence of a viral antidote that the killer would use to perk him up and then inject him with the virus again to prolong his death."

"So, Vadim killed him," Robert surmised. "Have we decided Vadim is the Organ Grinder with the monkey?"

"Maybe," Jack opined. "It's looking that way but, honestly, we're not sure. But more importantly, this killer was someone who had knowledge of how viruses work and the experience in developing an antidote. We have suspicions on someone other than Vadim, but then, of course it could be Vadim."

Alex's quick intake of breath startled her. Robert looked at her and said, "What, Alex? What's up? Do you know something about this?"

Jack looked at Alex intently, "This man, Syed, is most likely the man who beat your grandmother. We isolated his image on a camera near your house and a partial fingerprint places him there as well."

Alex said nothing, but merely stared at the floor. "I would think the Organ Grinder could have information about the virus. Especially since you are pretty sure he killed the terrorists."

She shook her head, "No, of course not." She tried to be convincing but Jack eyed her carefully. He could read her like a book. He knew she was aware the suspect was Ali. He continued to stare at her indefinitely.

Alex was paralyzed with indecision. She needed time to think. *Oh my God, did Ali kill that man. He's such a gentle boy and he'd been so helpful that day. They had worked for hours caring for the sick and injured people in the MASH unit. After the last ambulance had left, Alex had called Martin's Cab and they had given the young man a ride home. He had told her he had no family and that his brother had recently died. He'd seemed apologetic that day and admitted to her that he was Muslim. He tried to apologize for what had happened. Since then, she had learned he was one of Tim Smith's grad students at Tulane. She knew he'd done it. In her heart, she knew Ali had killed the evil sadist who had almost taken her grandmother's life. But, she didn't care. Syed had also killed Ali's brother and she believed Ali was the one who had sent messages about the Novichok to her phone and the FBI command center.*

As Jack continued to watch her shrewdly, she seemed to shrink into the chair. He decided to let it go. Finally he said, "Yvette, you're up. That's all I got." He gestured for her to take over.

Yvette reached for a file folder in her briefcase and shuffled through some papers. "Well," she began, "We've finally gotten the answers we've been looking for to identify the virus. It's a mutant viral form of Ebola and simian virus 40. It's taken us weeks to positively identify it."

"So, it's a monkey virus, correct?" Jack asked.

Yvette hesitated, "Yes, but it also has components of Ebola and, strangely, enough it is closely akin to the virus Dr. Mary Sherman was developing back in the 1960s."

"Really! How interesting is that," Robert exclaimed. "That's amazing, Yvette. Are you sure?"

"I couldn't be more sure and there's even more." Yvette's eye glistened with the anticipation of sharing her news.

"What, what is it. Spit it out Yvette," Jack roared. "We're tired of waiting and I want to party." Alex echoed her agreement and Monique gestured impatiently for her to continue.

"Well, she said, her voice a bit smug, "we know why the patients were dying from lung disease at CCMC. Remember, we thought it was some sort of pneumonia." Everyone nodded and she continued, "Well, they were actually dying from advanced lung cancer!"

"Lung cancer, how can that be?" Robert's voice was incredulous.

Yvette nodded her head. "It all goes back to Dr. Mary's Monkey virus. We, at the CDC, believe, the virus used in the attack last month was a highly mutated form of Mary Sherman's virus that actually caused advanced lung cancer. That's what was killing our patients, not the virus itself.

"But how do you know? We thought it was pneumonia, " Alex questioned.

"The histology showed us. Under electron microscopes, it became clear it was advanced cancer, not pneumonia."

The group was quiet for a moment considering Yvette's information. Monique asked, "But Monique, did Dr. Sherman's virus cause cancer?"

Yvette nodded. "We think it did. Remember how Bob Marley's friends swear he died from a "galloping" brain cancer after touching a rusty nail infected with the virus? Also, Jack Ruby died from a "galloping" lung cancer shortly after he was apprehended." It's believed, though the evidence is anecdotal, that both had been infected with Sherman's virus."

"Are you sure about this?" Alex wasn't convinced. "How do you know?"

"It's a matter of record," Yvette persevered. "Besides, we, at the CDC have injected the virus harvested here from New Orleans into lab rats and they are dying from advanced lung and brain cancers in a very short period of time. The more often you inject them, the quicker they die. The evidence is almost conclusive, but not quite. We still have a bit of work to do, but I can pretty much assure you that the virus that killed people at CCMC last month was mutated from the virus Mary Sherman was testing in New Orleans. It's all over but the shouting, folks. It's the same virus.

"Oh my God, what are we going to do? This is pretty bad news," Robert opined.

"Yes, it is," agreed Jack as he turned to Yvette. "Can I assume you have shared this information with the FBI and other federal agencies."

"Yeah, most assuredly," she replied. "All of them know and we're working on it."

Great, just fucking great, this adds another layer of complexity to fighting crime in New Orleans, Jack thought. He turned to his friends and said, "OK, everyone, now you know **the whole story,** so I insist, bottoms up and let's party. After all, this is the Big Easy and we love to party in New Orleans." With a flourish, Jack raised his glass and cut off his cell phone.

Everyone cheered, raised their glasses, and the party began.

Suggested Book Club Discussion Guide

Do you feel that the book fulfilled your expectations? Why or why not?

Did you enjoy the book? Why? Why not?

How did the book compare to other books by the author or other books in the same genre?

How did you like the plot? Did it pull you in; or did you feel you had to force yourself to read the book?

How realistic was the characterization? Would you want to meet any of the characters? Did you like them? Hate them?

If one (or more) of the characters made a choice that had moral or ethical implications, would you have made the same decision? Why? Why not?

Can you identify themes in the book? What do you think the author was trying to convey to readers?

How did you like the ending?

Would you recommend this book to other readers?

From Judith:

Many thanks for reading *Viral Intent*! I truly appreciate your support of my work. When you purchased this book, you contributed to the ongoing education of registered nurses across the world. Nurses are critically important to health care as they provide 99.2% of all health care hours offered to those in need. When you need a nurse, you will understand our work and what we really do to intervene in the lives of others.

To help spread the word, please:

Review my books and tell others about them. Each copy helps us help each other. I love reviews on Amazon and Goodreads.

Join my Blog at www.judithrocchiccioli.com and get periodic updates of my work.

Did you find an error or a misspelled word?

If so, I am so sorry :(. I have two professional editors and at least four others reviewed my manuscript, but all of us are human and when you are writing 77,000 to 110,000 words, there is always room for error. Please let me know by emailing me at judithrocchiccioli@gmail.com   or   writing   me   at www.judithrocchiccioli.com. I am always ready to hear from you with your thoughts, criticisms, and ideas.

Once again, THANKS for supporting Alexandra Destephano Novels! I Love my readers.

ABOUT THE AUTHOR

Judith Townsend Rocchiccioli is a native Virginian and holds graduate and doctoral degrees from Virginia Commonwealth University and the University of Virginia. She has been a practicing clinical nurse for over 25 years and is currently a professor of Nursing at James Madison University and the author of numerous academic and health-related articles and documents. Her first novel is based on her experiences living and teaching in New Orleans. When not teaching or writing, Judith is an avid silk painter and multi-media artist. She lives in the Shenandoah Valley of Virginia with her family and six dogs.